TEARSTONE

a novel

David L. Day

Copyright © 2023 by David L. Day

All rights reserved.

Print Edition ISBN: 978-1-958370-14-8

E-book edition ASIN: B0C9YLGR1W

Manta Press, Ltd.

www.mantapress.com

Cover Design by Creative Paramita

Third Edition

This book is a work of fiction. Names, characters, places and events portrayed within are either the product of the author's imagination or are used fictitiously. Any resemblance to actual persons, living or dead, events, institutions or locales is entirely coincidental.

No part of this book may be reproduced in any form or by any electronic or mechanical means, including information storage and retrieval systems, without written permission from the author, except for the use of brief quotations in a book review.

DEDICATION

For Denna, Logan, and Dylan.
You are still the reason.

FOREWORD BY TIM WAGGONER

Over a decade ago, I had the privilege of being one of David L. Day's mentors in Seton Hill University's Writing Popular Fiction graduate program. SHU's program is low-residency, which means students attend two in-person sessions at the school per year, and the rest of the time they work on novel manuscripts and get feedback from assigned critique partners as well as mentors. I got to read early drafts of *Tearstone* and comment on them – which was an easy job because David's novel was so good! Here's a sample of what I wrote on his final manuscript evaluation form:

The characters are strong, interesting, and engaging. The use of a large cast of characters and multiple viewpoints greatly strengthen the novel. They create a more richly developed setting. The town, in a very real sense, is its own character, much as in many of Stephen King's works.

I didn't invoke King's name lightly in my assessment. *Tearstone* did remind me of King's novels, especially *'Salem's Lot* and *Needful Things*, stories that revolve around communities dealing with a supernatural force that threatens their quiet existence. Plus, the sense of place is *huge* in King's novels, and it is in *Tearstone* as well. In fact, it's one of the novel's great strengths. I don't mean to suggest that David copied King – far from it. *Tearstone* is very much David's own story. What I mean is that David understands the secret to writing horror at long lengths, and I'm going to share that secret with you now. (Unless David reads this and says, *You can't divulge our clan's dark and sacred secrets, Tim!* and replaces me with someone else.)

Horror short stories work best when they focus on an individual – one person dealing with one threat, being pushed to their limits, and defeating it or, more often, being defeated by it. (And when characters do win, they are usually damaged by the experience, physical, mentally, or spiritually.) Horror novels, though, are – get ready for a shocker – longer than short stories. On a practical level, this means that you've got a lot more pages to fill, so you need more stuff to happen. But on an artistic level, it means you've got a much larger and grander canvas to work with. If you think of a story as a diamond (or maybe a stone?) a short tale is a single facet, while a long one can be *multi*faceted. In a short story, you can only give readers a glimpse of the diamond. In a novel you can show them the whole damned thing.

Stories – whether realistic or fantastic – are at their best when they're about people. And in many ways, this is especially true of horror. Even if a threat is external, horror happens *inside* a character. Horror is how a character perceives a threat, how they respond to it, and the choices it forces them to make. In a short story, you can only show some of these things as they apply to a single character, but in a novel, you can subject a larger cast of characters to the threat, allowing you to create a far richer story that explores the darker side of humanity in more depth.

Horror novels work best when they're about a threat to a *community* – a family, a group of close friends, a town . . . and what happens to this community as it attempts to deal with the threat. So, to sum up: horror short stories are about individuals, horror novels are about communities. David knows this secret, and *Tearstone* is proof. His novel is a glittering dark gem made of many facets, each illuminating a different aspect of what it means to be human – plus, it's a hell of a good read. The blurb I wrote for the original release of *Tearstone* says it all: "Enthralling and entertaining in equal measures, this is horror done right."

Back in the days when a craftsperson learned their trade through apprenticeship, the final work they created before becoming a professional was called a masterpiece – and that's exactly what *Tearstone* is: David's masterpiece.

Turn the page, start reading, and enjoy.

AUTHOR'S FOREWORD

It's been ten years since *Tearstone's* initial release. It remains to date the only novel I've published. It is not, however, the only novel I've written. I've published a handful of short stories. I still have a day job, although not the same one I had back then. I still have a wonderful partner and friend in Denna. And my sons now read and are way smarter than me.

The world at large has shared a lot of heartache and pain. I won't recount those common experiences here as they're well documented elsewhere. Instead, I'll share something only I can share. I've spent countless hours in therapy over the past ten years, therapy that I should have started as a teenager. It has helped me tremendously in processing the deep, complex scars left over from the years of abuse I endured as a child. I'm still a work in progress, but I'm in a much better place than I was when I originally wrote this story.

Tearstone was and is many things to me. It was a form of therapy, exploring the complexities of dysfunction in family systems. It was a safe place to express my deep-seated anger and self-hatred, emotions I didn't fully recognize at the time. It was, and is, something I'm proud of. It hasn't and won't win any awards or appear on any best sellers lists, but I think it still holds up well. And it serves as a reminder to me that it's not the truth of the story that matters, but the truth in the story. May you always find reflections of your truth in every story you encounter.

David L. Day
June 14, 2023

PART I

"Turning and turning in the widening gyre
The falcon cannot hear the falconer;
Things fall apart; the centre cannot hold;
Mere anarchy is loosed upon the world,
The blood-dimmed tide is loosed, and everywhere
The ceremony of innocence is drowned;
The best lack all conviction, while the worst
Are full of passionate intensity."

–The Second Coming, William Butler Yeats

TOM

Tom stood at the edge of the grave, head down, and stared at the mahogany coffin below. Pastor Talvery's droning prayer dulled Tom's mind, letting it drift in his lingering shock.

He still smelled the ocean, felt the Florida sun, and heard the waves lapping against the side of his boat. Settled in after returning from Peru, booked months out on fishing charters, and well stocked with beer and supplies, all snapped away by Aunt Harriet's single phone call.

Come home. Your father committed suicide.

The Keys seemed so far away.

The flight to Columbus and the bus ride through southeastern Ohio were not enough to clear his head. Even the familiar ground of Washington Heights failed to help him make any sense of the situation.

Dirt scraped the coffin lid as the pastor tossed in a handful. The service wrapped up, and the sullen crowd disbanded, moving with sloth-like grace toward quiet cars. A few patted Tom on the shoulder or touched his arm, sympathy stretched across their faces like latex masks.

Once most of the mourners had left, Talvery hugged Aunt Harriet, exchanged whispers with her, then approached Tom. "My condolences, son. No one I'd rather take a punch in the face from than Lewis Burton." He hugged Tom and strode off toward the parking lot.

What the hell did Talvery mean? Tom watched the pastor—a man he neither liked nor trusted—crest the hill and disappear with the rest of the crowd.

Aunt Harriet stepped up beside him, her polyester slacks rubbing at the thighs. She insisted he and Kyle call her Aunt Harriet even though they shared no blood. The boys saw her as a proxy mother, their own having died while giving birth to Kyle. She was a good woman, sensible, and always there when Pop wasn't. She'd even gone so far as to arrange a post-funeral lunch at the church. "Are you coming?"

"No, you go ahead." A thread of guilt ran through Tom, so he added, "Maybe I'll stop in a little later."

Aunt Harriet patted his arm. "You come when you're ready. No hurry at all."

Tom couldn't bring himself to look her in the eyes. She touched his cheek, then joined the pastor and the rest of the group. She should not have had to deal with all this. He looked up to watch her go, and he imagined her as the young redhead who used to babysit him and his brother while Pop went off to drink away the night.

Tom looked back into the grave and fixated on the casket, hoping for an answer to erupt into view. He needed something, anything, to justify Pop putting a Ruger to his temple. A few tears slipped down the side of his nose.

The darkness in the wounded earth seemed to grow and spill out to embrace the day around him, as if the very ground beneath the little town were poisoned. All he saw was the blackness of the great beyond, a place of only questions.

"I'm real sorry." A woman spoke to him from behind. A soft hand settled on his shoulder, and with that touch, the gloom receded, leaving gray daylight in its place.

"Thanks." Tom wiped the tears from his eyes and turned around to face a late-twenties blond with sea-green eyes. She pulled her hand back and offered a reluctant smile. He should know her. They were likely the same age and must have gone to school together, unless she was new to town. No one ever moved to Washington Heights, and no one ever left. Almost no one.

Tom searched for a connection and came up empty. "Were you a friend of my father's?"

Her smile faltered, though the compassion never left her eyes. "No, not exactly. You don't remember me. It's been a long time, huh?"

A courier bag hung at her side, and she fidgeted with one of the zippers. Tom could tell she wanted it to click, for him to blurt out her name. Nothing came. Her face was an amalgam of every stranger.

She glanced out at the graveyard. "It's okay. This is a pretty rough thing to deal with." She turned back with a renewed smile. "Cassy Fielding."

The pit of Tom's stomach tingled and his palms began to sweat. He wiped them on his jeans, hoping to look casual. He felt like an idiot anyhow. Was this some cruel trick or simple coincidence? Did Kyle put her up to this as a test?

Tom took a step back. Why was she here? Sure, he had things to tell her—maybe—but not so soon. He needed to talk to Kyle first about the land, and about what Pop's suicide might mean. "Sure, I remember. Alissa's cousin. Thanks for coming." He looked down at his hands and asked what he already knew. "Did they ever find out what happened to her?"

Cassy stopped playing with the bag. She shook her head slowly, eyes unfocused, then glanced into the hole behind

Tom. "I wanted to pay my respects. And see how you were doing." She shifted from one foot to the other, her little black dress fluttering in the breeze. "So, it looks like everyone's gone."

Tom peered over his shoulder in time to see the last of the mourners drive out of the cemetery. He should go to the lunch. There were people he should see, and maybe some of them could give him answers, a little inkling of what happened. But he lacked the strength to handle the pity-laden looks, the extolling of a flawed man, and the general bullshit nicety of a post-funeral meal.

"If you're not too busy after the lunch, how about a cup of coffee?" Cassy's hand went back to the zipper. "I'd like to talk to you for a bit."

He should have felt threatened by those words, but she delivered them with such earnest sympathy. The day felt a little brighter, and Tom felt a little less the stranger in his own hometown. And maybe, just maybe, this would help him decide what to tell her when the time came. If the time came.

"How about now? I think one person's all I can deal with."

Tom followed Cassy to Ornthal's Diner in his faded red Dodge pick-up, a loaner from Aunt Harriet. It sputtered when he killed the engine, settling to silence with a final bang.

Cassy waited for him by the door and let him open it for her. Tom followed her in and tried to keep the door from slamming. Oversized townsfolk stuffed the diner. More people than at Pop's funeral. No surprise there.

They made their way to a booth at the back. Tom slid in across from Cassy and fiddled with a napkin. Where to start? What was Pop thinking? Why wasn't Kyle at the grave or taking his calls? Then there was Cassy.

"So." He watched his hands work. The napkin looked like

a third-grader's origami project, and still he found no words.

"It's okay." Cassy placed her hand on his, stopping the chaotic paper folding. "Really. I don't mind sitting here with you for a bit. Take your time. If you want to talk, we can talk. If you want some quiet company, that's fine, too."

Her touch was gentle and smooth, and he found it easy to set the napkin down. He wanted to talk, but he knew better. He and Kyle had to agree on this. Tom glanced at her, then turned to stare out the window. "Thanks. I'm not sure where to—"

"Can I get you something?"

A young woman hovered over them, smacking gum like a starving horse, eyes fixed on a pad and pen.

Tom faced Cassy. "You go ahead."

"Coffee, black."

"Got it. Mister?" The waitress blew a strand of hair from her face.

"Same."

The waitress scratched away on her pad. "Two coffees, black. Got it." Then she was gone.

"She had to write down two black coffees?" Tom raised an eyebrow.

"That's Debbie, Charlie Ornthal's daughter. Usually a smart girl, by any measure." Cassy straightened her silverware. "She's going to college in the fall and probably has a lot on her mind."

"Sure." Tom brushed a jittery hand through his hair. "It just feels good to know I'm not the only one with head-in-ass syndrome." He craved a smoke, but he left his pack of Chesterfields back at Aunt Harriet's place. Pop used to smoke those awful Pall Malls. Tom could almost smell their rough stench. Did Pop have a cigarette right before he pulled the trigger?

Cassy cleared her throat. "You were saying?"

He had been staring at his hand, Cassy and the diner almost forgotten. She was so patient. Even so, he wasn't sure he could continue. Pop was in the ground, Kyle was AWOL, and there were too many questions for him to deal with.

"It's okay." Cassy slipped the courier bag from the booth to the table. "Take your time." She must have sensed the turmoil inside him.

Debbie reappeared with two cups of coffee and two plates piled with meatloaf, green beans, mashed potatoes, and gravy. She balanced them with expert grace as she transferred the meal to the table.

"My dad sent them over. They're on the house. He said to tell you he's sorry for your loss." She hitched a thumb over her shoulder. From the kitchen window, a hulking man with more hair than skin raised a paw.

Tom waved in return and told Debbie to give her dad his thanks. So many familiar faces and yet... he felt so different, so foreign.

"Sure." Debbie popped her gum and drifted on to the next booth, where she stopped to take an order from a withered old woman wearing a faded yellow dress, a gray shawl draped about her shoulders.

Cassy leaned over the table and whispered to regain Tom's attention. "You should eat what you can. Charlie's not known for his good graces."

Somewhere in the back, something shattered—a lot of something. Charlie's voice boomed through the diner. "Debbie. I need more plates, and don't stack 'em so close to the flat-top this time."

Tom poked at his meal, digging the fork through a splatter of mashed potatoes. Dishes clinked and voices prattled as he and Cassy sat in silence. The meatloaf smelled like Sunday dinner, and a deep longing for home settled into his chest. His stomach turned somersaults, so he set the fork back down.

He needed to see the house. Would it still be clean, as Pop always kept it? Would the rough odor of stale smoke still linger in the air? Or would an abandoned last meal be moldering in the sink, ripe with maggots, leaving the place smelling like fresh death? He wanted to curl up on the sectional where, on rare occasions, Pop would to read to him and Kyle while a fire crackled. Maybe he could pull out the old photo album to look at the father he abandoned and the mother he barely knew.

Why had he stayed away so long? Hadn't he been gone long enough for the wounds to scab over and heal?

"Okay," Cassy interrupted again. "I can see you're not much for company. And I don't blame you." She looked tired as she unzipped a side pocket on the courier bag, pulled out a business card, and pushed it across the table. "When you're ready to talk, give me a call. And for God's sake, try to eat something. They don't call it comfort food for nothing."

Before Tom could answer or pick up the card, Cassy slid from the booth and hailed Debbie. "Can you box these up for us? We need to get going. Tom's had a long day."

He wanted to talk. Didn't she understand he needed more time to adjust, though? One minute she was patient, the next she decided to leave. Why change gears so quickly?

As Debbie took their meals and boxed them up, he sat like a stone at the bottom of a pond. When she returned with two bags, he rose from the booth and picked one up.

"Thanks." He offered a hand to Cassy.

She took it, her skin against his, relaxing him a little. "Take care of yourself, okay?" Cassy turned to leave, then stopped. "Oh, I almost forgot. I have a couple things for you. From the scene... from your father's place." Cassy plopped the bag down, pulled out a college composition book, and tossed it on the table next to Tom. Then she pulled out an oblong shape wrapped in an old rag and placed it on top of the book.

"From Pop's house? Why do you have them?" He unfolded the rag and saw it cradled a stone, polished smooth as glass, the color of fresh cut grass and streaked with red.

"Look at the card." Cassy squeezed his shoulder, then turned and walked off, her black heels clicking on the linoleum.

Tom lingered by the table, and as the door shut behind Cassy, an overwhelming sense of pressure filled the little diner. He sat back down and flipped the card over. Deputy Cassy Fielding. Tom stuffed the card in a pocket. Maybe talking to her wasn't such a good idea.

The stone sat on the book, partially unwrapped. Something about it felt more familiar than anything else in this town, and yet it repulsed him. The mixed scents of limestone dust and old newspaper drifted up from it, along with an undertone of mildewed tea bags. He took the corner of the rag and dragged the stone off the book. His name was scrawled on the cover in Pop's jagged handwriting. Tom let out a sad chuckle. Pop knew he would come home.

The elderly woman in the yellow dress looked up from her lunch. "Don't be rude, boy. What you got there? What's so funny?"

He recognized her. She was older, but her raspy voice was unmistakable. He thought she should have been dead by now—or at least retired to somewhere nice. Tom supposed the old librarian might live forever.

"I beg your pardon, Ms. Lyons. Nothing's funny. Just a

couple of things Pop left me."

Elana Lyons peered over the booth to his table and adjusted her glasses, tightening her lips into a scowl. "Oh. The rock. Your father brought it to the library some time back. Couldn't tell me exactly where he found it." Despite her frown, she got up and came to his table. "Not from these parts, I'll tell you that." She reached down and picked up the stone. Her eyes glazed a little, as if errant and unusual thoughts flittered through her mind. "You find things like it—somewhat, mind you—across the world. In Egypt—"

Charlie appeared behind the old woman and plucked the stone from her hand. "I'm sure the boy doesn't want a history lesson. Go on. Leave him alone. He's just lost his father."

The librarian looked at the cook and tugged her shawl even tighter. "Well." She stared a little too long at the big man, then returned to her seat.

Charlie set the stone back down on the rag.

"Thanks." Tom wrapped the rock, then collected it, the book, and his to-go bag, and slid to the edge of the booth. Charlie blocked his way.

The cook scratched his belly through a greasy apron. "Look, I don't mean to be rude. You see, your dad had a tab here. I can't get your brother to pay. I thought you might make good on it."

Why couldn't they all leave him alone? Should he sit and argue or pay to be free? Tom didn't think long on it. Freedom always came with a price, so he pulled his wallet out. "How much?"

"Let's see..." Charlie looked at the ceiling as he struggled through some mental math.

"You know what?" Tom pulled all the bills from his wallet and pushed his way out. "Here's about a hundred bucks. If he owed you more, I'll have to get you later. Or maybe you can give me a job and I can work it off."

Charlie grabbed the cash and smiled. "Sure, thanks. A hundred ought to do it."

Tom hurried through the diner, out the door, and climbed in the old Dodge. He needed to see the house. After he stopped to get some smokes.

ELANA

Elana finished her BLT, left five dollars and thirty-three cents on the table, and shuffled out of the diner. She always left exact change—no tips for dirty little Debbie.

And did little Tom Burton think she didn't recognize him? She might have trouble finding her keys in the morning, but she never forgot a dirty worm. She never forgot the dirty birds, either. Daddy always said one day the good Lord Jesus would come back, and everyone would pay for their sins. Their privates would drop right clean off and blood would pour from all the dirty holes in their dirty little bodies. She was nigh on seventy-three and still a virgin, pure as the day the good Lord brought her into this world. She would be just as pure on the day he returned to take her out of it.

Elana tottered down the street. At the corner, scruffy twin boys huddled around a third who held open a paper bag. They whispered among themselves. She only caught snippets. No matter. She knew what those little scoundrels were about. She scuttled toward them. "Shane Hanlon!"

The boys fell silent and straightened into a line. Shane hid the bag behind his back, and though he shifted on uneasy feet, one corner of his lips turned up and his eyes brightened.

"What's in the bag, boys? Do you think I don't know? My Mr. Meshach has been missing for nearly a week now. He never stays away long. Can't go more than a day without his Fancy Feast." Her face flushed and tears threatened to spill down her cheeks. "I know you did something to him!"

Long fingers gripped her shoulder with kind authority. "Is there a problem, Ms. Lyons?"

Paul Carson stood next to her. She sized the young deputy up, doing her best to maintain a scowl. A part of her warmed to his touch against her best effort. She mustn't think that way, though. The Lord Jesus was watching. He was always watching.

"We weren't doing anything, sir." Shane mocked an innocent pout. "Just standing here, honest, and an old iron-box comes screaming—"

"I never." Elana's stomach rolled. These little boys needed a lesson. She turned to the deputy. "Are you going to stand there and let them talk to me this way?"

"Now take it easy, ma'am. What is it you think these boys did? Near as I can tell, they're just hanging out. They're kids, not criminals."

A streak of fire ran down her spine. These kids were hoodlums. Could there be any doubt? Darn near the whole town knew it.

"I'll tell you what they did. My Mr. Meshach has been gone for a week, and I'll kiss a hog if they don't have some firecrackers in that bag. You know it as well as I do. These boys have been killing critters." She wanted to shake the man and slap both cheeks red. He knew. They all knew. And what about poor old Mr. Meshach?

The deputy put his hands on his hips. "Boys, can you show me what's in the bag?"

Shane looked at his brothers, uncertain conspiracy written all over their faces. "I'd rather not, sir. It's some candy is all."

It was clear from the look on Paul's face he didn't believe the little scoundrel. Well, good for him. Maybe he wasn't such a dullard after all.

"Son, you're going to give me the bag, and if there's candy in it, then I'll give it right back. If I find anything else in there, I'm keeping it."

The three boys shifted in an uneasy jitter.

"You heard the man." Elana smiled. Squirm, little worms, squirm. "Hand it over."

Shane looked from one twin to the other again. "Go!" He threw the bag at the deputy and all three bolted down the street.

Elana rose to her toes as she shouted. "You dirty worms. You'll have to answer to Jesus for what you've done. Do you hear me?"

The deputy picked up the bag and checked inside. "Well, looks like we might have something here." He shook the bag a bit. "M-80s. Enough to do some real damage."

"I told you they did it. They hurt my little Mr. Meshach and you have the proof right there." She stared at the deputy, wearing her best visage of triumph. When Paul didn't respond, she added, "Well, don't just stand there. Go on, arrest them!"

Paul rolled the bag up and tucked it under an arm. "I'll have a word with their folks later. I'm not going to arrest three boys for having fireworks. Have you ever known a boy who didn't have fireworks? It doesn't prove anything. If you find Mr. Meshach lying dead next to an M-80, then maybe I'll take it as proof and I—"

"Oh, don't you talk down to me." She prodded his firm chest with a brittle finger. "You don't want to arrest them, fine. Don't say I didn't warn you. Those boys are trouble. You never know—maybe your cat's next."

She turned and continued down the street. No way would she give him the satisfaction of talking down to her. No one talked down to Elana Lyons. No one.

She heard him mutter something as she walked away. It didn't matter what the deputy thought. He might be charming, but as far as Elana and the good Lord were concerned, he was just another dirty worm.

She fumed as she walked the remaining three blocks to the library. When she arrived, Elana told her assistant—a mousy little girl whose name escaped her—to stay at the desk while she took an extended lunch. Those boys drained her tolerance clean away. The back office doubled as a nice little chapel where she could kneel on cold linoleum and pray to her man, Jesus, for strength.

SHANE

A block from their run-in with the old bookworm and the deputy, the boys slowed to a shuffle. Shane led, with younger brothers Alex and Lonny trailing behind.

Bitchy Bookworm and Deputy Dawg may have cost them their 'works, but Shane was a resourceful twelve-year-old and knew plenty of other ways to have fun.

Little stones skittered by him as one of his brothers kicked at gravel. Alex, the smarter twin, spoke first. "Stupid librarian. Who cares about her stupid cat?"

"Yeah," Lonny added. "The furry little ball of shit probably ran away. Who'd want to live with the old hag anyhow?"

Shane stopped at the crosswalk even though there were no cars in sight. He fingered the plastic lighter in his pocket, the one he cribbed from the kitchen drawer where mom kept her Virginia Slims, then turned to face the twins. "You wussies still want to see my surprise?"

They looked at each other, splotches of doubt and fear mixed on their faces. Shane knew the value of fear. A stinging belt across the ass, a rough palm across the face, or even the right words spoken the right way get attention.

Lonny ran a hand through sandy hair, long from the summer months, and cringed as he spoke. "You mean it wasn't the fireworks?"

Shane punched Lonny's shoulder, knuckle out so it dug deep into the muscle. That would leave a huge bruise. Shane liked the dumb one, even though sometimes the kid acted like an idiot.

"Nah. Anyone can get fireworks. Those M-80s would have been awesome, but I got a fan-fucking-tastic idea. We need to make another stop."

Shane turned and crossed the street. He knew they would follow. If they didn't, he would pummel them both. Alex might threaten to tell, but he wouldn't dare get dad worked up. All three boys knew shit ran down hill in the Hanlon family.

Lonny caught up, still rubbing his arm. "Are you going to tell us?"

Shane thought the slow one might burst apart, bouncing as he walked. Part of him was tempted to let them in on his secret. How could they not think this the coolest thing since the Wii? Another part of him saw the dark streak running through his plan. Telling them too soon would be risky. His two instincts wrestled with each other as the boys walked. At last, he squinted one eye and curled his lip. "Nope, you'll have to wait."

Alex shuffled up on the other side. "Come on. You have to tell us. At least say where we're going, will you? How far? What's better than M-80s?"

"Sorry little dude. You still have to wait."

Alex slowed and popped out his lower lip. Lonny put an arm around him and pouted as well. As long as they didn't start whining like babies. Goddamned little wimps. Why couldn't they trust him?

The three boys reached the corner and turned onto Krikton Avenue, where the town blended to a smattering of Gothic homes detached from the street by huge swatches of yard. A few more blocks and they would reach the elementary school.

Shane stopped and his brothers crowded in on him, hungry for the promised super-secret surprise. The perfume of their sweat mixed with the stench of bubble gum washed over him as he looked from one to the other. He put a hand to his chin and rubbed, raising an eyebrow for effect. "Okay, I got it. I'll give you a hint. You ready?"

Both boys nodded as if their heads were mounted on springs.

"How do you make a cat sound like a dog?" That should keep them busy for a while.

The bobble-heads stopped. Alex's brow knit into a deep furrow. Lonny repeated the riddle to no one in particular.

"You boys chew on that one." Shane turned and continued toward the school. They walked in silence, except for the two times Lonny made idiot guesses. He'd never get it. Alex might, given enough time. Even if he did, he probably wouldn't say it right out loud.

They reached the school and wandered around back. The desolate playground looked like a cartoon relic, stark wood beams decorated by brightly colored plastic. At the far end sat the maintenance shed, once painted electric lime, now mottled with rust. Someone left the doors open.

"What are we doing here?" Lonny asked as they cut across.

Shane turned with a mind to land another punch, but stopped short. Stupid little prick, he wouldn't know a firecracker if it was shoved up his ass. "Shhh. You want him to hear us? I'm betting old Chronic Murphy's in there doing his thing. Follow me."

The boys changed direction and walked to the far edge of

the playground, where it backed to a patch of woods used for nature walks during the school season. From there, they worked along the tree line and stopped when they faced the back of the shed. A thick odor drifted from the little building.

Shane filled the boys in on his plan.

"Got it?" He hoped the little water-heads wouldn't mess this up. Lonny nodded, which didn't mean crap really, only that he heard the words. Shane turned to Alex. "Do you get it?"

"Yeah, I get it. Nothing to it." Alex bent down, grabbed a couple of large sticks, and handed one to Lonny. "Let's go." He swatted his twin on the ass, yelled "En guard," and chased him toward the shed.

Shane dropped his head. They already fucked it up. They were supposed to get to the shed first.

The twins broke out into a play sword fight, and when they reached the shed, they rattled the corrugated siding with their sticks. Alex started to chant, "Chro-nic Mur-phy sitting in his shed." Lonny joined in, "Smo-king blunts till he's fucked in the head." They circled the building twice, singing at top volume, until Murphy emerged.

"What the hell's going on out here. Can't a guy get no rest?"

Shane watched as the dumpy middle-aged man, dressed in Bermuda shorts and a faded Hawaiian shirt, rounded the corner of the shed. Now, Lonny. Make for the jungle gym.

As if by Shane's will, Lonny did as he was supposed to. Might be hope for the chucklehead yet.

Murphy joined the chase. He yelled after them through what sounded like a mouth full of cotton. What should have been "Stop it" or "Come back here" came out as "Schtoph it" and "Come bacsheer."

As the twins reached the jungle gym, Alex caught up to Lonny and shoved him hard, sending the other boy to the ground and skidding through dense playground mulch. All three froze, and the playground fell silent. Then Lonny let loose with a major wail.

The cry was supposed to be fake. It sure sounded real, though, the way it came just a little too loud. Shane didn't have time to feel bad—only a minute, maybe less—so he moved fast, as any twelve-year-old could when something super cool was at stake. He reached the shed, grabbed the handle of one open door to slow down, and swung inside.

The air was hazy and reeked of sweet-smelling smoke. The old dude was probably bombed out of his fucking mind. Probably wouldn't remember shit. Shane coughed and drew his shirt over his mouth.

Two five-gallon gas cans sat against the back wall by several smaller ones. Easy targets. Shane hopped over the lawn mower and grabbed the nearest one. Empty. It clattered against one wall as he tossed it aside and grabbed the second one. Full. And heavy. He paused to listen.

Outside, Lonny still wailed, not quite so loud as before. Alex kept saying, "I'm sorry, it was an accident. You okay?" Murphy grumbled on about calling the ambulance and how the school nurse wasn't on duty today—no shit, Sherlock, it's summer.

Shane sprinted from the shed, following his first instinct to run to the woods. Halfway there he stopped and looked at his brothers. The twins had a clear view of him. Murphy's back was to him. He waved a hand. Lonny gave a thumbs-up and Alex nodded.

Shane ran again, this time toward the south end of the playground, which would lead him around the school and back onto the street.

Murphy's voice cut across the grounds. "Hey, what you got there? Little brat, you stealing my stuff? You think my tools are for little boys to play with? What the..." Shane rounded the school building.

He set the can down and looked around the corner. Alex and Lonny disappeared behind the far side. Murphy slowed down and looked from one end of the building to the other.

Too easy. Shane wasted no time, though. He picked up the can jogged to the front of the building. Alex and Lonny waited for him at the sidewalk, still catching their breaths.

"Good work, fuck-nuts." He handed the can to Lonny. "Let's get going. Try not to drop it."

Shane's day looked better. Who needed M-80s? There was more than one way to skin a cat.

TOM

Tom pulled the pickup to a stop in front of the house, its white paint and wrap-around porch looking fresh as the day he left. The building's shadow stretched across the field as the sun worked its way toward evening. He got out of the truck, a chill breeze wrapping him and stealing his warmth.

He climbed the steps and found the front door locked, knocked, then peered through a window. The rooms inside appeared lifeless and dull, forgotten snapshots.

The papers were dead weight in his pocket. He pulled them out, shuffled the contract to the rear, and reread the letter. No contact for almost a decade, then Kyle leaves these empty words for him with Aunt Harriet. Who did his brother think he was?

Tom stuffed the papers back in his pocket, wrinkling them a little. A childish thing to do, but cramming them away made him feel a little better. He got out his cell phone, called Kyle's office, and started back toward the truck. "C'mon. Pick up the phone."

He kicked and scratched at the gravel driveway, pacing in a tight circle as he listened to the phone ring. "Damn. Where are you? Why won't you answer? What the hell—"

"Hello?"

"Kyle?"

"Who is this?" Kyle sounded annoyed, maybe a little indignant.

Tom stopped circling. He needed to slow down and stay calm, not start an argument. Kyle knew damned well who it was. Tom played the hand anyhow. "It's your brother. Can we talk?"

"Sure."

Kyle's voice strained in irritation against the single word. It bore something heavier as well. Pity? Maybe. Regardless, already Kyle's tone grated Tom to the very soles of his feet. "I know it's been rough, and I've been away for too long. Can you listen to me a sec, though? I'm out here at the house and it's locked up solid. I got your letter today—a fucking letter? That's how you let me know you're going to sell the place? A goddamned fucking letter? We have to work this out. You can't pawn this land off without talking about... you know." So much for staying calm.

"It's for sale. Pop has been going over the edge for a long time. I thought about this for months. Had you been around, I would have talked to you about it. That's what brothers do—talk to each other. You weren't here. I met with the Lodge board. They had their chance to buy the land. They weren't interested. No one is. The house is old, the Lodge building's a burden, and with Pop gone... well, it's time to unload it all and move on. I don't plan to stick around long enough to find out what else happens."

Tom circled the pickup once, lit up a smoke, and tapped the lighter on the hood. "Yeah, sure. Let's forget the whole thing and move on. Pop put a... a *bullet* in his head and you hear a starting pistol. Is that it? Time for you to start your life now? You stayed. Not my fault. I had to leave."

He pulled the phone away and looked across the field at

the old brick Lodge, squatting in shadows like a dark reflection of the farmhouse. This wasn't going well. Why couldn't he keep his cool?

Tom sat down hard in the gravel and took a long drag from his smoke, burning it almost to the filter. Should he mention his run-in with Cassy? Probably not. It might get him an upper hand. More likely Kyle would hang up. He was doing a fine enough job of pissing Kyle off already. And what did he expect? Did he think Kyle would welcome him home with open arms and relinquish the house? No, of course not. "Shit." He let the smoke drift away with the curse, feeling stupid and cold, like the plastic in his hand.

Tom raised the phone again. "I'm sorry. Are you still there?" Silence. He leaned his head back against the pickup, closed his eyes, and flicked his butt across the driveway. "For Christ's sake."

"I'm still here." Kyle no longer sounded annoyed, only angry. "I don't need this from you. Whatever your deal is, I don't want anything to do with it.

"We should have let it go sooner. I don't like it any more than you do. I've been here the whole time. I'll say it again. Where the hell have you been?"

"If you don't like—"

"Don't say anything more. I don't care. Sign or save it for the probate judge. I already made my case. You can do the same. It's going. I have a buyer lined up. This train was rolling long before you got to town. Me, I'm done with it. Time to cash out and move on." The line clicked. Just like Kyle to get the last word whatever it took.

Tears threatened at the edges of Tom's eyes. He dropped the phone and rubbed at both temples. This wasn't what he wanted at all. Maybe he should have gone to Kyle's office instead. Then what? Would the conversation have turned out any differently? Probably not. He lit another cigarette, his mouth still dry and funky from the last one. He needed to think. Sitting in the cold gravel smoking until his lungs hurt wasn't the way to do it. He pitched the smoke and took a final look at the house. Unable to do anything more, he climbed in the truck and left for Aunt Harriet's place. Maybe she had beer.

KYLE

yle hung up. What a great day. He oversold the Thompsons on life insurance then his brother's call came along and killed the buzz. He swiveled his black leather high back away from the window to his desk where a slightly used bottle of Maker's Mark stalked an empty plastic tumbler.

Fucked up families were the sort of thing drinking was made for. Kyle poured a double, recapped the bottle, and slid it back into a drawer. The whiskey burned his throat. When it struck his belly, the warmth was heaven.

What the hell was Tom doing? The loser was going to screw everything up. Why wouldn't he sign the contract?

Kyle got up and went to the door of his little office. His agency was a small section in the strip mall on the edge of town no bigger than a closet. It was enough, though. Selling insurance didn't require a lot of space, just a place to make people wait and a place to close deals. He poked his head out into the waiting room, where the secretary's desk guarded his office from two chairs, a magazine-littered coffee table, and the front door.

"Cheryl, knock or buzz when my last appointment shows. No calls." He flashed his perfect whites and added a little wink as he shut the door. The door muffled her response. He didn't understand what she said, nor did he care.

Kyle locked the door and returned to his desk. He took a pair of scissors from the desk and spun around to face a framed stock photo of the President hung low on the wall. Once removed, the picture revealed a patch in the drywall, recently painted to match the rest of the room, still a little too fresh to blend in.

He wanted answers. He hated not having them, not knowing what's going on. The land, the house, and even the old shit-worn Lodge were so close to turning into his lottery ticket. So close.

Kyle took the Monte Blanc from his breast pocket and sketched a cartoon face on the wall—Tom's face as he remembered it from years ago. He slid the open scissors across the drawing, scratching a bright line of white from one round eye to the other, then picked at the gash with his free hand, pulling paint away in little chips.

Kyle pictured the house, the old Lodge, and Pop on the unusually warm February evening when they had it out. Had Pop already planned to spread his brains across the barn wall even as they stood there arguing? Or did Pop wait until later to come up with his solution?

Kyle drew the scissors across a second time, not half an inch from the first. The blade cut a little slower as he dug a little deeper, and a few more chunks of white and brown fell away. He felt better, but not great. He pulled the bottle of bourbon back out and took a big swig, steeping in the heat.

The bottle sat uncapped as Kyle turned back to face the wall and cut a third time. There were no thoughts to go with it, only a primitive desire to fight for what he believed was his. More spackle and paint fell to the floor, and Kyle imaged the chunks as fresh drops of blood. Then a gaggle of thoughts emerged from nowhere, bringing with it fluttering paranoia.

Had Tom talked to Cassy? Was that his game? His brother wouldn't spill his guts, would he?

Kyle slammed the scissors into the wall, point first, striking a support beam and digging in deep. He bit back a scream as he pulled the scissors out, then drove them in again and again, trying to rebalance his mind with each new blow, until he convinced himself Tom wasn't that stupid.

Cheryl knocked and jiggled the handle. "You okay? Mr. Petersen is here." Her voice came through the door, distant and muffled.

"Tell him I'll be right there." Kyle pulled the scissors out of the wall, nicking his palm as his hand slipped from fresh sweat. One more thing to bring this day down. He found an old box of Band-Aids and sealed the little cut, then cleaned the scissors with an old napkin and rehung the picture. He snuck a final sip from the bottle before tucking it away.

Kyle crossed the room and looked at himself in the full-length mirror hanging on the back of the door. He practiced a smile and ran both hands through his hair, smoothing it to perfection. "Who's a winner? You are." The smile wasn't his best, but it was damned well good enough for cheap-ass Petersen.

He spied a couple drops of blood on the palm of his hand, licked them away, and smoothed his hair a final time.

"That's right. You're a goddamned winner." He winked at the mirror, opened the door, and stepped through.

"John Petersen, how have you been?" Kyle was all teeth.

CASSY

assy pulled her Hyundai off Outpost Road and up the gravel drive. She cut the engine and stared at her little ranch house. A sink full of dishes and a needy iguana waited for her inside those chipped gray walls and filthy windows.

Seeing Tom again stirred something inside her. She thought it wouldn't, hoped she would be okay. She was wrong. The sight of him made her warm in spots, and she no longer knew for sure which parts were angry and which parts were... otherwise.

The surrounding woods cast long shadows over the house and driveway as the afternoon grew late. She rested her eyes and enjoyed the coolness of the shade for a few minutes, then dragged herself from the car and went inside.

She hung the courier bag next to the gun belt on the coat rack, slipped off her shoes and cast them aside. Her feet were thumping heat. How long since she'd worn heels? Not long enough.

A pile of mail lay on the floor by the door. She scooped it up, headed to the kitchen, and tucked her leftovers in the fridge next to a carton of soured milk. She sorted out the junk and put the only good thing—the new issue of Guns & Ammo—on the dinette.

Cassy took a mug from the sink, rinsed it, and poured herself a cup of cold coffee from the pot brewed before work. She sat down at the table and leafed through the magazine as she sipped her drink, stopping on an article about the new Beretta Storm. Reading did not keep her focus long.

Where did Tom go for all those years? Why didn't he keep in touch? When she questioned Kyle, he claimed ignorance on Tom's whereabouts. What awful thing happened to cause even his own family to lose track of him?

Cassy gave up on the magazine and went to her bedroom where her best buddy Herbie lived in a little aquarium atop a worn dresser. She took an orange from a bowl, peeled it, and tossed in a few pieces. The thick iguana crept over and gnawed on a wedge.

Cassy sat on the edge of her unmade bed and ate the rest of the orange, trying to ignore the manila folder on the nightstand. She promised herself earlier she wouldn't look in it, not today. She needed to settle and get used to the idea of Tom being back in town.

The simple little folder called to her.

Herbie let out a heavy breath.

"You said it, buddy." Cassy scooted back on the bed, crossed her legs and, unable to stop, grabbed the folder. She fanned the contents out on the bed: a missing persons report, an old school photo of her cousin Alissa, and Sheriff Monterey's notes detailing the investigation.

Everything about the case looked solid. The whole family thought Aunt Sandy was a grade-A nut case. Their reasons ranged from too much bible-school as a child to too much liquor and sex as an adult. No one spoke of Alissa's father— who or where he was. The sheriff's report contained notes on alleged sexual abuse by her mother. No hard evidence ever surfaced, though. Family lore and gossip served as facts in the case, unverified snippets of tribal knowledge. In the end, the sheriff figured Alissa ran away.

Monterey's conclusion never sat right with Cassy. She knew her cousin, knew there were problems, sure, but she also knew Alissa loved her mother in spite of everything. The girl wasn't one to run away.

Cassy picked up the school photo, taken their junior year, and looked at the little blond girl in it. She remembered the day it was taken. Alissa showed up in her usual outfit—charcoal dress, white socks, and black shoes. At lunch, the girls went to Cassy's house where they picked out a denim skirt and pink oxford for Alissa, teased her hair, and did her makeup. Once Aunt Sandy saw the photos, she refused to pay, and Alissa missed three days of school. When Alissa finally returned, she claimed the flu. None of the kids believed her even if the adults did.

How much alike they looked as they got older. The memory of the rumors spread around school brought tears to Cassy's eyes. Had they shared a father? Cassy never worked up to confronting dad. Asking would admit there might be some truth to the stories, and just putting the question out there would dent too many relationships beyond repair.

Cassy gathered the pictures and papers, tucked them in the folder, and put them back on the nightstand. A cool gust of air blew through the window and called to her. She stripped out of the dress, put on some running shorts, a loose t-shirt, and her Nikes. A long run should clear her head, so she headed outside to lose herself.

SHANE

The boys stopped at the edge of the highway, pausing as they always did to soak in the dark mystery of the woods before them. Without speaking, they worked their way down the bank and entered the flats, a muddy expanse of wetlands separating route 56 from the Ohio River. Washington Heights had only one shitty video store and was miles from the nearest movie theater, which left the river as the prime hangout spot. A boy could get lost for days in discovery of the murky creatures writhing and wiggling for survival in the mud on the riverbanks.

Shane led as Lonny and Alex stayed a good distance behind. They trudged through the woods for almost an hour, stopping to rest only when the fat afternoon sun played near the horizon and every shadow stretched out for miles. The town lay forgotten behind them, the buzz of mayflies and the screech of katydids the only reminders of life.

Shane set the gas can down in a lone patch of mud. The muck burped as the can sank a little. That was one heavy mofo, as dad would have said. He should have made the dumb one carry it the whole way. No matter. He earned honors on this one. Maybe he would let one of them carry the crispy prize back to Ms. Lyons. Or maybe he would make one of them eat it.

Alex stood a few feet off, unzipped his pants, and pissed on the withered remains of a tree.

Lonny sat down on a log next to Shane and pulled off a sneaker. He tipped it and a couple little balls of hardened clay rolled out. "What are you laughing at?"

"Guess you haven't figured out my riddle yet." Shane watched as wires misfired in Lonny's head. He knew the kid would never get it, at least not until he saw the other half of the puzzle.

"I think I got it." Alex shook and zipped up. "I don't see any cats or dogs out here."

"More than once and you're playing with it." Shane laughed again. "And you're right. You don't see any cats or dogs out here. It's just you, me, Lonny, and five gallons of gas." To make the punch line, he picked up the can, spun off the top, and splashed a little gas on Lonny's leg.

Lonny jumped up. "Hey, watch it!" He hobbled away from Shane, sneaker still in hand, trying not to get his sock muddy. He found another log and sat down. "Great, you asshole."

"Put your shoe on, you pussy." Shane flipped Lonny a double-barreled bird.

Lonny did as he was told. The shoe went on, and he grimaced as he tied it in a double knot.

Alex shuffled over and squatted next to Lonny. "It's not so bad. I got gas on me once. Remember? Dad let me run the pump at the Sunoco, and it spurted out all over my hand. Stunk like hell, stung a little, too. It stopped after a bit." Alex ran a hand across the cuff of Lonny's jeans.

"Enough, you assholes. Get your hand off him. He'll be fine. Do you want the surprise or not?"

Lonny and Alex both looked at him. Good, that got their attention. The little pricks would sit there all day fawning over each other if he let them.

Alex stood up. "Okay. Where's the cat? You got Mr. Meshach stashed here, don't you? You know if dad finds out, it's the collar for you."

Shane hated to have his bubble burst. Alex wasn't supposed to say, and the way he asked without asking—like dad—really pissed Shane off.

Shane spoke quietly. "Yeah, I got the cat. And dad isn't going to find out. Who's going to tell? If he does, we'll *all* wear the collars." He sat on a stump and glared at Alex.

Something rustled in the hollow of the stump. His hand slipped in and searched about until he felt the old crinkly plastic grocery bag hidden there earlier that morning. A rough claw swept across the bag and dug into the tender flesh between the thumb and forefinger. Now it puts up a fight? The little fucking cat had been so easy to catch. A can of tuna and you're every kitty's friend.

Shane slapped the bag and a soft howl clambered out into the cooling late afternoon. Not caring if the cat lived or died, he clenched the bag, along with a lump of furry meat, and dragged it out. The little beast inside writhed and yowled as Shane chucked it to the ground.

"You can't." Lonny paled. "Dude. It's a cat. It's somebody's pet."

"Yup." Shane kicked the bag and the creature inside yelped. "It is definitely a cat."

Before either of his brothers could move, Shane hefted the can of gasoline and sloshed a healthy puddle onto the bag. He was going to torch the fucking thing. Nothing short of a flash flood would save it. Gas coated his hands and dribbled down his shirt. He dropped the can and more fuel splashed onto his pants. "Do you remember my riddle, Lonny? How do you make a cat sound like a dog?"

The twins jumped to their feet. Alex made for the cat while Lonny scrambled to get the gas can. Shane kicked the can, sending a plume of gasoline into the air and showering back down on all three.

Shane pulled the lighter from his pocket.

Emaciated shadows twined and stretched around them. Shane saw dark flames in them, gray upon gray, wrapping and warping the landscape.

He wondered why on earth this seemed like a good idea? The thought slipped away slick like a river toad before Shane could stop himself.

He flicked the lighter.

Alex shouted.

Lonny scuttled away.

Trails of gasoline blossomed in all directions. Fire burned up from his feet. Flames engulfed Lonny and Alex. One boy ran into the woods—which one was impossible to tell through the pain and fire—the other toward the river.

Shane screamed.

LEWIS

June 14, 2007

Dull summer heat lingered in the evening air. Lewis Burton sat on the Adirondack in his yard sipping iced tea. Kyle dropped by for dinner earlier. He left as soon as his plate was clean. Even though he never stayed long, it was nice to see the boy outside Lodge every now and again, nice to believe he still had a little something left for his old man.

Lewis rarely slept more than five hours during the long summer nights. Maybe allergies kept him awake, or maybe too many cigarettes. The night felt like it might stretch on for days. The tea made things worse, but damned if he couldn't enjoy a nice drink now and then.

He stared across a quarter-mile of field at the dark building. Most of the sheep were down for the night. A few bleated and straggled between him and the Lodge.

Loneliness settled in. Tom would have made a good farmer—great with animals, a true caregiver. Kyle needed more than farming. He had no connection to the land or any sense of the surrounding creatures.

Lewis turned his attention to the Lodge to fight off old regrets. Most of the sandstone foundation was patched and covered with concrete to stem off erosion. One section of the east wall remained untouched where a fresh opening appeared some months ago in the crumbling sandstone. He should have covered it right away. For some reason he found it difficult to start the work. Maybe sealing the hole felt final, like closing off a last hope. Or maybe laziness came with his old age.

Lewis sipped more of his tea. To hell with it. He pulled out a pack of unfiltered Pall Malls, the kind that made a man feel like a man. Doc told him to quit at every check-up. At his age, with nothing much left to lose, what was the point? Smoking made him feel good, even with the occasional coughing fits.

The sun slipped down as he smoked his cigarette and drank his tea. A smattering of light painted the front of the Lodge and glinted off the bronze Square and Compasses set above the doors, poking holes in the evening.

Lewis wanted to see the Lodge. He didn't want to go back in the house, filled with ghosts of his boys and long–dead wife. An empty darkness moved in there years ago and threatened to swallow him every night with cold, clammy hands.

He rose and went to the pole barn where a seldom-used workshop lay at the back. He shimmied past a rusty Ford tractor, cleared off the workbench, and dug around in an old wooden toolbox for a flashlight. Sometimes the cracks ran deep.

The flashlight beam danced across the clover as Lewis crossed the field toward the Lodge. The last light of day continued to trickle away until darkness washed down the face of the old building. By the time he reached the front steps, his bones ached to the marrow, forcing him to squat on the stoop for a spell.

Old fool. What was he doing? He lit another Pall Mall. Half-way through it his lungs raised a phlegmy protest, making him toss the butt onto the gravel driveway. Arthritic joints complained as he rose and went inside.

The foyer lights sputtered a few times then settled into a soft fluorescence. A pool of shadows beckoned as he approached the stairs and descended. At the bottom, Lewis turned on the row of hanging lights, casting the basement in a dirty glow. Sandstone from the foundation coated everything with a fine dust, and the pillars, placed at regular intervals, made the space awkward—a hollow cavern used to store broken furniture and forgotten memorabilia.

Lewis meandered to the back wall, where the foundation was split open wide enough for a man to slip through. Two bags of Quikrete sat propped against the wall next to a big orange bucket, a mixing paddle, and an electric drill.

Sandstone crumbled away under hand as he steadied himself against the wall and bent to inspect the crack, piercing it with the flashlight beam. Somehow, the damage looked wider and deeper than when he brought the concrete down.

The split ran through the foundation and into the limestone bedrock on the other side. Beyond, Lewis saw only grayness, like an early morning fog. The rift ran deep and wide.

The fit looked tight—like stuffing a two-pound bag with three pounds of manure. Sleep was a stranger tonight, and if left idle, Lewis would drag himself down with melancholy. If he did not peek, he would come back in the morning with different sensibilities and plug the thing up, always left to wonder what was back there. The troublesome thing looked like it might widen and split until the whole damned building collapsed.

Muscles complained as Lewis hunkered down on hands and knees to work his way in. He exhaled and held his breath to make himself thinner. The foundation stones crumbled anyhow as he squeezed through to the bedrock.

The opening widened a little, enough so he could breathe again. The rough rock scraped through his old tee shirt, ripping it in spots, the flesh beneath yielding thin beads of blood. His jeans held up only slightly better. The rock still chewed at them as he worked forward. He felt like the worst kind of idiot. He would get himself stuck like a rabbit in a fence, and there was no one around to hear his death scream. Backing out was probably a good idea.

His eyes adjusted to the light as he scooted backward. Able to see the far end of the crevice was within reach, he changed direction once more.

Lewis worked forward, shuffling the flashlight ahead, wiggling against the rough stone, and becoming numb to the pain. It felt like 10 minutes, claustrophobia knocking on his ass. Then he was out.

He knelt several feet up from the ground on a pile of broken limestone and shale. What opened this hole? Earthquake? No memory of tremors in the area. Then what? The land was old. No telling how long the crack had been there. Maybe it was always there, waiting for the last of the sandstone to fall, waiting for the right person to come along.

Rocks scattered as Lewis swung his legs around and stretched them out. He sat still and listened as the chunks of stone settled. Then, convinced everything would hold, he shone the flashlight around.

Brown and yellow limestone walls curved away on either side. Dampness permeated the air and soft dirt covered the ground. Lewis sat on the cusp of a large circular chamber with a solid stone table in the center. He swept the beam up the walls to the smooth, low-hung ceiling. Not a chisel mark anywhere. His palms began to sweat and the muscles in his neck tensed. The room swam, so he put a hand on the wall for support until the vertigo passed. The surface felt glassy, like the face of a statue carved by a master craftsman.

Despite the stale smell, the air was breathable, like the heavy scent of the sheep barn. It was cool as well, almost pleasant as a slight breeze from the crevice tickled his neck. He shone the light across the room and weaved it back and forth until it came to rest on a north-facing archway. The ravine lay somewhere beyond the opening, maybe a hundred or so yards. He was reluctant to go through, knowing what he might find at the other end. He kept it as an option, though. If the situation turned sour, at least there was another way out.

More rocks scattered and kicked up a sizable cloud of dust as he scooted down. The debris gave way, and Lewis lost control and shot down the remaining few yards. Both feet hit the cavern floor and he toppled over, landing face first in the dirt. The flashlight rolled forward and clanked against the base of the table.

He got to his feet, spat out gritty saliva, and pounded dirt from his clothes. Damned idiot. Should have turned back. He was going to hurt himself if he wasn't more careful.

Fresh pain forced Lewis to limp as he retrieved his flashlight and examined the table. In the middle sat a smooth oblong stone, green with streaks of dark red. The shadows it cast wavered, as if the light bent to avoid touching the tiny obelisk. He reached out, unable to resist. The air around him felt tense and electric, like right before lightning strikes. His hand tingled as it drew near the stone.

A penetrating cold swept through Lewis as he grasped the rock and struggled to work it loose. God only knew how long it had sat there.

A fine layer of dirt coated the stone, and the smoothness of its surface made it difficult for Lewis to get a good grip. At last, after twisting with what little strength his gnarled hands still had, the cursed thing scraped free.

His strength drained away, and a flood of ill memories surrounded him as he fell to his knees. Kyle's birth and Charlene's death; the face of every animal he put down; a poor bloodied girl who never had a chance. Then the images vanished back into the one safe room in his mind where painful thoughts were imprisoned, leaving him dry and empty.

Lewis regained his feet and turned the heavy stone in his hand, rubbing a thumb across its surface. Maybe Elana would be interested. She might even find something about it in all her books. If he ever got out of this stinking hole.

He swept the beam of the flashlight up to the archway. The beam petered out into nothingness even though air flowed from the crevice, through the cavern, and out the doorway. Which way?

Lewis swung the beam back to the threatening debris. Maybe it would break his bones and leave him there to die by inches from starvation or dehydration. The archway must come out on the bank of the river.

Only one way to be sure. He turned off the flashlight, letting the obsidian shadows engulf him. The very air pressed down. The flashlight felt heavy and the stone even heavier. How long before he was certain? A minute is a minute the world over, but that next minute dragged on as he counted out eternal seconds in a slow, steady rhythm. Where the crevice should have been he saw a whisper of light offering the kind of comfort he used to find in bourbon.

Eyes now adjusted, Lewis turned back to the archway where the darkness thickened into a heavy fog. He counted off the last ten seconds and, as he got to sixty, shadows upon shadows unfolded. The emptiness reached toward him, a thin hand with dark skin pulled tight over darker bones, and with it came the distant buzz of angry insects.

He turned the flashlight on again, and light splayed across the stone. Whatever reached out to him disappeared. He scanned the opening and spotted a small nest in the corner— the familiar organ-pipes of mud daubers. The well of the archway still resisted penetration from the light. It didn't matter—he wouldn't be able to bring himself to go through it even if the walls started to collapse.

The pile turned out easier than expected. His feet found all the right spots, his legs held steady, and his balance stayed true even with both hands full. The crevice was a bigger challenge, but manageable. As he worked through it, the rift opened to let him pass. The flow of air, too, pushed him from behind and prodded him outward like a dusty old womb ejecting the last of its brood.

He stood once again in the basement, flashlight in one hand and a chunk of something he didn't understand in the other. What was this strange little stone?

Lewis turned to face the foundation crack, fighting off intense disorientation. Did he come from there? He gazed down at the rock. Had it fallen from the crack or did he crawl in to get it? Maybe. Or maybe the caffeine and nicotine were too much for him this night. Maybe he should take Doc's advice and give up the last few invigorating things in his well-worn life.

Lewis returned home with the stone and tucked it away on the upper shelf of his bookcase. The stone made one brief journey the next day when he took it to share with Ms. Lyons at the library. She refused to touch the oddment or let Lewis leave it in the building, snapping a Polaroid instead to use in her research. He returned it to the shelf, where it sat until the first Lodge meeting in the fall, where he presented it as a gift, only able to recall finding it in the basement while patching a hole.

TOM

The smell of fresh-baked carrot bread greeted Tom as he entered the little cottage. The television played low in the living room, and Aunt Harriet hummed Amazing Grace in the kitchen. If only Kyle would let him stay in the house, maybe he could get some peace and quiet. No doubt, Harriet would want to talk.

He slipped by the kitchen and down the hallway to the spare bedroom. Once inside, he shut the door as quietly as possible and dumped the makeshift journal on the bed. He held the rag-swaddled rock, and it emanated the sickening-warmth of a feverish child, so he tossed it next to the journal.

The sight of them made his stomach churn, and yet he couldn't bring himself to tuck them away. What was Pop doing? He knew he should read the journal. He couldn't bring himself to the task yet. Though it might hold some answers, the thought of seeing those last words felt so... final. Instead of squirreling them away, he moved them to the edge of the bed, kicked off his shoes, and settled back.

Before Tom could close his eyes, Aunt Harriet knocked. "You okay? I thought I heard you come in... We missed you at the lunch. People asked about you."

Why couldn't she let him rest? She of all people should know how rough his situation was. Tom rolled his neck to ease some of the tension.

"C'mon, honey. Open up and let me in. You can't hide forever." She knocked harder. "I brought you a little something to eat."

"Okay, already. I'm coming." Tom put the journal and stone on the nightstand and answered the door.

The old woman greeted him with one eye squinted and lips tight-pressed. "Well?"

"Come on in." He stepped aside, and she waddled in with a plate full of carrot bread in one hand and a cold six-pack in the other. She handed them to Tom, brushed a t-shirt from an old recliner, and plopped down.

Tom tried to stay polite with the old woman. Despite knowing he was lucky to have her, every nerve in his body fired in triple time. All he wanted was to settle back, soak in alcohol, and drift away.

"What do you want?" His voice broke on the last word.

"It isn't healthy, honey." She plucked a piece of bread from the plate. Crumbs tumbled down her chin as she took a bite. "You've been holed up in here for almost two days. Today's the first I seen you outside these four walls, and I thought you might finally be getting some legs under you about this whole thing.

"I know it's been difficult—nothing tougher, I suppose. You can't keep all that sorrow bottled up. Besides, this old house isn't the place to improve your mood. You spoke with the Fielding girl after the service. Why don't you call her, honey?"

Tom slumped onto the bed and opened a beer. "Shit." He took a swig then caught himself. "Sorry, Aunt Harriet."

"Well if I'm going to listen to you curse, you may as well offer me a beer."

"Of course." Tom felt a little embarrassed as he twisted the cap off another beer and handed it over. She was right. She shouldn't have to listen to his sailor's mouth.

Harriet pushed herself from the chair. "These old bones ain't what they used to be." She took the beer, sat back down, and took a big drink. "Ah, good stuff." Thick spittle flew from her lips.

"I suppose I could call her." Tom pulled out Cassy's business card, got the phone from the nightstand, and started to dial.

Harriet reached over and clicked the receiver. "Honey, not right now. Tomorrow, maybe. You're in no shape to sell yourself. You look like one of old Chuck's poop bombs. He sure pushes out nasty stuff, and you're acting like you ate some of it."

Tom hung up the phone and lay back on the bed. Of course he shouldn't call right now. Hadn't Cassy walked out on him at the diner? He needed a little space and Cassy seemed to know it.

They sat in silence. Harriet nursed her beer while Tom stared at the ceiling. Outside the window, crickets chirped and trees rustled. Tom closed his eyes to let his mind slip away. It was nice not to think about anything.

Harriet broke the silence. "What's really troubling you honey?"

Tom didn't want to drag himself away from the emptiness. The question overwhelmed him. What wasn't troubling him would be an easy one. There were simply too many pains and fears, and he didn't know where to start. He shrugged.

If Harriet noticed, she didn't let on. "Can't say I'd have good advice, but I can listen a bit. Like my pappy used to say, 'If you got beers, I got ears.'"

Tom sat up and took a big drink. He ran the cool bottle across his forehead to fight off the feverish feeling. "I don't know where to start. I'm not sure you'd understand. Hell, I'm not sure I understand."

"It's okay. Start at the beginning." Harriet emptied her beer, pulled a piece of carrot bread from the plate, and nibbled at it.

Tom took Kyle's letter from his back pocket—the one from the court authorizing sale of Pop's land, the one asking for Tom's signature—and handed it to her. "I called him, tried to reason with him. He wasn't having any of it. Kyle's going to sell it all off and he won't even talk it over first. He's such a..." Tom stopped himself short, not wanting to curse again in front of dear old Aunt Harriet.

She slipped on the pair of tortoise-shell glasses hung around her neck and read the papers. When finished, she set them on the nightstand. "So what? Your dad's gone sweetheart. As for the old Lodge building—I say let someone else have it. Nothing good ever came from it."

Heat flashed across Tom's face. He chugged the rest of his beer and bought a moment to cool off before saying something he might regret. What could she know anyhow? She lived here since God was a child and she spent a lot of time with the Burton boys, but did she really know them? Some secrets we even kept from ourselves. Kyle's letter was about more than Pop. It had to be. He opened another beer, considering what to say next.

"While you're up." Harriet waved her empty bottle.

Tom handed her another, this time unopened.

"Makin' me work for them?" She struggled with the cap.

"It's not right. He shouldn't sell the place. Kyle was working on this before Pop... before, you know. I mean, how could he? I never cared much for the old Lodge. Dad had a real thing for it. Kyle did too, I thought. I mean, it's family in a way, along with the house and this town. We grew up here. Kyle has no right. Once they're gone..."

Once they're gone, what? He had nothing left here. Why should he care? A person can't leave a place for a decade and expect everything to stay the same. Even so, a part of him still regretted not coming home sooner.

Harriet twisted the top off at last and took a sip. She kept the cap in her free hand. "Honey, I know more than you might think. The Lodge was the place to be back when you were where just a firefly in your daddy's eye. I never had the notion to join any of them clubs, but I spent some time working at the Lodge on the side. I met your folks there. Even made it to a good number of parties, and they threw some zingers." She stopped there and gazed at the bottle cap. A faint smile traced across her lips then disappeared as she gripped the cap tighter.

"Sweetheart, you ever wonder why we put a building up one place as opposed to another? What makes one spot better? Oh sure, many things—practical reasons, my pappy would say—make it easier to build somewhere. This isn't some strip mall we're talking about. Let's suppose one spot *is* as good as the other. What then?" Harriet relaxed her hand revealing a perfect imprint of the bottle-cap on her palm.

"Something in the land, maybe." She spoke quietly— almost to herself—then looked at Tom. Her gaze slipped right through him, made him feel thin and insufficient like a hospital gown. "Let it go. There isn't anything good for you there. There isn't anything good for any of us. The world has moved on." She slipped the glasses from her nose and let them fall to her breast. "Tell me, if it weren't for your dad, would Kyle have joined?"

Tom studied her face. Why was she talking about where the Lodge was built? Did it matter? He didn't have an answer for her, so he shook his head a little and shrugged.

"Sweetheart, I know you think you have something special up there, some deep roots. Your dad, for one. We all want to be like our mommies and daddies. You need to let it go. Things in this town aren't what they used to be."

Tom felt hot tears on their way and swallowed hard.

Harriet shrugged and drew a ragged hand across her plump face. Her eyes were a little red and puffy. "Bygones. The past is the past, honey."

Tom nodded and lowered his head. "I suppose. It's just—"

"Well ,what do you have here?"

Tom looked up at the old woman. Her empty beer sat on the nightstand, and instead of the bottle, she held the wrapped stone in one hand and the journal in the other, eyes fixated on the rock as if it were a chunk of gold.

"Cassy gave them to me. They were at Pop's." Even though he wanted to shout at her to put them down and get out, he needed her to stay. "Please put them down."

She peered at him. "Well I'm not going to hurt them, sweetheart. I'm curious." She set the stone on her lap and opened the journal. "Looks like a diary. You read it yet?"

Tom shook his head. "I don't want to know what's in there. Kyle says Pop was going crazy toward the end, and Pop never was much for writing. It's probably either some anger-filled rant at me for leaving town or a bunch of nonsense."

Harriet read a little. "Then I don't suppose you'd mind if I borrowed it." She took the stone from her lap, rose, and headed for the door.

The question came out before Tom could stop it. "Aunt Harriet... did you and Pop ever have a thing?"

At the door, she paused and looked back at Tom. Her eyes twinkled. "The past is the past, honey. Good night."

57

DORTHEA

orthea's eyelids fluttered open. Harsh sunlight poured in between the curtains and pounded her eyes. Sleep evaded her the night before, as it did most nights as of late, and though still tired and drained, she forced herself to rise.

She rolled out of bed, mindful of her tremendous belly. The loose, sweat soaked nightgown clung to her body, and her damp hair sagged to her shoulders in thick, dark locks. She stopped wearing panties a couple of months ago, unable to fit in the ones she owned and too goddamned poor to get new ones. Jessica offered to buy her some maternity granny-panties several times. What was the use, though? Dorthea had nowhere to go until this little bugger came out.

She padded from the cramped bedroom she and Jessica shared. Her feet felt like balloons filled with maple syrup, and fresh bruises ached with each tentative step. God, how did she wind up pregnant? She was always so careful.

The light aroma of blueberry pancakes mixed with the heavier scent of spiced sausage filled the combined kitchenette and living room.

Jessica cooked at the dual-burner stove, clad only in a tank top and boxer shorts. "I thought you might be up soon." She flipped a pancake. "There's a short stack and links on the table. No milk left. I used the last on these, so you'll have to make do with water. I'll pick some up on my way home tonight."

Dorthea envied Jessica's firm ass, plump breasts, and abdomen tight enough to bounce a quarter. Aside from hair color, she and Jessica used to be a matched set. Now look at her. No guy would ever pay to see her dance again. Hell, no guy would ever look at her for free again. She walked over, rested her belly in the small of Jessica's back, and hugged with sweaty arms.

"Okay, enough." Jessica peeled away. "You're going to get me all yucky, and I already showered."

Dorthea grunted and stepped back. Was she so ugly? Women were supposed to glow when they were pregnant, weren't they? Sure, the body got all bloated and lumpy. Even so, wasn't the new life growing inside supposed to bring out a special beauty? Maybe this baby missed the memo, because this fat hard lump in her belly siphoned off every bit of energy, giving nothing back.

In spite of the constant thrum of nausea, Dorthea felt hungry. She sat at the table and shoveled pancakes and sausage down her gullet. Syrup in one hand, fork in the other, she devoured her breakfast in the space of minutes. When finished, she looked up to find Jessica engrossed in the show.

"Well, hungry hippo, do you want more?"

Dorthea nodded. Although her stomach pressed against her lungs, she felt hungrier than when she sat down. Something deep within her churned and bubbled in agreement. Then something in there moved. "Oh! He kicked!" She waved Jessica over.

Jessica brought a second stack of pancakes, set them on Dorthea's empty plate, and pulled up a chair so they sat side-by-side. She rested a tentative hand on the Dorthea's belly, feeling for the baby, and they both waited in silence. A few seconds later, the baby kicked again.

Jessica blushed. "I felt it. She's a strong little sucker."

"Or he." The baby kicked again, and this time Dorthea felt a little foot connect with a rib. She yelped and rocked back. Several more kicks followed, each connecting in painful ways with organs or ribs. She stood to let gravity stretch her guts into a more comfortable place.

"Damn, that fucking hurt." Dorthea rubbed her belly through the threadbare gown.

"Yeah, about those pains." Jessica stood and offered an arm for support. "You have to go to the doctor. We've put this off long enough. There's the hospital over in Charleston or Doc Crandall's clinic out near Washington Heights. He owes us after the way they treated us at the bachelor party. Look at you. You're beyond huge, way too big for the second trimester, I think. Aren't you worried? She's been kicking the crap out of you for weeks, you haven't been eating right, and... Well, honestly, I want to know."

The kicks subsided, leaving Dorthea feeling as if she had gone three rounds in a cage fight. She withered back into her chair. "I don't want to know. We're going to need money for after the baby comes, and I don't want to go anywhere near Washington Heights or creepy Doc Crandall. I know you insist no one touched me—except you, of course—but Jesus... If I didn't get pregnant at the party, then where?" The baby erupted in a fresh round, and Dorthea slipped from the chair to the floor. Before Jessica could help her up, Dorthea hiccupped and vomited a steaming pulp of blue and gray onto the linoleum.

Dorthea's throat stung as she coughed and spat to clear out

the after-taste. Even though she also tasted blood under the acidic bile, she said nothing. Jessica would insist on an ambulance.

Jessica brought a glass of water. "Here, drink this while I clean up."

Dorthea chugged in spastic gulps. Sweat poured down her face, the hum of nausea grew to a roar, and every muscle in her body twitched from exhaustion. "Help me back to bed, please."

Jessica finished wiping up the mess, then struggled to get Dorthea to her feet and back to the bedroom. Dorthea flopped down and stretched out on her left side to try to find some relief. No luck. Nothing she did helped the overstuffed feeling or her strained muscles.

"Just let me rest. I'll be better when you get home tonight." Dorthea offered a weak smile.

"Okay," Jessica said after giving her a long, uncertain look. "You rest. I'll be home late. I'm gonna work the club after my shift at Hooters. If you can, try to eat something. There are some chips in the cabinet and cold pizza in the fridge. Definitely drink some water." She stood to leave, stopped at the bedroom door, and looked back.

Dorthea thought Jessica looked like a movie star as soft sunlight played in her blond hair. She wanted to kiss her, but if Jessica pushed her away again... No, she couldn't deal with the possibility of rejection.

"And," Jessica added with a fresh smile and a wink, "stay the hell out of my beer."

Dorthea laughed as Jessica left and the baby set into another flurry of kicks. It all hurt so much.

SHANE

eat rippled over every inch of Shane's body, caressed every nerve, sinking into the pit of his brain. When he was four, a deep fever took him. The memories were little more than faded watercolors, painted in broad strokes and tacked askew to the walls of his mind.

The fever arrived during a warm winter bath. Mommy sat on the floor next to Shane and, as the burning crept through, the world became play dough. He remembered staring at his fingers. So far away, too large, thick with blood.

Water enveloped Shane as he slipped back and choked against the tide, trembling, lost in raging internal flames. Mommy scooped him out, bundled him up, and took him to the couch.

Mommy cradled and comforted him as Shane fought against the stifling heat of the towel and blankets. Daddy told him later the fever reached one hundred and three degrees. He remembered being torn from the harsh comfort of mommy and carried outside. So much glaring whiteness stung his eyes.

Daddy spoke incomprehensible words in harsh tones. Then stiff coldness fought back the fires as he dumped Shane in a snow bank.

Tonight the fires returned one hundred fold. Would they ever stop? The world—and Shane—once again turned into

Silly Putty®. Every inch of flesh squirmed and danced as his surroundings stripped away to darkness. Time dripped from every branch and rippled with the flow of the river.

A soothing hand touched Shane's forehead. Mud, cool and thick, smeared across his face, his arms, his torso. He coughed as chunks of it dripped into his mouth. A rough finger swiped his lips clean, and fresh cool air swarmed in.

Shane lay in darkness, hearing only his rough uneasy breaths and the chattering katydids as the heat seeped away.

"You will be fine." The voice sputtered and cracked. "Relax." Words of cold comfort, like daddy said so long ago as Shane lay in the snow bank.

"Thirsty," Shane whispered. Slow footfalls padded away and panic tickled at base of Shane's spine. He tried to move. Streamers of pain licked away at the raw, mud coated flesh. Another scream tried to escape him, failing to pass through his dry mouth. Shane wept without tears.

Whoever had arrived to help still lingered close by. Shane heard a kick, a grunt, and the crumble of clay underfoot followed by a distant splash. His saviour returned and trickled cool water on his lips.

Something heavy plopped down on the ground. Shane tried to open his eyes, his lids unable to break the cakes of mud gluing them shut. Rough hands returned with more mud. Thick words, senseless crowded syllables, seemed to pack down with the clay. Soon the sludge and voice crushed down upon him. Would they ever stop? Oh, please stop...

Handful after handful of sludge continued to pile upon him.

The washed-out memories of mommy and daddy oozed away as a new flame took hold. Who was doing this? Why him? Where were Alex and Lonny, why wouldn't they help?

A thick chunk of something warm and wet pushed through the muck and wedged between his lips.

"Eat."

Shane groaned and chewed the hunk of meat. The taste of copper and raw steak filled his mouth, making him gag. He lurched and heaved. The flesh worked its way down Shane's throat as if alive. As it slid down his gullet, the mud leeched away the pain. He swallowed, then struggled to speak again. "Who are you?"

"I am... no one."

The speaker rose and walked away. Shane waned toward unconsciousness.

Time froze. Mud dried.

He awoke an eternity later. Hardened clay held his mouth shut. A deep, dark shadow wrapped around his heart. The raw smell of earth filled him as the ground embraced him with the comfort of the grave. The heart of eternity beat once, a singular, infinite sound.

At last, rough hands cracked away the cocoon.

Stars glittered through the trees, each one cradled in an aura of red, the space between them cold and uninviting. A soft wind crept through the flats, rattling every branch it touched.

Shane blinked away the caked clay as an old man cleared the last of it. Charred flesh crackled—or was it still mud?—as Shane stretched out and propped himself with shaky elbows. At his feet stood the ghost of a boy dressed in a t-shirt and jeans.

"Do you see it?" The old man's words sputtered.

Shane turned to stare deep into gray eyes, rimmed with red, set deep into an ashen face. The old man smiled, showing a mouth full of wicked teeth tainted yellow and brown.

"Who is he?"

The old man stood, smoothed out his soiled tank top and faded green cargo pants. Filth coated him from top to bottom in one continuous smear. "He is you. Or was."

Shane looked back at the spirit as it wavered and folded in upon itself. The image collapsed like a punctured lung and disappeared with an almost audible pop. "Where'd he go?"

Shane struggled to stand. Although his flesh cracked and flaked, he felt no pain. Soft ash crumbled from his burnt lips as he licked at the dryness, his rough tongue only scouring the flesh. Shane stared at the shadows of the flats rushing to fill in the space where the ghost stood mere moments before.

The old man had not answered. Shane turned to ask again. Something in his saviour's smile made the words stop short of his lips. Did he really want to know?

"Do you remember much?" The old man raised a faint eyebrow. He held one hand in the other. A finger, the pinky, was missing and fresh blood dribbled from the wound.

"A little..."

"You had a name once. Would you like a new one?"

Shane shrugged. He searched for some feeling, some emotion about this whole thing. He found nothing. He had a body, a charred and peeling mess. There was also the ghost that had just vanished. What was he now? Shane Hanlon? Everything confused him and he blanked. A name? Which one gets the name—the ghost or the body?

The old man tore a small strip from his shirt and bound his hand. "How about we forget the name? Or you could stick with Shane." The words crackled like flames.

Even if this old man thought names unimportant, Shane felt lost without one. Names mattered. Things without names were nothing, weren't they? Maybe he wasn't Shane Hanlon any more. He was someone, though. Wasn't he? His body moved, words came from his mouth, and breath—although stale and cold—crossed his lips.

"A name? Please?"

The man stooped down and picked up a flat stone. "Nice skipping rocks you got here." He threw it out toward the river. The rock disappeared into the night followed by the soft plinks of several nice skips.

"C'mon. I have to have a name." Shane's skin crumbled and flaked as he shifted. One crispy toe cracked loose.

The old man picked up another flat rock and a short stick. He stepped toward the boy. "Then I will give you a name." He jabbed Shane's chest with the stick and began to write.

Shane jumped at first, surprised, then held still. There was no pain. Pus and blood, now boiled to a thick ichor, trailed down the makeshift stylus as the old man scratched out a series of letters. Shane just watched, eager for his new name.

When the old man finished, he dropped the stick and skipped the other stone into the darkness. "Now you have a name: DUGGAE."

Invisible threads wrapped around and bound Shane. What should have been scary as hell felt more like being smothered in blankets by mommy—harsh yet somehow comforting.

"When you finish my work, I will tell you what it means."

Shane nodded. It would be okay. He had a name, and for now, having a name was enough. He would do whatever the old man asked.

The old man leaned down and whispered into his ear.

KYLE

Dust floated in the sunlight streaming through the window above Kyle's king-sized bed, and the air reeked of sweat and stale beer. His head ached. His mouth tasted of cotton soaked in tar. Then there was the chick next to him. Shit. Why did he do this?

Kyle slipped out of bed, went to the bathroom, and took a leak. He flushed then realized the door was open and pulled it shut. They weren't supposed to stay until morning. Why was she still there?

The hateful mirror showed a tired man with red-rimmed eyes and thinning hair. Kyle splashed cold water on his face and fought the urge to cry, winning a temporary victory. What sick game was he playing? The poor girl was at least ten years younger than he was.

Kyle put on yesterday's boxers, slipped into a robe, and made his way to the kitchen. The automatic coffee maker brewed away, half full. He poured a cup and stood at the kitchen island, looking out across the great room and through the massive wall of windows onto a balcony. There was a spot on one of the sliding doors. A smudge. Maybe a fingerprint.

Kyle kept an eye on the stain as he walked to the great room and sat down on his leather sectional. He wanted no trace of her in this place, and though he was unsure whose fingerprint marred his door, the very idea of it being hers hurt. He flicked on the news as a distraction. It didn't work. The fingerprint still felt like a blemish on his heart.

Nothing got through the thick fog in his head as he watched. The coffee tasted bitter and burned his lips, and his skull buzzed like a nest of wasps. A half-full bottle of bourbon sat on the coffee table, calling to him. Not even pretending to argue with himself, Kyle gave in and poured a healthy shot into his coffee.

"Hair of the dog?" The unwelcomed bitch stood in the hallway door wearing one of his shirts—a turquoise Van Heusen, wrinkle free, with perfect collars. More of his stuff, fucked up by an outsider. Christ, he would have to wash more than the sheets today.

Kyle set his coffee down and struggled to remind himself she was not Alissa. Whatever he did last night, he did for all the wrong reasons. Just like all the other times. Alissa was gone—why couldn't he stop torturing himself?

"Take it off."

The girl looked at the loose shirt. "What, this?" She moved into the great room and smoothed the shirt down over her breasts and stomach. "I like it. It's so snug. Shows off the best parts, don't you think?" She smiled. Her blond hair hung in loose tangles on either side of her face.

"Please, just... take it off." Kyle's hand trembled, and sweat seeped from his forehead. One more smudge, one more stain in his life to clean away. Even though part of him wanted to beg forgiveness and let her know this wasn't her fault, he wouldn't give in to the feeling. Any leeway he gave might split like a crack in a dam, and he was afraid of what else might come rushing through. "Really, take it off now. Please? There are some sweatpants and t-shirts in the bedroom."

She ignored him and came closer. "Well, I see you ain't wearing much." Her voice dripped with seduction and the sound of it made him ill. "Why don't we get rid of these clothes? Here, I'll go first." Her hands slid up, and she started to unbutton the shirt, taking a little step with each button she popped.

Kyle stood before she got too far. "Really, I'm glad you're taking it off, but please put something else on. There are some old clothes back in the bedroom you can wear."

She stopped, and the smile evaporated. She undid the remaining buttons with quick, angry flicks. The shirt fell open revealing a great pair of tits and rock-hard abs.

Kyle's body mutinied as the shirt slipped from her shoulders and fell to the ground. He cringed, feeling like a schoolboy at the chalkboard with his first hard-on. Before he could say anything more, the young woman turned and marched back down the hall to the bedroom. He picked up the shirt, carried it to the washer, and dropped it in with a waiting load.

The girl returned—what was her name?—wearing gray sweats and an old Motley Crew t-shirt. She sat down next to him to watch TV.

Kyle felt a barrier between them, and somehow it made things a little better. The dam would hold.

A few moments later, she rose and went to the kitchen. Cabinet doors banged as she rooted around.

"The cups are hanging over the sink." Kyle propped his feet on the table.

The young woman said nothing. She continued to rustle, making too much noise, at last coming back with half a cup of coffee. She sat down and reached for the bourbon.

Kyle plucked the bottle before she could. "You know

you're not staying, right?" He couldn't look at her. Maybe she could stay. Would it be so bad?

"Who's Alissa?" She slurped coffee and watched him over the top of the mug.

"Again, you're not staying." This girl had no right to say her name. What did he tell her last night? Kyle's hand trembled.

"C'mon. You pick me up, bring me back here, play your stupid little game, and you won't even tell me who she is?" She slid up right next to him and leaned over so they were almost face-to-face. Her blue eyes shot holes in him. She looked so much like Alissa.

Part of Kyle wanted to reach out and touch her face or feel her hair. Another part wanted to scrape a chunk of broken glass across her neck. "Forget it. Not your business." He shifted over and tried to watch the news around her.

She would not be ignored. She leaned over more, eyes narrowed, face tightened.

She stared. He watched the news. Quiet shadows stretched across the room.

The girl broke first. She popped up from the couch and stomped her way to the bedroom. Halfway there, she stopped and marched back. "Fine. You're an asshat. You think I'm some stupid slut because you picked me up after a few drinks? You drive me back here in your corvette, you got this nice big house way out in God-knows-where, you dress like a fucking corporate drone, and you think I didn't know what this was? I wanted a fuck, you know? I wasn't asking for marriage or a date. You didn't even have to kiss me first. I'm young and damned cute. I like having fun as much as anyone else." She grabbed the bourbon, took a swig, and plopped it back down on the table. Kyle sat back too quick, upsetting his mug and splashing hot coffee down his leg as he fumbled to keep it steady. "You don't have to be such a dick about the whole thing. God, you're such a mean, depressing little shit. Who the fuck died anyhow?" She spun around and marched back to the bedroom.

Tremors ran through Kyle, joined by an overwhelming urge to grab her, mash her, and beat her. Instead, he went to the kitchen, dried his leg with a hand towel, and poured a little more coffee in his cup. He called a cab for the girl, which he should have done in the first place, then sat down to square off with another round of bourbon.

Kyle swallowed the last of his drink and was about to make another when the chick returned, dressed in her denim skirt and tank top still wrinkled from the night before. She stood in the hallway and glared. "So, will you at least give me a ride home?"

"I have to leave for work in a bit. I called you a cab. It'll be here soon. Sit, stand, do what you want. Just don't talk anymore. Please." Kyle handed her a fifty. She took it and repaid him with an icy stare. "Don't touch anything. I need to get dressed." He headed to the bedroom, undressed, and climbed in the shower.

Kyle still couldn't remember the girl's name. He guessed it might be some mental block. Sure, the booze didn't help much, but he didn't have trouble with names. Ever. Being good with names was part of his business.

The night before was a jumble. Some of it showed up like images in a fogged mirror—the call with Tom, the end of his day, skipping dinner and driving down the highway until he found a bar, any bar, a quiet place to hide. Why was he hiding, and from what? He had no idea what took him there last night.

And this girl, she was so like Alissa. But Alissa was long

gone. Memories of her rose like the morning tide and washed away whatever beachhead he'd built up.

Once cleaned and dressed, he returned to the great room. The girl was gone, the smudges remained. He sat down for one more drink before leaving. As he sipped his spiked coffee Alissa's name repeated in his mind, and bourbon-laced tears spilled down his cheeks.

TOM

Tom walked into the kitchen to find Harriet at the stove. "Smells great. What's for breakfast?"

She turned around. "Morning, sweetheart. It's nothing fancy, just some steak and eggs." She poured him a cup of coffee. "You take a seat, and it'll be done in a jiffy."

Tom sat down and sipped his coffee as Harriet returned to her cooking. He noticed the stone sitting on the counter next to the sink and remembered his question from last night.

"Aunt Harriet, I..." He looked down into his mug.

"What'd you say?" She filled a plate and brought it to the table. "You always were a little too quiet. You got something to ask me, sweetheart, ask." She made herself a plate and sat down across from Tom.

"No, no more questions. I wanted to say I'm sorry. I mean about asking if you and Pop... well, you know."

She covered her steak and eggs in hot sauce and took a huge bite. "Mighty tasty if I do say so myself." She spoke through a mouthful. "The steak really makes it."

Tom looked down at his plate. The eggs looked fine. The steak looked greasy and stringy, and smelled heavily peppered. Something about the meat wasn't right, so Tom continued instead of eating. "About you and Pop? I'm sorry."

Harriet cut off another piece of steak, dribbled more hot

sauce on it, and swept it through some egg yolk. "No need to apologize. You're old enough to know the truth. There wasn't any love between us, but you know... we all have needs. Now go on, eat something."

The stone drew his attention again then he looked at Aunt Harriet. She chewed away on another big bite, eyes closed. She looked thinner and weaker, like she had stayed up all night. "Did you read Pop's journal?"

She swallowed and looked at him with flat eyes. "No. I came out here and fell asleep in my chair. Don't know what came over me. I got so tired. It's out there on the television."

Tom avoided the steak and took a reluctant bite of egg. It tasted fine, so he swallowed and took another forkful. "What's with the stone?"

Half done with her breakfast, Harriet set her fork down and drank some coffee. "Well, I don't know. Had it on my lap when I woke up. Been carrying it around all morning. It feels nice in my hand. Now enough about the stone, let's talk about Lewis. I kept all your postcards. Never shared a one with him, though. I did tell him you were okay now and then." She shoveled another mouthful in and Tom was thankful she chewed and swallowed before continuing. "He sure was a sad man, missed you an awful lot. You know, he never would tell me why you left. Said he didn't know. I never quite believed him." She set down her fork again.

Tom didn't like where this was going. He finished his eggs as Harriet stared at him across the table. Something in the kitchen changed. He no longer sat across from dear old Aunt Harriet. Spite and accusation flashed across her eyes as she watched him eat.

At last, Harriet took another sip of coffee and looked away. "Are you going to tell me why you left your poor old

Pop and brother? What were you running from?"

Maybe it was time to tell someone. Maybe suicide was Pop's way of releasing him and Kyle. Tom took the last bite of egg, still wary of the steak, and washed it down with coffee. He should talk to Kyle first.

"I wasn't running from anything." Lying came hard. Tom could not bear to look into Aunt Harriet's eyes so he looked at the stone instead. "I guess I needed to get out of this town. Always knew I'd come back some day. Not like this." He looked back at her and was relieved to see the familiar compassion return to her eyes.

"I understand. You'll tell when you're ready. Maybe not me, but you'll tell." She stood and took her plate to the sink. "Now, if you'll excuse me, I need to clean up and get my day started. We're having a bake sale at the church tomorrow and I want to try this new idea for meat pie."

Tom rose and joined her at the sink. The rag Cassy used to wrap the stone in lay on the counter. Harriet picked it up. Tom plucked it away before she could scrub her dish with it and hugged her tight. He felt six again, visiting with dear old Aunt Harriet. "Thank you."

Using the rag, he grabbed the stone and wrapped it up. "I need to go call my brother. Maybe I'm in better shape to talk today, and maybe he's in the mood to listen. I'll see you later."

She kissed his cheek. "You go on, then."

CASSY

C assy's seatbelt tightened as the cruiser bounced over a washed-out pothole. The last remnants of morning dew hung in the air and the cool breeze made the trek almost pleasant. "Watch it, would you?" She unlatched her belt and gave Paul a look as the car beeped in protest. "You should have let me drive."

They pulled around a bend and entered fifty acres of woods. The Hanlon family lived in a four-room cabin another hundred yards up the road. Paul stopped the cruiser. "Put your belt back on. What's your problem this morning?"

It was a fair question. Cassy's mind couldn't sit still, flipping between Tom and the dredged-up memories of her cousin. Paul wouldn't understand either of those things. Straight-laced Paul, no worries in the world. "Not enough sleep." She snapped the belt and silenced the grating warning pings. "Why are we both out here anyhow?"

Paul drove on. "Not like you got anything better to do."

"True. I don't like doing the crap work, either. You just don't want to talk to these people. Admit it."

Paul mumbled.

"What? Can't hear you." Cassy leaned over.

"I said you're right. Feel better?"

She settled back in her seat. "A little. Well, no. Thanks

anyhow."

The trees gave way to a small clearing where a log cabin sat amidst a rusted out Bel Air, a patchwork dog kennel, and other bits of backwoods cast-off. It amazed her how, even out here in the woods where life was supposed to be about simplicity and frugality, people still weighed their lives down by accumulating useless stuff.

Paul pulled to a stop short of the Bel Air. Off to the left, tall grasses rustled as something crawled toward them. He looked out his window. "You bring the bribe?"

Cassy grabbed a to-go box from the floor—her leftover meatloaf from the diner—and passed it over. "Is this really necessary? I mean, it's a dog. Never heard anything bad about him." She couldn't resist pushing his buttons.

"Go on, get out if you want. The mutt's got it in for me."

Cassy got out and walked around to the front of the cruiser. A Doberman popped up his head, sniffed the air, then sat down, his slick tongue lolling in the wind. "Good Zak." She crossed her arms, leaned against the car, and called to Paul. "You coming out? He's fine."

As soon as Paul opened the door, Zak sprinted toward him. Paul slammed the door. Zak jumped up, placed a front paw on either side of the door, and tried to stick his head in as Paul rolled up the window. "I swear he's laughing at me," he shouted. "Crazy smiling dog."

Cassy patted Zak's head. "Down, boy." Zak backed away from the door a few steps then sat, tongue flapping as he panted.

Paul pulled the meatloaf from the box, rolled down his window, and threw it out into the yard. Zak took off after it, giving Paul a chance to get out of the car.

Cassy patted Paul on the back. "You know he only gets

excited because you bring him munchies. If you stop feeding him, he'll stop expecting you to feed him. Eventually."

As if in agreement, Zak barked and startled Paul. The deputy stumbled on a rock and toppled over backward, landing on his ass with a thud.

Cassy laughed and put out a hand. Paul took it and laughed a little too as she helped him up.

"I suppose. At least this way I know he's getting fed."

They approached the cabin. Cassy paused by the Bel Air and checked her watch. Her surroundings felt wrong.

Paul stopped. "What is it?"

The woods were too quiet. The Hanlon boys should be running around like mad apes by now. She should at least hear them nearby. "It's almost nine. You ever sleep late as a kid?"

Paul shrugged. "No, but it doesn't mean much. They could be anywhere." He continued on to the cabin.

She let it go. Paul was right. Those boys were probably miles away, maybe at the flats or terrorizing some poor farmer's livestock. She joined her partner at the door and knocked. "Dune? Emma?" The woods chittered as they waited, and she was about to knock again when the door opened.

Emma Hanlon stood in a t-shirt and shorts showing a little too much skin. Red hair cascaded about her shoulders in wiry tangles and her eyes were puffy slits of fatigue. She held a cup of coffee in one hand. Relief swept across her face. "Come in. Thank God you're here."

"Is everything okay?" Paul asked as they followed her in.

Dune, a well-tanned scarecrow of a man, sat at the dining table. A cold bowl of cereal sat in front of him, neglected, bloating in its milk. He nursed a cup of coffee as well. Neither he nor Emma looked as if they had seen sleep for days. Emma joined her husband at the table and motioned for the deputies to sit.

Paul took a seat. Cassy remained on her feet. The cabin was far from tidy—a few toys littered here and there among discarded t-shirts and shoes. Nothing out of the ordinary. Still, the silence bothered her. "Do you need some help? Where are the boys?"

Emma and Dune exchanged looks. Then both looked at Cassy, deep confusion sketched on their faces. Emma poked Dune in the ribs. "You mean you didn't call? I thought you'd finally come to your senses."

Dune shook his head. "I figured you did."

Paul started in. "I don't know what you two are talking about. We're here about these." He pulled the bag of M-80s out of his pocket and tossed them on the table.

Cassy tensed. Always so discreet. Couldn't he see something was wrong here?

"I got these off your boys yesterday."

Emma looked at the bag, then at the deputies. "You saw them?" Her voice cracked as she spoke. "Where were they? Are they okay?"

Cassy rested a hand on Paul's shoulder. "Well, ma'am, Paul saw them outside Ornthal's. They're not here?"

Dune reached across the table and took the bag of fireworks. He peered in, then huffed in disgust as he rolled the bag closed and tossed it aside.

Emma reached over and wrapped a hand around her husband's arm. She trembled, on the verge of tears. "Boys ain't been home since yesterday." She rubbed Dune's bicep. "We've been waiting for them. Lost track of time. You want some coffee?" Without waiting for an answer, she went to the kitchen counter and filled a couple of chipped mugs.

"You didn't call anyone?" Cassy watched Emma return to

the table. Their eyes met, and Cassy's guts knotted. She knew what was going on. They were in shock, thinking the worst against their will. Maybe the boys camped out for the night or maybe one was injured and they couldn't go for help. Or worse, maybe someone—someone they knew—scooped them up and...

Cassy stopped herself from finishing the thought. She knew what it meant to have someone close disappear.

Emma put down the coffee and took her seat. "No. We talked about it. They stay out late sometimes. Boys. You know. Never all night, though."

Dune looked at Emma. "They're kids. Fireworks and comic books are about all they need. They'll be fine. Least until they get home."

"Yeah," Paul said. "About the fireworks. Monterey sent us out here. Dune, you have to keep those out of their hands. You want one of your sons blowing his fingers off?"

Dune's narrowed his eyes and clenched his teeth. He stood and shouted down at Paul. "Did you hear a goddamned word we said? Our boys are missing, and you want to preach to me about firecrackers?"

Paul stood up. "If you're so worried—"

"Okay, no need for shouting." Cassy moved to stand between the men. "Paul, why don't you wait outside."

Dune stepped around the side of the table. Paul backed up a pace. Cassy held her ground between the two men as they glowered at each other. "Dune, sit your ass down." She turned to her partner. "Paul, get your ass outside. I'll finish in here."

Paul turned around and stormed out. Cassy never understood why he played the hard-ass at all the wrong times. He was a good cop. He was not always good with people.

The door shut and Dune sat back down. "I think my boys

are more important than a bag of fireworks. I think my cousin would agree, don't you? Now why don't you get on out to your little cruiser, drive back to the station, and do whatever it is you do to round up a search party."

Cassy took Paul's chair and sat down. "You're right. We will start looking for those boys. I still need one of you to come down to the station and fill out some paperwork as soon as you can. You have to understand, we follow a process for something like this, part of which is a report. The sooner you file it, the sooner we can escalate. You know, get some outside help if we need it."

Dune and Emma exchanged looks. Then Dune nodded. "Sure, okay. Give us a little bit and we'll be down."

"It would really be best if one of you came down with us. Now. The other can stay here and wait for the boys." Cassy hoped they would listen. The looks on their faces told her not to expect much.

Emma spoke this time. "Well... let's give them a little more time. Besides, we could both use a little sleep. Should be easier knowing you're looking into it. Noon, maybe?"

Even though Cassy hated the idea, she understood the need to hang onto hope. They still believed their boys would come bursting through the door at any moment. They could be right, but she didn't think so. Maybe a couple of more hours would convince them, and if they didn't show up, she or Paul could come back out.

Cassy stood to leave and extended a hand to Dune. "Well, if you change your mind, come on down."

"Sure, we'll stop by." Dune shook her hand.

Emma got up, came around the table, and gave Cassy a hug. "Thank you, deputy," she whispered. Cassy could feel the fatigue as the poor woman's body leaned into her.

As Cassy turned to leave, a loud thump came from the porch followed by Paul's muffled scream. "Get off me, you damned mutt." She ran to the door and threw it open to find Paul pinned down and getting a good face licking from Zak. She couldn't help but laugh as she stepped around them.

Dune followed her through the door and kicked the dog in the rump. "Get going, beast. That's no way to treat the law." He gave another swift kick to the ribs. Zak yelped and fell off the porch. Dune jumped down and got in one more kick before Cassy intervened.

"That's no way to treat a dog, either." She took Zak by the collar and led him around the side to the kennel. Zak limped in, circled twice then lay down and whined. As Cassy latched the door, she noticed four short leashes staked to the ground, prong collars at the end of three. Maybe she underestimated these people. Maybe the boys ran away. Or maybe her imagination ran a little wild. She would mention it to Monterey when they got back.

Cassy came back around to the front of the house and joined Paul as he walked to the car. They got in the cruiser—she drove this time—turned the car around and headed back to the station.

They rode in silence for a little while. She knew Paul would speak his mind sooner or later. She wished it had been later.

"Fact is I don't think their boys are missing. Not yet, at least. It's only been one night. Hell, you ever stay out all night without telling your folks?"

Cassy remained silent. Maybe Dune and Emma would come to the station. It would help if they filed a report. Details solve crimes. She doubted they would show. When it came down to it, most folks in Washington Heights liked to solve their own problems.

SHANE

Shane detoured from finding the pregnant lady. She would wait. As he wandered out of the flats, trying to guess the meaning of his new name, an unseen prong-collar tightened around his neck—a sense memory unaided by images, driving him toward a different goal.

He reached the dirt road to the Hanlon's cabin, unsure of where he was or why he ended up there. Even as the morning sun broke through the gloom, the chill of night still lingered in every fiber of his baked body.

As he drew near the cabin, a dog barked from somewhere in the tall grass, and a car approached from the road behind.

Shane slipped into the woods and watched as the cruiser pulled to a stop. Two deputies got out. The man paid off the dog with meat—Shane smelled it from where he stood—and the pair made their way to the cabin.

The dog licked away at his prize as Shane worked through the brush toward the cabin. Leaves and branches scoured off bits of skin as he circled around and emerged from the woods behind the dog kennel. Muffled voices drifted from the little house, and the glint of four prong-collars on short leashes caught his eye.

The conversation from the cabin faded into the background as those four shiny bands of metal consumed

Shane's attention. The dull tightness around his neck became sharp and choking. He wanted to ask daddy to stop, promise he would be good. Shane put a hand to the pain expecting to feel cold, unforgiving metal. He found only skin, cracked and cool and raw. He stepped toward the kennel, drawn to the glinting chrome, then stopped at the sound of footsteps on the porch. Someone came back out.

The dog sprinted from his hiding spot in the grass, pounced onto the porch and out of view. The man from the car cursed as the dog landed on him. Shane slipped around the side of the kennel, through the open gate and grabbed one of the collars. It felt wrong, so he let it drop and grabbed another. The second one resonated with him. He unhooked it from the leash and gripped it tight.

As more people emerged from the cabin, Shane slipped out of the kennel and back into the woods. He hid among the crosshatched shadows of the trees.

More arguing on the porch. Then the woman from the car came around the side of the cabin with the dog. She helped the poor creature in and it circled around then lay down. The dog stared into the woods at Shane and whined. Shane whined softly in response and watched as the woman returned to the front porch. He wanted her to stay. Maybe if she stayed he could stop himself. He could tell her about what his father did to them, about the collars. She could help.

Shane felt the cool collar in his hand as it hummed and buzzed with a life of its own. His throat ached in an itchy, naked sort of way. He looked at the wretched piece of metal then put it to his neck and latched it in place.

The dog stopped whining and buried his head beneath one paw.

Shane listened to the crunch of gravel as the deputies

drove away. He waited for the sound of the car to fade and crept around to the back of the cabin, pausing at the kitchen door. Shane stood on the tips of his toes. Another brittle toe cracked off as he peered through the window. Mommy and daddy sat at a table, daddy with his face buried in his hands, mommy staring into her coffee cup.

He knew they missed him in their own way. He should miss them too. A sudden flash from a snowy channel in his memory. Yesterday morning, five of them sat at the table eating pop tarts, laughing because Lonny still ate his boogers, and Emma cringed as his brother gobbled up a meaty one.

Shane should walk away and tend to the pregnant woman. He smelled her on the wind. The old man saved him to help her, not to come back here. Whatever control the old man held over him weakened at the corners while Shane was here. He didn't want to go, not yet. Shane dropped back down from his toes and stepped away from the door. Stay or go?

The wind scurried around the side of the cabin and brushed through the remnants of his hair. Shane walked back to where Zak cowered in the kennel and crept back inside. The dog raised his head and lapped at the spot where toes used to be as Shane gathered two more of the collars. He bent down and hugged the dog, brittle skin flaking off and showering the dog like volcanic ash. "Good boy."

When he returned to the kitchen door and looked in, he once again saw his parents sitting at the table, talking to each other in low murmurs. What were they talking about? Him? The twins? Were they sorry for the shit they'd done, or were they trying to figure out how long to keep the boys in the dog house this time.

Shane had no plan. He walked in. Dune looked first, slack-jawed and stupid. Emma looked next with dull confusion.

Shane thought of the cold chrome strapped around his neck and the poor dog in the kennel, working up a tremor of tears. "Mommy? Daddy?" He sniffled, the air wheezing through his dried and cracked sinuses.

Dune's face crumpled into confusion. "Boy? What the hell happened?"

Emma stood and rushed toward him. "Oh my God. What happened? Are you okay? Where have you—"

"I'm okay." Shane tried hard to sound lost and scared. "We had an accident."

"Where are the twins?" Dune got up as well and took a few tentative steps toward him.

Emma knelt down and tossed her arms around him. She felt warm and rough, her touch scouring like hot sandpaper. Shane pulled away.

Dune saw the collars in each of Shane's hands. "What you got there? You been fucking with the kennel?" His voice rose. "You hurt my dog?" Any hint of relief at seeing Shane dissipated. Dune took another step forward and raised a fist.

"Oh, daddy," Shane wailed, his voice the rough whistle of a desert wind. "I'm sorry, I'm so sorry." Shane rushed to Dune and held his arms wide. "Daddy, please, I'll be good. See, I already put mine on. I'll be good."

Dune's fist hung in the air for a few seconds as mixed emotions battled on his face. Then the fist lowered and broke open. Dune knelt down and looked into Shane's eyes.

"What the hell happened to you? How did you get here?" He reached a hand out to touch the boy's face, pulling back at the last moment. "Emma, call the clinic. Have them send the ambulance."

Shane lurched forward and wrapped his arms around Dune. "Hug me, daddy. Please?"

Dune steadied himself and hesitated.

Shane held on tight. From somewhere behind him, Emma stifled a sob. Dune relaxed then slowly hugged the boy.

Before Dune's heart struck another beat—so close, so warm—Shane wrapped one collar around Dune's neck and drew it as tight as it would go. He latched it as Dune pushed back and lurched to the kitchen table, scratching as the unyielding prongs dug deeper into his throat.

Emma yelped and ran out from behind Shane.

Before she could get by, he grabbed her hand and held tight. "Mommy? Please let him go. He made me wear this. Remember? It was him."

Emma struggled to pull free. Shane held tight. Dune worked at the collar, unable to find the latch, unable to breathe.

Emma would not fall for the same trick. Shane yanked as hard as he could, and she fell back onto the floor. He scrambled on top of her and pressed the second collar around her neck. Even as she beat at his face, scraping burnt skin and exposing raw flesh, he managed to draw hers tight and latch it. He rolled off in time to miss a wide swing.

They wouldn't die right away. He didn't want them to. Dune, who had started to pale, knelt down next to Emma and fought to undo her collar. She swung again, apparently unaware Shane sat well out of range, and connected with Dune's nose. Rivulets of blood dripped from one nostril as he reeled back.

Emma kept a broom by the fridge, mostly for messes, sometimes for scooting the boys out of the house. Shane scuttled back from his parents, got to his feet, and grabbed it.

Dune and Emma danced, limbs scrabbling as if pulled by an unskilled puppeteer. Were they scared? Angry? Did they see how much they deserved this? They looked scared. They didn't look scared enough. Shane stepped in and jabbed the bristles of the broom into the fray to confuse their attempts to remove the collars.

Dune managed to get a hold of Emma's collar. The boy flipped the broom around and came down hard with the wooden handle. Something cracked, and Dune pulled his hand away with two fingers twisted at odd angles.

Emma, now on her feet, stumbled toward the front door and she collapsed to her knees. How long before she choked? Which one would go first? Shane saw a welt forming on her throat where the broom had connected. Did the blow crush her windpipe? That would be more awesome than the cat. If only Lonny and Alex were here too.

Dune staggered toward Shane, his wide eyes pooled dark with hate and fear. Shane swung the broom once again and landed a blow across Dune's cheek. Dune's head swung to the side, he lost balance and toppled to the floor.

Both Dune and Emma's movements slowed.

Shane sat on the floor, knees drawn to his chest, and watched as the man and woman died. When all movement ceased, when he no longer heard the faint rhythms of their hearts, he removed his collar.

He took his time, dragging the bodies to the bathroom, finding the biggest knife he could, gathering up some plastic containers. The old man suggested sheep. Shane didn't need sheep. These two would do just fine.

Now he could get on with business.

TOM

Tom arrived at Ornthal's early and waited out front, trying to look casual. The truth was, he felt lost and jumbled inside. Nothing looked familiar, and though a few faces he thought he recognized passed out of the diner—each offering a smile or a nod—the town still felt like a foreign land. He held the rag-wrapped stone in one hand, tapping his thumb against the side. Maybe Kyle knew something about it. Or maybe, as crazy as it sounded, the thing held some value to his brother. Maybe, just maybe, this weird little chunk of rock would give Tom some leverage in the situation.

Kyle arrived late, carrying a newspaper and manila envelope. At least he showed up. He passed by Tom without a word, opened the door, and looked back. "You coming?"

"Not even a hello?"

"Not here. Let me get a drink at least, okay?" Kyle continued into the diner. Tom had no choice but to follow.

Two men about Tom's age chatted away at the counter over messy plates and coffee rings. Like everything else, he couldn't quite place them even though they looked familiar.

"Debbie, two coffees and a large tomato juice." Kyle took a little table by the front window, plopped the envelope on the table, and opened his newspaper.

As Tom joined his brother, one of the men looked over

and nodded without a smile. Tom raised a hand, then lowered it almost right away. The nod was probably for Kyle. He recognized the guy now as Davie Crandall, the doctor's boy. Not one of Kyle's friends, not exactly, but they had hung out a few times as kids. Definitely not one of Tom's friends.

He took a seat opposite his brother, the newspaper standing between them like some cheap fence. Debbie arrived with their drinks and asked if they wanted something to eat. Food was the last thing on his mind, so he declined. Kyle grunted.

"Holler if you need anything." Debbie retreated to the kitchen.

"Hey, little brother." The words came out all wrong despite Tom's attempt to get them back to some sort of solid ground, somewhere familiar where they could talk like family. His thumb once again tapped the stone on his lap.

Kyle folded the newspaper neatly and placed it on the table next to the envelope. Even as he smiled, his eyes betrayed wariness. Something else as well... Guilt?

"I need to get to the office soon." Kyle pulled a contract from the envelope and slid it across the table. "Let's keep this short. Are you ready to sign?" He took a long drink from his tomato juice and chased it with a sip of coffee.

Kyle never could make things easy for anyone except himself. Tom looked around the diner to collect his thoughts. He wasn't ready to take this head-on yet. He turned back to Kyle. "You look good. Been keeping up with yourself?"

Kyle put the contract down. "What do you want? Really."

The bell on the diner door chimed. An older woman in a yellow sundress and straw gardening hat approached the register and waited. She wiggled her fingers in a little wave and brightened the room with a smile for Tom.

"I asked you a question." Kyle knocked on the table. "You listening to me?"

Tom returned the woman's smile. He remembered cookies and juice and sitting cross-legged on the carpet listening to stories, and he felt a little more at peace seeing her even though he couldn't place her name.

He turned back to his brother and set the rock on the table. "Any idea what this is?" He flipped the rag open to expose the stone.

Kyle jerked his hand from the table, looking as if Tom had put a dead dog there instead of a lifeless hunk of rock. The fear passed quickly, and Kyle's eyes went cold and dead as he met Tom's gaze.

"Yeah. It's a rock. Now are you going to answer me or—"

"What do I want? Maybe I wanted to see my little brother. Who doesn't show up for their own father's funeral? I made it, why the hell didn't you?"

Kyle leaned forward, eyes watery and glazed like those of a drowned man, his breath smelling of bourbon. He spoke quick and low. "I had to work. I don't know what kind of shit you're playing at, bringing that thing here. It's nothing to me. Yes, I know it was Pop's, and yes, I know he had it when he did himself in. You asked why I didn't go to the funeral. I had to work. Nothing more."

Tom crossed some sort of line. This wasn't what he hoped for at all. He looked away, face flushed, forehead hot.

The woman from the counter stood behind him now, peering at the stone on the table. She smiled again and spoke in a voice roughened by decades of cigarettes. "You have a mighty fine piece there. May I?"

Tom turned back to Kyle, eyebrow raised. Seeing his brother's initial reaction to the stone made him think letting her handle it wasn't such a good idea. Kyle threw up both hands in surrender and shook his head.

Tom covered the stone. "I'm sorry, ma'am—"

"Oh, call me Jess. You probably don't remember me. I used to teach Sunday school at the church. I'd recognize you two anywhere."

"Okay, Jess. Kyle and I are having a little family discussion—"

Kyle huffed, then chugged the rest of his tomato juice.

"—and maybe now's not the time."

Jess's smile broke down. "Sure. I'm sure you boys have lots to talk about. My condolences, by the way. If you get a chance, come on down to the antique store. I'm sure Teddy would love to see it. Might even give you a hundred dollars for it."

"Maybe I will. Thanks."

Jess walked back to the register, where Debbie waited with two to-go cups and donuts wrapped in paper.

Tom leaned back in his chair. "You want the point? I want some time in the house. I need a place to stay. Even though Harriett put me up, I don't want to stay there. It's not home. At least let me stay at the house until it's sold. We're going to have to clear Pop's stuff out anyhow."

Kyle put away the contract, tucked it and the newspaper under his arm, and got up. He stood over Tom and looked down, thick bags under his eyes. "I shouldn't. You don't deserve it. Maybe if you'd been here, Pop wouldn't have..." Kyle's lip curled at one end. He pulled a key ring from his pocket and held them out.

At last. Maybe Kyle was coming around after all. This was some sort of progress, wasn't it?

As Tom reached for the keys, Kyle pulled them back. "I'll

never forgive you for leaving. Welcome home, brother." He dropped the keys into Tom's open hand, turned and walked a few steps, then paused.

"Call me when you're ready to talk about something other than Pop. You've been gone a long time, and we do have some catching up to do. Don't forget, I've been right here. "

Tom watched him go. The pit of his stomach turned, and he struggled against an unwanted memory creeping out from some dark hole in his mind, one he couldn't ignore: Kyle, covered in blood, cradling a young woman.

He rubbed his eyes to clear the image and fought the urge to run out of the diner after Kyle. More words would only make things worse, so he wrapped the stone and finished his coffee. Maybe he should let Jess have the rock, for all the good it seemed to be doing.

Debbie arrived with the check. Tom paid, left the diner, and walked a few doors down to the antique shop. He remembered the place as he stopped at the door. A stylized sign hung above the entrance, the words "Antique Shoppe" carved into brown wood. He could still see the faint outline of the original sign on the building, "Swap Shop" in block letters. He went in. Even though the sign had changed, the place remained filled with the same old junk.

Several people, out-of-towners by their looks, picked over Washington Heights' finest trash: lamps, clothes, furniture, and tin signs among the more interesting pieces. The place smelled of dusty relics left too long in a forgotten closet.

"Be with you in a minute," Jess called from somewhere in the back of the store. An older man behind a counter glanced up at Tom then returned to his crossword puzzle.

Maybe selling the rock wasn't such a good idea. This place felt wrong for it, like throwing an arrowhead in the trash. He held up the stone and peeled back the rag to take another look. The greens and reds brightened and cast the rest of the store in sepia tones. He couldn't leave it here to sit among the ruins of this town until someone with enough money came along. Suppose no one ever did? It would lie here forgotten, and although it may be a mystery to him—and may remain forever so—it was among the last things Pop handled and much more important than a chair or a grandfather clock or any other random prop from his family's history.

"I see you brought it." Jess stood in front of him.

Tom jumped and nearly dropped the stone.

"Oh my, didn't mean to startle you. Hey Teddy, come take a look." Jess took the wrapped stone from Tom and folded back the rag before he could stop her.

The man at the register set his pencil down and came around the counter. "What's this you're yelling about?" He sized Tom up then looked at the stone.

"I told you a few minutes ago. Did you forget already?" Jess handed the wrapped stone to her husband. "Looks like it could bring in a lot, huh? I mean if the right buyer comes along."

A young woman dressed in a tennis outfit, smelling of Jasmine, brushed by Tom and asked about a coffee table. Jess excused herself to help.

"Well now, what exactly is this?" Teddy turned the stone over in his hand once then rubbed its smooth surface.

"Don't know. It was my father's." The shop closed in on Tom as Teddy continued to caress the stone. Something about the way the other man touched it made Tom's stomach turn.

"Tell you what. I'll give you, say, fifty bucks. Sound like a deal?" Teddy looked at Tom with eyes like two chips of obsidian. He continued to rub the stone as he smiled. "Fifty bucks is a lot of money for a rock."

Tom felt more certain this was not the right place for it. Teddy looked too eager. Tom spent a fair amount of time over the years haggling and trading, and he knew when someone was trying to pull one over. "Well, I don't know." He said no more, curious about where Teddy would take the conversation.

The old dealer examined the stone again. "Feels warm..." He stroked its surface. "If you could tell me its history, I might give you more."

"I told you everything I know."

"You say your father found it. Whereabouts? It isn't local. Mostly limestone and granite around here. And coal, of course. Nothing like this... How about a trade? We have some nice stuff here."

"I think I'll pass, actually. Sorry to waste your time." Tom reached for the stone. "I thought—"

Teddy pulled the stone away. "Whoa, not so fast, son. We can make a deal, can't we? I mean, the more I look at it... Tell me what you want. You smoke? I got this nice Victorian walnut smoking stand here, cast brass details. Got it for a couple hundred at a swap meet. Circa 1900. I bet it would look nice in your house." Teddy locked eyes with Tom.

Tom reached out, more slowly this time, and flipped the rag back over the rock. "Really, I think I'll leave now." Teddy offered no resistance as Tom took back the wrapped stone.

The old dealer leaned in. "You like girls? Older women, maybe? I'll give you anything for it. Just don't take it away, okay? You can sleep with my wife, or watch me and her do it, or..." Teddy's voice dropped to a whisper. "Or maybe you like boys. What about me? You can do me nice and easy." Beads of sweat popped out on his forehead, like a meth addict looking to score.

Tom backed away a step. What on earth about this thing would make an old man stoop so low? He couldn't be serious.

Jess returned and took Tom's arm. "Tell me you're not leaving us. The old coot try to trade me away again?"

Tom relaxed a little. Maybe it was all a joke. Something in Teddy's voice suggested otherwise. "I don't know enough about it to deal."

Jess patted his arm. "You say it was your father's? Can't ask him now, can we." She frowned as she thought. "I don't suppose—"

"Damn it, woman!" Teddy tried to grab the stone. Tom pulled away, letting the dealer's hand grasp at empty air. "I want the stone, you little fuck. Now you give it here." He trembled as he stared at Tom, teeth bared, hand held out.

A few of the customers looked up from the knick-knacks. One woman scowled and pulled her bored son along as she left the store.

Jess pulled a tissue from her pocket and dabbed Teddy's forehead. "What's gotten into you? You never curse, except when you're working on your crosswords. Look at you, you're practically drenched." She pulled a chair over. "Now you sit down and leave this boy alone."

Teddy faltered, then sat down and rubbed his forehead. "Sorry, son. Don't know what got into me."

Jess gave her husband a sour look then turned back to Tom. "As I was saying, I don't suppose you asked your brother about it? Stands to reason he might know. Tell you what, why don't you leave the pretty stone here, go get him, and come on back." Jess crept closer as she spoke. Sweat formed on her brow.

Tom smelled her sour breath and realized she now stood within reach of the stone. He tucked it in a pocket, looking from one to the other. "Thanks, really. I got it." He turned and left before either could respond.

LEWIS

October 11, 2007

Blood slicked the floor and steps behind Lewis as he helped Mac down the stairs to the banquet hall. Christ, the man was heavy. The broken shaft of a deacon's wand, an archaic ritual prop closer to a spear than a wand, stuck out from the left side of Mac's abdomen. Blood and spittle dripped from his mouth. He grew paler by the second, and Lewis grew more worried, praying this little fiasco wouldn't end in death.

At the last two steps, Mac stumbled a bit, and the ragged edge of the wooden shaft scrapped across Lewis's back. The burning pain made him stagger as well. He couldn't keep hold of Mac to stop his old friend from tumbling the last few steps onto the floor.

The pastor's scream resounded in the foyer. "Little fucking asshole. What the hell." Mac rolled to his good side. Lewis felt a hole open in the pit of his stomach. Less of the wand protruded than before and fresh blood trickled out from around it.

A group of men huddled in the foyer. No one moved to help the pastor to his feet. They stared, some with mouths hung open, others whispering.

Why wouldn't they help instead of standing there like a bunch of dumb-ass rubber-neckers? Lewis's face was hot, sweat trickled down his back, and his breath came in short bursts. He was too old for this shit. He took the last two steps and bent to help Mac up. The pastor took his arm as best as he could, and together they strained to get the big man back on his feet.

Lewis couldn't keep his mouth shut any longer. "Why are you all standing there? You're like my goddamned sheep. Oakstone. Crandall. You're young. Get over here. Help a brother out."

The two young men he called out exchanged looks. One fidgeted—Lewis didn't know which, could never tell them apart—and replied in a quiet voice.

"My dad told us to stay put. He went to get his med kit from the car. Should be right back."

"Great. I don't suppose you'd want to get your ambulance, would you? Maybe give old Mac here a lift to the hospital?" Lewis had to force the words out as he strained to help Mac to the banquet hall.

The worthless little doctor wannabe shrugged as they walked by. "Dad said not to. This is Lodge business. We don't need any bad press."

Great, so they would keep this all under wraps. And if Mac bled out, what then? Would they throw him in the ravine out back, or maybe dig a shallow grave if they had the time?

Lewis got Mac into the banquet hall and helped him onto a table where the old pastor stretched out. With each movement came another cry of pain. Tears streamed down poor Mac's face.

"Easy, big fella, easy. You'll be fine. It only looks bad with the shaft sticking out." Lewis grabbed several cloth napkins from a serving station by the door and packed them around the wooden handle. He soaked the blood up as best he could, the warm liquid making his skin crawl. A lifetime of sheep farming made a man immune to disgust from bodily fluids. It didn't prepare him to watch a friend's lifeblood trickle away.

Mac cried out again. "Leave it. Goddamn, where's the doctor? Where are the cops? Did you call the cops? I want him locked away for this."

"No cops, not yet." Lewis exchanged soaked napkins for fresh ones. "We have to get you taken care of first. I want you to blast a fiery sermon on Sunday, do you hear? You're going to be fine."

A commotion arose in the foyer and Lewis frowned despite himself. Maybe Mac wouldn't notice. Men shuffled down the stairs, voices whispered. They must be escorting Victor out.

The men were too loud. Mac strained to sit up. "Let me back at him. I'll pull this stake right out of my side and shove it up the little fucker's ass. Bet he'd like—" Mac erupted in a coughing fit and fresh blood seeped from his wound.

Lewis forced the pastor to lie back down. "Hold on to your rage for Sunday, Mac." Lewis ground his teeth as his nerve endings frayed. He shouldn't feel so angry. He knew a man in pain needed sympathy and a strong hand to help. He couldn't continue to give either. Lewis was at the edge of his good graces. Something about the way Mac moaned dug at him.

Mac reached out, grabbed Lewis by the upper arm, and gripped it tight. "Damn it hurts. Where the hell's Doc?"

"Davie says he's coming. He'll be here. Loosen up on me a little. Goddamn, you've got some grip."

Mac looked at Lewis, eyes wide and bloodshot, like he

hadn't slept in days. His breath reeked, and stubble peppered his face. The silver hair on his head dripped with sweat.

Those bloodshot eyes felt accusatory and bitter as they scanned Lewis's face, leaving him itchy and tense.

Lewis twisted a little and dug away at the pastor's fingers with his free hand. "Mac, I said loosen up." The pastor wouldn't let up. He stared and strained, lips peeled back against clenched teeth.

"Did you know, Lewis? Did you?"

"Goddamn it, Mac, I said let—"

Doc Crandall arrived and hefted a big orange medical kit onto the adjacent table. "Okay, let's take a look, shall we?" He unzipped the bag, dug around until he found a pair of latex gloves, and snapped them into place. He poked and prodded at the wound. Lewis looked away and reminded himself this was no different than one of his sheep getting caught in the barbed-wire fence.

Mac let go. "You fucking knew, didn't you Lewis?"

Lewis turned back ready to argue. Instead, he forced himself to stay silent. Yelling at his friend would help nothing. Pressure built in his head, around his eyes, and across his forehead. His nerves sang, his skin itched and burned, like salt and sandpaper on an open wound. His hands balled into fists, nails dug into the palms.

The doctor continued, either not hearing or not caring what the pastor said. "Well, this'll come out nice and easy, Mac. I got something here for the pain, I'll stitch you up, and it'll be good as new. Looks like he missed every—"

"Fuck you, Lewis. You knew this whole fucking time, didn't you, and you never said a word to me."

The accusations were too much. He didn't know shit.

Lewis was horrified with himself even as he pulled back a

fist. He was unable to stop from swinging hard across the pastor's face. There was a dull, meaty thump and a sickening, satisfying snap as he landed the single blow. Mac's head flipped to the side and bloody spit sprayed onto the floor.

Doc Crandall staggered back a few steps and held his gloved hands up. "Whoa. Nice one."

Lewis turned on the doctor. His every fiber yelled out to take another swing, to strike the stupid physician standing in front of him. By some miracle, his self-control returned, and he relaxed his fist.

The doctor smiled, oblivious to the rage spinning inside Lewis. "Man, you got him good. No problem, I'll take care of the broken nose, too. Free of charge."

No one ever fought in Lodge, ever. Lewis wanted no more part of whatever brought this on. He closed his eyes and took a deep breath, fighting to keep control. Lewis Burton did not go around striking people. Not anymore. He opened his eyes. "Doc, fix him up. I got to get out of here."

He walked by the doctor and paused in the foyer by the group of huddled men. They parted in silence, letting Lewis pass between them and out the front doors.

The air outside lacked the electricity he felt in the Lodge and an alien calm prevailed in the coolness. Lewis's skin still itched, although not so goddamned deep as before.

Kyle sat on the bottom step, a cigarette in hand, his back to the door. Lewis sat down, and Kyle offered a smoke. The nicotine dulled the sparks in his nerves as he took a first drag.

"What's up, Pop?" Kyle spoke as if it were a Sunday afternoon cookout in the park. Had something pulled the plug on all Kyle's senses as well?

"Mac's got it pretty bad. I think Doc Crandall can get him fixed up..." Lewis took another drag from his smoke.

"Yeah, I saw. Not pretty. Victor's good with that spear thingy. It's the damnedest thing." Kyle flicked his cigarette. "Do you think he practices at home in front of the mirror?"

Lewis chuckled and coughed out a cloud of stinging smoke. "Did you hear how it started? I mean, we're sitting there while the ballot box is being passed, then I heard them talking. Then the screaming started. I couldn't make any sense of what either was saying. Next thing I knew, Victor skewered the pastor."

Kyle lit another smoke and gazed at the horizon. The last light of day faded from purple to gray, and Lewis wondered if his son would answer. At last Kyle spoke. "He said Victor's been sleeping with his wife."

Lewis took a final drag from his own cigarette and chucked the butt into the grass. "Isn't Victor...?" He couldn't get the last word out. Never should have let someone like Victor join.

"You can say it, Pop. He's gay."

TOM

Tom left the antique shop, hands trembling. He glanced back at the shop. Jess and Teddy watched him from the window, eyes dull and round, mouths like Oreos. What a sorry old pair.

The stone in his pocket felt warm and heavy. He hated the feel of it, did not really even want the thing. Neither did he want anyone else to have it. It was like some awful stubborn magnet refusing to let go, attracting all the wrong kinds of attention.

He wanted to get as far from the store as possible and find a safe place to collect his thoughts. He needed a few minutes to settle down. Maybe those two in the shop were sick or something, or maybe he remembered Jess through rose-colored glasses.

Aunt Harriet's place might be safe. More likely, it was filled with the cloying scent of baked goods. His belly tightened at the thought, so instead he walked through the town square. A Golden Retriever ran toward him, pursued by an overweight woman wearing a smiley-face t-shirt and a pair of cut-offs two sizes too small. Tom snagged the dog by the collar and knelt next to it, petting its smooth coat. The poor thing quivered under his hand, whimpering as it sat and watched the woman chug up to them.

She stared at Tom as if he had stolen her purse. "You got

my dog."

The golden whimpered, bowed its head, and leaned against Tom's leg.

Tom stroked the dog again. "Poor thing's scared. What happened?"

The woman shook her head. "None of your..." She bent over, coughed, and hocked a thick wad of spit. "Not your goddamned business. You gonna give me my dog back or not?"

"A simple thank you would be enough." Against his better judgment, Tom released the collar as the woman grabbed it. Her sweaty hand brushed his, feeling like a cold dead snail. The dog looked at him with sad eyes. Tom glanced down at his hands. He did not want to get involved in another tense situation. When he looked back up, the dog was lurching along obediently, eyes forward. Tom watched the woman drag it off down the street, hoping her mood would change by the time she got it home.

A few people in the park stopped and stared, not at the brusque woman, but at him. The collective weight of their icy glares made him feel all the more unwelcome. Not wanting any more attention, he ducked his head and continued walking, picking up his pace.

A few blocks south on Congress Street, the businesses petered out into a mix of small homes and duplexes, most looking abandoned. Muffled shouts came from one of the more dilapidated houses as Tom approached. As he passed, loud crashes rang out followed by more shouts mingled with a child's wail. A dog began howling from behind the house, and a few others across the neighborhood joined in.

Tom moved faster.

He reached The First Holy Church and stopped, thinking it

might give him a little refuge. The structure sat well back from the street, nestled between two run-down Cape Cods, its front doors hidden in the shadows cast by an overhang. He stood at the walkway to the church, wondering if it was open.

A voice snaked out from the gray. "Come to play?" The words felt greasy and dirty, like whispers from a Peruvian hooker. Tom's stomach sank and his bowels felt heavy.

He took a tentative step toward the building. "Hello?"

The shadows moved and bulged, and Tom thought they might reach out to pull him in to God-knows-what. Then the darkness coalesced from patches of black on black into the recognizable form of Mac Talvery. "Did you come to pray?"

Tom relaxed a little. Some small part of him remained alert, ready to run. He fingered the string of beads around his neck. "Pastor. I didn't see you there. Funny, for a minute I could have sworn you said—"

"Said what?" Mac tilted his head and stepped to one side. The shadows no longer concealed the entryway, and Tom saw the doors stood open.

"Well, I haven't been to church in years. Honestly, I think the last sermon I heard was yours, back before I left town." He ticked a thumb from one bead to the next. Sitting in a church alone was one thing. Having the pastor with him was another thing entirely. Still, the day grew hot, and he was more than a little tired. "Can I come in and sit for a while?"

Mac stepped from the shadows and down the first step, robes fluttering like so many angry ravens. "Please, come on inside. I'm glad you came. We can talk about your father, pray if you like, or you can have a little quiet time."

The heat and humidity of the day beat out Tom's hesitation, and he joined the pastor on the steps. "Maybe for a few minutes." This was a church after all, and no matter how reluctant Tom was to trust Mac, the man was a Pastor. That had to count for something.

Mac's face lit up. "I'd like that. Come on in." He led Tom through the narthex, into the sanctuary, and took a seat in the front pew. Tom sat next to him. A wooden cross with a plaster Jesus stared down at them from behind the altar.

Tom stared back at the image of the Savior and wondered if Pop's suicide was a sacrifice of sorts. Pop wasn't exactly the giving type. Still...

He turned to the pastor. "Do you think it hurt?"

Mac gazed up at the cross. "I'm sure it hurt like hell. Can you imagine? Nails through the feet and hands, thorns—"

"No, I'm sorry." Tom shifted so that he faced the pastor more fully. "I meant Pop. Do you think it hurt when he pulled the trigger?"

Mac turned back to Tom. "Oh. Well, I think your father hurt for a long time. You know, he and I went back a ways. One of the first friends I made when I moved to town. Signed my lodge petition. He used to be happy... I guess you'd say he changed when your mom died."

"You mean he started drinking."

Mac put a hand on Tom's shoulder. "Yes, he started drinking. There was something more going on. He kind of closed up shop on the inside." He squeezed then let go, dropping his hand to his lap and looking back at the plaster Jesus. "Even though your father was rough on you boys at times, he loved you." Mac touched the cross at his neck. "He stopped drinking. You probably didn't know. About three years back, he got into a program over in Charleston."

Tom shifted as he pulled the stone from his pocket. "You knew Pop pretty well. Did you know anything about this?" Tom held out the stone and flipped open the rag.

Mac glanced at the relic then turned his gaze back to Jesus. "You best get rid of it. I'd rather you not bring it into my church again, at least." The pastor sat stone still.

"What's the deal here?" Tom shoved the rock closer to Mac. "All I get are weird reactions from people with this thing. It's only a rock, right? I just want to know why Pop had it when he died. Look at it. Please?" He shook the rock. "Look at it!"

Mac finally turned back to face Tom. He avoided looking down at the stone itself. "I hadn't spoken to your father in months. I stopped going to lodge back in October last year when I got this." He unzipped his robes, opened them up, and lifted his shirt, exposing a scar the size of a half-dollar on the side of his abdomen. "It's not serious." The pastor traced the scar with the tips of two fingers, then dropped his shirt and zipped his robe. "Things got hairy in the lodge. Your father found it somewhere on the grounds—he never could say for sure where—and gave it to the Lodge to display in the meeting room along with some of the other historic stuff."

"What happened to you? Are you saying this—"

"There was a fight. A bad one. I got hurt in more ways than one." Mac's eyebrows knit as he thought for a moment. "I'm not saying anything, mind you. I'm only telling you what happened. Let me ask you something. Do you believe some objects have power?"

"No." But the rock felt too warm, so Tom set it between them on the pew and put a hand to his necklace. "I don't."

Mac raised an eyebrow. "You don't, huh? We talk of the power of the cross all the time."

Tom ticked off a few beads with his thumb then dropped his hand and glanced at the plaster Jesus. "That's not real power, though, is it? The cross is a symbol of the first resurrection. The power's in the minds of those who believe Jesus rose from the dead." Tom shook his head. "I lost my faith a long time ago. Sometimes a situation strikes too deep and uproots any faith you thought you might have—faith in family, faith in friends, faith in God. There's no power in the cross." He faced Mac again, expecting a look of disapproval, finding instead a soft smile.

"Jesus' resurrection wasn't the first in the bible. There were others before him. Take Lazarus, for instance."

Tom looked at the wooden cross again. "See, that's kind of my point. We don't have churches dedicated to Lazarus, do we? He came back from the dead and it seems like no one really cares much. Jesus is a different story. Even the power of the cross isn't about resurrection, it's about the belief people attach to it."

Mac shrugged. "We know what happened to Jesus after his resurrection, and we know what it meant. No one really knows who Lazarus was or what happened after he came back from the grave. Sure, there are some wild theories out there. Some say he went on to earn great riches, others say he became a powerful cabalist. I even met one man at a conference who thinks Lazarus is still alive, destined to walk the earth until he can bring about the rapture. Me? I like to think he led a happy, normal life. His resurrection wasn't about him, though. It was about Jesus as well."

Tom pinched the bridge of his nose. This conversation wasn't what he wanted. Nor was it what he needed. Christian philosophy and dogma were not going to give him any meaningful answers.

Mac must have noticed Tom's frustration. "Okay, so you don't believe in the cross, or the resurrection if you prefer. What about those beads at your neck?"

Tom touched his necklace again. "They were a gift from an Urarina Shaman. I spent a lot of time in South America, and I lived with his tribe for a while." He pulled them forward and looked down at the beads, red and black swirled on each in a natural yin-yang pattern. "They're Huayruro seeds. They're only a reminder, no different from the cross." He tucked the necklace back into his shirt. "So I believe the power of an object lies in the mind, not the object itself."

Mac glanced at the stone. "I suppose you might be right." The pastor reached for the rock then stopped, letting his hand hover mere inches away. His eyes glazed over and his breathing slowed.

Tom waited for the pastor to finish. The silence became too much. "So, what exactly happened to you? Who cut you?" He looked down at the stone, and when the pastor still didn't respond, Tom reached out and took the man's hand. "Mac? What happened?"

The pastor shook his head, as if awakening from a nap, and met Tom's look. "Sorry, I don't know what came over me."

"The scar. What happened?"

Mac withdrew his hand. "Oh. Well, I haven't really talked about it with much of anyone." He looked to the cross again. His eyes glazed and wrinkled at the corners, showing a different kind of scar. "A friend betrayed me. He..." Mac dropped his head to his hands. "He was going to leave. I lied about him, and—"

"Honey?" Mac's sparrow of a wife called from a doorway in the north transept. "The Sanderson's will be here before long. Did you forget?" She approached with a mixed look of concern and suspicion. "Mac? Is everything okay?"

Tom grabbed the stone and tucked it away in a pocket as

Mac looked up. They both stood as Mrs. Talvery reached them.

"Yes dear, everything is fine." The pastor rubbed his eyes with both hands then smoothed his robes. "This is Lewis's oldest son, Tom. You must remember him. Tom, this is my wife Cynthia."

Tom held out a hand. "Pleased, ma'am."

Cynthia shook it briefly, still looking suspicious of him. "Well sure. Stay as long as you like, but we have a christening here soon."

"Of course." Mac patted Tom's shoulder. "If you'll excuse me. Maybe we can talk more later." The couple left through the north transept, leaving Tom alone with the rock, his beads, and a plaster Jesus.

PART II

"Surely some revelation is at hand;
Surely the Second Coming is at hand.
The Second Coming! Hardly are those words out
When a vast image out of Spiritus Mundi
Troubles my sight: somewhere in sands of the desert
A shape with lion body and the head of a man,
A gaze blank and pitiless as the sun,
Is moving its slow thighs, while all about it
Reel shadows of the indignant desert birds.
The darkness drops again; but now I know
That twenty centuries of stony sleep
Were vexed to nightmare by a rocking cradle..."

–The Second Coming, William Butler Yeats

TOM

Tom pulled up to the cottage, drove around a rusty Cavalier and a Chrysler station wagon, and parked off to one side. Inside several women sang along with the radio. The sound of their voices cheered him a little, and although he did not intend to stay, for the time at least he was glad to be back.

"Aunt Harriet?" No one responded, so he followed the music to the kitchen and stopped in the doorway.

Aunt Harriet and two of her friends sang at the top of their lungs. One woman stirred batter in a massive bowl, another flicked flour across the table and rolled out dough, and Aunt Harriet scooped filling into a pie pan. She waved as he came in. Tom had to smile as he leaned against the doorjamb. "How much have you all had to drink? And can I get some?"

Aunt Harriet tossed a final scoop of filling into the pan, set it aside, and picked up a half-full wine glass, singing along with the radio. She snatched the dishtowel from her shoulder as she approached and twirled it around his neck as the song finished. "You don't recognize it? Skeeter Davis? Ah well, before your time, I suppose." She gave him a little peck on the cheek and turned the music off. "Wine's on the counter, glasses are over there." She took a sip and exchanged glances with her friends.

Something about their look whisked away Tom's moment

of joy and replaced it with the urge to leave again.

"Or there's beer in the fridge, of course." Aunt Harriet returned to the pie pan and took it to the counter.

"Here, let me." The dough-roller went to the refrigerator and got a beer. She dug a glass out of the cupboards, filled it, and handed it to Tom.

Aunt Harriet began arranging fresh-cut dough slices into a lattice-top crust. "Honey, you remember Mrs. Dumfry." She finished laying strips cross-wise and began weaving in the remaining lattice.

The batter-stirrer winked. "My, you've grown."

The woman standing by Tom wiped a hand on her blouse and held it out. "And I'm Mrs. Janus. Last time I saw you, you were knee high to a grasshopper. Please, call me Rhonda." She laughed. "No need for formalities."

Mrs. Dumfry set down her bowl and joined Rhonda. "And you can call me Charlene."

The women crowded Tom, and he coughed as the odors of overripe cantaloupe and hand-lotion enveloped him. He sipped the beer to help clear his throat.

"Oh dear, sounds like you're coming down with something." Rhonda put a wrinkled hand to Tom's forehead and the crevices in her face deepened as she frowned. "You feel a touch warm, too."

"I'm fine, just tired." Tom took a step back into the hallway.

Rhonda stepped forward. "Of course, you are dear, what with the funeral and traveling and all." She took him by the hand and pulled him back into the kitchen.

Charlene stepped up, took the beer, and held his other hand. "You must be exhausted. Why, where are our manners?" The women led him to the table. One pulled out a chair and the other ushered him into it.

Charlene set the beer on the table. "Here you go, honey, you drink this up, and then you can go lie down for a nice nap."

Aunt Harriet finished weaving in the last strip of dough, put the pie in the oven, and joined her cohorts. The three of them surrounded Tom, watching him, smiling like star-struck groupies.

Rhonda wiped spittle from the corner of her mouth and spoke to no one in particular. "He looks so much like his father."

The other two murmured in agreement.

Tom chugged the beer, couldn't get it down fast enough, and when he finished, a loud burp caught him by surprise. He blushed and excused himself, then rose to go. "If you don't mind?"

Aunt Harriet rushed around the table and took him by the arm. "Well, there is one thing actually. I was telling these women about the items Lewis left you. I showed them the journal, but couldn't find your pretty little rock. Is there any chance we could see it? We'll give it right back."

The damned stone again. It felt like a hardened tumor in his pocket. Maybe this was a chance to be free of it. Aunt Harriet was acting weird. Maybe she always acted this way around her friends. Nothing erodes inhibitions like age and booze, and these women had plenty of both.

"Why not." He pulled the stone from his pocket. The rag fell away as he held it up, and he wondered if this was the first he'd actually touched the damned thing. The stone felt smooth and slick, as if coated in fine dust or oil, and the colors demanded attention.

"What is it?" Charlene put a hand out, stopping short.

Tom shifted focus to the three women who now encircled him. Each ogled the stone with an eerie affection, and even Aunt Harriet acted as if this were the first she saw it.

Rhonda reached out and took it. "Don't know what it is, but I'll tell you what I'm thinking. I'm thinking it's been a long time." She laughed and placed one hand on Tom's arm as she turned the stone over in her other. "Yes it has." Her dry tongue flicked across cracked and wrinkled lips, and she winked at Tom. "Know what I mean? Can I borrow this for an hour? Unless you're not busy." All three women cackled and passed the stone around like modern country witches.

The stone stopped at Harriet and she looked deep into it, as if searching for some lost secret. Rhonda rubbed Tom's arm, Charlene reached over and rubbed his shoulder, and he felt powerless to stop either.

Aunt Harriet began to hum an unfamiliar tune, half gospel, half Gregorian chant. She unfastened her apron, slipped it from her neck, and let it fall to the floor.

The tune buzzed through Tom's head and the world around vibrated. He touched the beads at his neck, more from habit than intention, and as Aunt Harriet reached for the zipper on the back of her dress, whatever spell rode on the waves of her song broke.

He grabbed the stone and backed away from the table, sending a chair skidding across the floor. "Stop. What are you doing?"

Aunt Harriet froze. Rhonda and Charlene stared at Tom. A slow grin spread across each of their faces and they fell into a fit of giggles.

"Why, we're only playing, honey." Aunt Harriet scooped her apron from the floor and put it back on. "Just some women having fun, you know."

Rhonda nodded as she righted the chair. "We're flirting with you, honey. The pickings get slim at our age."

Charlene picked the rag up and handed it back to Tom. "Can't blame a girl for trying, can you?"

"Can't blame you for trying?" Such total bullshit. What where they trying to do, start a foursome? Even if they weren't twice his age, there was nothing arousing about the situation. They made him sick.

Tom wrapped the stone and put it away. He looked at the three of them standing there as if he just walked into the room and interrupted them. After a long silence, he stepped around the table to Aunt Harriet. She had the same look as Jess and Teddy had after he left the shop. He couldn't stay mad.

"Look, I don't know what kind of game this is. I really came home to pack." He pulled the keys from his pocket and jingled them.

Aunt Harriet raised an eyebrow then a more familiar smile spread on her lips. "Well blessed be, you got them. Kyle's not going to sell?" She gave him a quick hug and although the moment was no longer tense, he still resisted. He would no longer see her as the woman who had cared for him and his brother.

"Well, not exactly."

Tom explained the deal as the other women returned to their baking. "So I really want to get over there. I hope you're not offended by the short notice." Those words came out uneasy. After what she had done, she should apologize to him.

"Oh no, honey. You go on. Keep the truck. I've no use for it any time soon. I expect you at the bake sale. Promise?" She returned to the sink and began cleaning up.

"Sure. Thanks for everything, Aunt Harriet. I mean it."

As he left, Rhonda and Charlene replied in unison, "Don't be a stranger." The three women fell into a fresh round of laughter.

CASSY

Cassy plopped down at her desk and rubbed her neck. What a morning. Why did every nut job in Washington Heights pick today to come out to play?

Paul came up from the basement. "Got Ferguson locked up. You can drive him up to Coopersville later."

"Why don't you drive him?" Being stuck with all the crap work irritated her to no end. "It's bullshit."

"Language." Monterey came out of the bathroom and joined the deputies. "Be professional. We're police, not sailors."

"Yes, sir. Sorry. It's been crazy out there. We've had twelve calls since leaving the Hanlon place. A couple of extreme domestic disputes. Jeppeson's wife found him stringing his own sheep up in the barn, and we caught Ferguson chasing his daughter with a pick-ax. Said she was fooling around with her own brother. We put him in holding for now. And—"

"Cassy volunteered to drive him up to Coopersville tomorrow." Paul shot her a smile.

"Fuck you very much Paul." She sneered back. "As I was saying, there were also a whole slew of vandalisms, cars and windows mostly, and someone spray-painted a giant penis on the high school. They even trashed the trucks at the Fire House, cut hoses and wires in the engines. Drew from the shop is on his way out to see what he can do. He's not hopeful. Those are special machines. Thinks he'll have to order parts. We need a few minutes to catch our breath."

"Don't get comfortable. I haven't heard from my cousin yet, so I'm bettin' his kids are still missing. I want you two out looking for them."

Cassy stretched and stood up. Of course, the Hanlon's hadn't come in. Dune was probably out with his double barrel roaming the woods right now. Or with dog collars. She didn't bother saying any of this, though. The look on Monterey's face said she stood no chance of arguing. "Can I at least grab a soda or something?"

"No. Get your asses out there. Now." Monterey sat down and rolled a smoke. He popped it in his mouth, picked up a tattered copy of *Who Moved My Cheese*, and buried his face in it. "That's an order. You're lucky you're not still in here answering phones."

Paul came around the desk and tugged her sleeve. "Come on. Let's get moving."

As they reached the door, Monterey called over his book. "Oh, and Cassy, there's a file missing. You know which one."

She looked at Paul and he rolled his eyes. She knew what he was thinking: not again. Cassy turned around. "I—"

"I have it, sir." Paul stepped forward. "I was reviewing old cases and must have left it at home. Won't happen again."

Monterey looked from one deputy to the other, one eyebrow raised, smoke drifting from his cigarette. "Well, if that's how it is. I didn't see your name on the sign-out sheet."

"I was being—what's that you like to say? Empowered. Yeah. I was taking some initiative." Paul turned around and made for the door. "Let's go, Cassy."

"Empowered doesn't mean sloppy," Monterey called after

them.

At least Paul waited until they got in the cruiser before he unleashed. "What the hell are you doing?"

Cassy slammed the door and Paul pulled away from the station. She felt tears welling within her and fought them down. She wouldn't let him see her cry. "I can't let it go. She's blood."

"The case closed how many years ago? Christ, that alone should say hands-off. What's more, it was also Monterey's case. Are you trying to get fired? He knows you think it was sloppy work, and you might be right. Fact is, it's been over with a long time. Leave it be. You bring me the jacket tonight. Or better yet, when things calm down, we'll go and get it together. You're like a goddamned little kid."

"Fine. Truth is, I don't know why I took it. I won't say I forgot about her, but I had let it go. I made my peace with her disappearance long ago. For some reason, it's been eating at me again for almost a year. Little things, you know? I see Kyle Burton sometimes, and it makes me think of her. Or the girls braiding their hair and jumping rope in the town square. Sometimes she pops into my mind, and I almost see her, as if she were standing right in front of me, asking for help. Jesus, if I didn't know better, I'd say she was haunting me. Something's changed and I don't know what or why. I'm all stirred up inside."

Paul glanced at her and his look softened. "Man. I had no idea." He pulled into the school. "Well, we'll get the file back, and you leave it alone. I mean, make a copy if you really want it. Don't let Monterey know. He did his best, and you're making him feel guilty. You think he didn't want to find her?" He stopped the cruiser and climbed out.

Cassy scurried out. "I think he didn't find her. And what

are we doing here?"

Paul slammed a hand on the hood. "You're right, he didn't find her. He tried, though, right? And we're here because kids mess around at schools. Last I saw those boys, they were headed this way. So, let's take a look and then move on. Get it?" Paul walked around the side of the school.

Cassy chose not to stir the nest any more. Paul was right, after all. Monterey had no reason to leave Alissa's case unsolved. She followed and caught up with her partner at the playground. The jungle gym and slides looked like cartoon monoliths. The deputies walked along the side of the school, surveying the grounds for anything suspicious.

The schoolyard was well-used, and she couldn't see the point. "Finding anything out here is going to be impossible."

Paul grunted and continued walking.

Cassy stopped. She thought she saw movement at the back of the yard. As her gaze passed by the little shed, a familiar head poked out then disappeared back into the shadows.

"Hey," she whispered.

Paul stopped and looked back.

"The shed. Guess who."

Paul nodded and joined her, and together they walked through the yard to the old metal outbuilding, stopping short of the door.

Murphy dug around at the rear of the shed, his back to them. "Damn. Where the hell is it?"

Cassy tapped a knuckle on the shed door. "Excuse me."

More clanging echoed from the shed. "Son of a—"

She knocked again and spoke louder. "Hello?"

Murphy looked over his shoulder, scowled, then straightened and came out.

"Oh, hi deputies. I didn't see you there. I was looking for...

um, looking for...” He glanced back at the shed. “Oh yeah, the gas can. Looking for the gas can. “

“Gas can?”

“Yeah, you know, for the lawnmower.” Murphy fidgeted a bit as Cassy sized him up, his bloodshot eyes twitching from one deputy to the other. “I’m supposed to cut the grass today, here and at the church, but all the cans in there are 2-cycle mix.”

“Uh, huh. Well, I’m sure it’s around here somewhere.” She caught a whiff of weed and wondered if Paul smelled it too. “Look, some kids are missing and we thought they might’ve come by here. The Hanlon—”

Paul took a step forward. “What’s that I smell, Murphy? You smoking in there? Again?”

Great. Cassy dropped her head. Couldn’t Paul see this wasn’t the time for his bad-cop bullshit? She bet this was exactly the kind of distraction that kept Monterey from finding her cousin. She grabbed Paul’s arm. “Not now, please? We can worry about Murphy’s smoking habit later.”

Paul said nothing more as he pulled away. Ever since Murphy ran over some poor kid’s cat with the mower, Paul made a game of busting the stoner every chance he got. “Take your own advice and get over it, okay? No games, not right now.”

Paul hitched his belt and puffed his chest. “You’re lucky she’s with me. You should thank her.”

Murphy wiped his grimy hands across his shirt and held one out. “Sure will. Thank you, sir... er, ma’am... deputy.”

Cassy ignored the gesture. “Missing kids, Murph. Stay with me. Three of them, last seen yesterday. Any ideas?”

Murphy nodded then stuffed his hands in his pockets. “Sure, three kids. Lemme think. Yesterday.” His eyebrows knit as he looked around and mumbled.

"Murphy?" Cassy looked in to catch his eyes. "Still with me?" She hated to give up. If those kids came by here, he was sure to have seen them.

"Yes." He held a hand up. "Yesterday, three kids. My gas can. They came by and stole my gas, ran off south. Probably used it to burn up their little GI Joes—or whatever kids play with these days. Little bastards. Did I mention they stole my gas?"

"You did and thank you." Cassy patted Murphy on the shoulder. "Now I suggest you get rid of whatever might give my partner here a reason to bust you. We have to find these boys now. I'm sure Paul will head right back here when were done."

Murphy eyed Paul then looked back at Cassy. "I will, ma'am, and thanks again." He put a hand out again, then pulled it back and nodded instead. "I will."

Cassy turned to leave. "Come on, Paul, let's get down to the flats."

ELANA

lana finished with her afternoon meditation. Her aching knees creaked as she stood. She paid no mind to the pain. Until the good Lord saw fit to strike her lame, prayers would continue. A small filing cabinet served as an altar where white votive candles encircled a hefty brass crucifix. She blew out the flames sending gray tendrils of smoke puffing into the air then kissed a finger and smeared it on the frozen face of her man Jesus. "Amen."

An old metal desk huddled against the wall under a bulletin board. A single photograph of the curious stone hung there, taken almost a year earlier and given to her by Lewis Burton. Photocopies of various artifacts from throughout history clustered around it dangling from pushpins: Hindu Lingam, Greek Omphalos, Native American Totem Poles, Egyptian Benben, the Washington Monument, and many more.

None matched the deep green jasper streaked with red, polished to a smooth oblong. A year of research failed to uncover any trace of the stone's history. She was prepared to call it a fluke, some rough act of nature without meaning or consequence.

Still, something bothered her, and she was unable to rip the pictures down and throw them away even though recent months of reading turned up nothing new. She surveyed the images, looking for some unseen connection to spark an epiphany.

Her eyes hurt from all the dirty worms. History and archeology held a deep fascination with the phallus. Why would Jesus let such nasty symbols exist? Elana sat on the rough wooden stool, closed her eyes, and rubbed her neck, visualizing the stone as a singular teardrop shed by her Savior as he suffered on the cross. That felt closer to the truth than any of those other dirty penis pictures. It was a blessed teardrop sent to cleanse the world.

Her skin grew warm, almost feverish. Her heart raced, and a chill ran through her body. Cold, metallic hands settled on her shoulders, massaging, working their way down her back and around her side toward her breasts, crossing her abdomen, down, down, down. The room filled with the same pungent odors she used to smell in her parents' bedroom when she sneaked in late at night to snuggle down in their warmth, pressed close to her daddy's chest. A miniature solar flare erupted within, then the sensations disappeared. Her man Jesus spoke to her through the singular sweet burning. The cold hands vanished, and she once again sat alone in her empty office.

Elana slipped from the stool, straightened her blouse, and marched through the door into the stacks. Where was that no good girl? "Kathy!" She emerged from the stacks to the checkout area.

"Ms. Lyons?" Kathy scurried out from behind the front desk and rushed over. "Is everything okay? Do you need an ambulance?"

Why was an ambulance the first thing offered whenever she needed something? "No, I don't need an ambulance. Now cut the act. Where are they?"

Kathy looked around. "Where are what?" A few people

wandered from the stacks to watch the commotion.

"Don't play dumb with me, girl." Elana became aware of the onlookers, grabbed Kathy by the wrist, and led her back to the front desk. Her voice dropped to a hoarse whisper. "Not what. Who. Your sex-crazed friends. I smelled it all the way back there."

Kathy slumped and frowned. "My what? Sex... Ms. Lyons, look around. This is a library, there's no one having sex here. Is this some kind of joke?"

"I do not joke, young lady. If I say there's someone doing something inappropriate here, then there is. Now are you going to stand there like a lost kitten, or are you going to help me find them?"

Kathy shook her head and backed away. "Ma'am?"

"Oh, never mind you, useless girl, I'll take care of this myself. I better not catch you doing anything indecent. Don't think I don't know what you kids like to do in here, all hands and mouths and heavy breathing. When Jesus comes back—"

"I know." Kathy's voice quivered. "We're all going to be turned into deformed eunuchs. I haven't seen anything. I've been at the desk all afternoon checking in books and filling the pushcarts. It's what you hired me to do, remember?"

"If you had any sense, you would keep a better eye on the library, too."

"If I had..." Kathy withered in place, tears welling up. "I'm supposed to work the desk. How can I watch the place if I'm stuck behind the desk?"

"So, you don't like working behind the desk?"

"No. I mean yes. I..." Tears worked themselves free and raced down Kathy's cheeks. "What do you want me to do?"

More people popped out of the stacks. Most headed for the exit, and none dared interfere. How could they with her man

Jesus on her side? Elana still burned from forehead to sagging breasts as the little girl tried to make a fool of her. The townsfolk may come and go, borrow a book or watch a movie, but by squatter's rights, this place belonged to her. "Keep your voice down. Stop crying. People are staring."

Kathy continued to weep, stifling her sobs with both hands.

Elana wagged a finger. "Now you get back to work, useless girl. I'll deal with you later. Oh, and only men can be eunuchs. Women will have their clitorises gouged out." She turned around to address the onlookers, donning her best matronly face and clasping her hands at her bosom. "It's okay, everyone. We had a little misunderstanding. Go on back to your books." Most of the remaining patrons hurried out the door as she finished.

The air felt hot and dense. A teenage boy on the sofa buried his face behind a book. She let him be for now and walked the length of the library, checking down each row. Aside from her, Kathy, and the young man on the couch, the only other person was a bohemian girl decked out in a patchwork dress, hair in cornrows and laced with beads, earbuds plugged in deep.

Elana returned to her office door, glanced down the row of study carols, and slipped in. Her man waited in there on his brazen crucifix, gleaming in the fluorescent light, soaked in a strange aura of yellow and brown. Soft shadows seeped from behind the frozen messiah.

She looked away and her gaze happened upon the images stuck to the bulletin board. The stone in the center burned with greens and reds as indiscernible syllables burrowed through her eardrums deep into the center of her brain. The words made no sense. They didn't have to. Elana grabbed a set of keys from the hook by the door, stuffed them in her pocket, and took the brass Jesus from his home atop the filing cabinet. She held him up and prayed for guidance. The room grew cold. A dark tongue of flame coalesced from the shadows and descended, kissing her forehead before evaporating.

Her feet moved as if by the Holy Spirit, and she found herself standing at the front door, slipping the key in, clicking the deadbolt home. Through the window, the sky darkened to crimson, and the sun became a darkened well among the clouds. Could it be? Was the end approaching?

She could see it. The horsemen galloping into town, swords drawn. Mr. Kanetti, who complained of her attitude and tried to get her replaced, would go first. The lazy Sheriff, who never lifted a finger when she reported stolen books, would be next. Then maybe the Doc, or Charlie. Neither paid their fines, and it wasn't as if they couldn't afford it...

"Ms. Lyons?" Kathy ventured out from behind the desk.

Elana blinked, and the world outside was once again the familiar grainy postcard of Washington Heights. She gave Kathy a sidelong look. "Never mind, girl. Closing up a little early is all."

"What's with the cross?" Kathy retreated.

Elana looked at the lump of brass, yellows and browns seething behind it like a bed of earthworms. Jesus had something to say and needed to say it now.

"I'll be back here in a few minutes. You stay put."

She turned around and stormed by the young man reading on the couch. He peeked over the top of his book, and she returned an icy glare. "Maybe you want words with the man Jesus here?" The boy shook his head, got up and scurried to the front desk. Elana continued toward the rear of the library, chased by the whispers of the two up front. She would leave them alone. For now.

The study rooms were nestled in the back, opposite her office. All three doors were shut. Soft light glowed from beneath one.

Elana opened the doors of the darkened rooms and found them both empty, filled only with the smells of industrial cleaner and hard plastic. She paused at the door of the third, pressed an ear to cold wood, and listened to the soft slurping and rough scuttling inside. Her sex grew warm.

This was her library and damned if she had to knock on any door. The cold knob felt obscene in her hand, so she turned it quick, threw the door open, and stepped in.

A couple of teens—a boy and a girl—sat at the desk, books open. The brass in her hand grew hot and heavy, and the image pulsed into a mess of arms and legs writhing on the table, snippets of clothing littering the floor and draped over the plastic chairs. The air was a soft haze of yellows and browns, and the fresh odor of body juices assaulted her.

"You dirty little worm! You dirty little bird!"

The conjoined teens on the table wiggled in surprise.

"What the—"

Elana brought the heavy cross down on the boy's head. Blood flicked and splattered across the room, speckled her face and blouse. The young girl screamed and swung out, connecting loosely with one of her knees. She faltered, then the burning within bolstered her up, giving her the strength to stand and bring the cross down again. Silence permeated the room.

Elana watched the shallow rise and fall of their bare chests. They wouldn't stay still for long.

Outside of the room, next to the copy machine, stood a small worktable. On it sat a dark green paper cutter, and Elana conceived a new use for it. As she snatched the board, Kathy called out. "Ms. Lyons? Everything okay?"

She stepped over two rows and peered down the aisle. Kathy and the young man stood in front of the checkout counter looking concerned. The bohemian princess was nowhere in sight.

Kathy gave a little wave.

"We thought we heard a scream," the young man added.

Elana waved back. "Everything's fine, I'll be there in a minute."

The pair at the desk exchanged looks. Why couldn't they mind their own business?

Kathy leaned over the desk. "Is that blood?"

"I said I'm fine. Get back to work." Elana didn't wait for a response. She returned to the study room where the slumped teens struggled for breath, slipped in, and shut the door.

The boy and girl were not as she left them. Both were dressed and sat in the chairs. Elana paid no attention. It was just the devil playing tricks. Her man Jesus had his say. She had a little something more. She yanked the boy from his chair to the floor and pulled his pants down. She set the crucifix on the table so Jesus could watch, knelt down, and placed the cutting board on the boy's thighs.

His semi-erect penis glistened. She pulled a face as she grasped the head between forefinger and thumb. It felt rubbery as she slipped it under the arced blade and pulled it taught.

The young man groaned, fluttered his eyelids, and struggled to sit up. "What the..." He looked down and saw the board. "Ms. Lyons?"

Elana brought the blade down, but lacked the strength to get through in one clean cut. The boy's holler rose to a buzzing howl as she brought the blade down a second time. The member slipped clean, and she tossed it across the room.

The young man writhed on the floor. Blood streamed from between his legs and smeared the cutting board. He kicked and wiggled, sending the board scurrying across the floor. Elana grasped the crucifix, stepped over the boy, and brought it down on his head—again, again, again—until he fell silent.

"You got words for man Jesus? He doesn't shed tears over dirty little worms. At the end-of-days, your privates come off, and you got to answer for all your sins."

The semi-conscious girl groaned, and Elana turned. "You got something to say, dearie? I think not." The heavy brass smacked down on her skull twice, erupting a fresh flow of blood, and quieting the girl once again.

She pulled the girl from the chair to the table, drew up the skirt, and sliced away the cotton panties with an arm of the cross. "Let his spirit fill you up, little lady."

The girl's legs parted easily, giving Elana plenty of space to work with. She held Jesus by the base and slipped him into the dirty little bird. An arm of the cross caught on the perineum, so she pushed harder until the crucifix sliced through with a pop.

The door opened, and the young man from the couch stood ashen, jaw agape. "Ma'am? Are they—"

Elana gave him no time to finish. She slipped the cross from the minced womb, turned to the boy, leveled the cross and charged. The brass drove deep into his gut. Jesus filled her with his strength, and she twisted and turned, blending the boy's internals to chum. His yells, even his fists striking her face and neck, were not enough.

A sticky, crimson mess covered the floor. The young man slipped and fell into her, helping drive the cross deeper. His scream fell to a gurgle cut short by a cough, sending fresh blood over her shoulder and down her back. So hot, so wet, so warm.

He crumpled to the floor and clawed at her ankles as she stepped over him and out of the room.

Elana slipped along the wall, looking down the rows of books, listening to a scurry of whispers from the front, broken by the sound of someone rattling the doors. She paused at an aisle and peered around the corner. Kathy stood at the desk, facing the exit and speaking to whoever shook the doors.

She pressed against the end of a row, held the smeared cross up, and prayed once again. Ice touched her deep inside, writhing through every vein. Something was wrong. Was she mistaken? Was it someone other than her man coming? She held Jesus's crimson-tainted gaze. Wrong or not, it was too late to matter. She and Jesus would finish what they started.

She crept across two more aisles and spotted the hippie girl rattling the doors. A fierce flame replaced the ice, and she charged a second time. The little bohemian never saw her coming.

Jesus dug deep into the base of the girl's neck and a pop rang through the brass as Elana thrust it deeper. The girl twitched, slipping from the cross, and fell to the floor in a heap of colorful fabric and hair beads.

She turned to the desk and held the cross for Jesus to get a good view. "Now we're ready to deal with you, dear girl."

Kathy screamed, grabbed the phone from under the desk, and dialed. Elana marched over, holding her crucifix out like a shield. She marched around the counter swinging the cross.

Kathy ducked, receiver still pressed to her ear, speaking frantically. "Help! I'm at the library, Ms. Lyons is—"

The crucifix found Kathy's temple.

Kathy sunk to the floor, still conscious, and scrambled like a drunk to get away.

Heat flowed up and down Elana's body, something deeper and more intimate than the flare from before. It reached her dry, withered crotch, and juices held at bay her entire life began to flow.

Kathy still struggled against the floor, a thin trail of blood stringing out behind her. She hitched and hawed, taking breaths in big gasps, unable to gather enough wind for a scream. Did she think she could get away? Did she think herself so different from the others?

Elana rubbed the cold slick crucifix against her crotch, the perfect mixture of warm blood, cold metal, and the stink of fear bringing her to climax.

Kathy stopped and wilted into a heaving mess.

A few more steps and Elana towered over the dirty little bird. "Come now, girl. It's better this way. Though the end-of-days are upon us, there's no need to suffer through the hell to come."

Kathy rolled over. "Why?" The word stumbled out, weak and beaten.

Elana brought the cross down, Jesus first, into Kathy's abdomen. She stabbed and stuck, mincing the girl to a pulpy mess.

Her work nearly finished, Elana stood, smoothed the blood and chunks from her blouse, and returned to the phone. She heard several faint hellos from the receiver as she wiped her ear clean and raised the phone.

"Hello? Kathy? Talk to me. What's going on?"

Elana panted. "It's Ms. Lyons. Kathy stepped away."

"Ms. Lyons, are you okay? It's Sheriff Monterey. Do you need an ambulance?"

With a sharp, thick arm of the cross pressed into her neck, Elana replied, "Yes I do." She punctured the skin and drew a ragged gash. Warm blood spilled from the wound as the receiver tumbled to the desk.

CASSY

Paul and Cassy drove along route 56, following the wetlands stretched miles south of town until they gave way to grasses, then scrub brush and gradually trees. Paul swung the cruiser across the road and parked in the breakdown lane. He took a flashlight from the glove box while Cassy checked her Glock 17 9mm.

"Do you really need that?" Paul got out.

Cassy came around the car and clipped the pistol into its holster. "Be prepared, right?"

"We're just looking for kids, but whatever makes you feel safe." He surveyed the woods. "Let's get to it. We have a lot of ground to cover, and I'm hungry."

She pulled an energy bar from her breast pocket. "Didn't they have cub scouts where you come from? Here."

He tore into the bar and mumbled thanks through a mouthful, stepping into the woods.

The woods buzzed with katydids and locusts while the fat, lazy river rippled in the background. A rough, earthy scent hung in the air. She called Monterey with their location then traipsed into the woods.

The deputies walked for over thirty minutes, spread out between the road and the river, keeping each other in sight. They stopped to check out the occasional cluster of beer cans or burned-out fire-rings. Nothing seemed unusual until Cassy reached a shallow hole.

"Over here." She waited, stricken by déjà vu, as if she once again stood by Lewis Burton's grave. She knelt and touched the hardened clay.

"What's this shit?" Paul stood next to her and kicked at the lip of the hole.

"Fire pit?" She knew it wasn't right even as she said it. She didn't want to entertain her first thought of a grave.

Paul laughed and kicked the dirt again. "No embers. Too big, anyhow. Hello, what's that? You stay here, I'll be right back."

Paul moved out, and she looked on ahead of him. A mound broke the landscape some thirty yards off. "Careful."

"It's dirt. It might be odd, but it's still only dirt."

She traced the lip of the hole once again. Something out here felt wrong, and she didn't trust Paul on his own. "Wait up, okay?"

Paul stopped short of the mound. "Got another one up there. Why don't you go look and I'll check this one out."

Cassy's stomach dropped. "Three of them?"

"Oh, go on. Don't think crazy." Paul waved her on as he knelt and began picking at the mound. He held a clump up as she passed. "See? Dirt." He cast clotted earth into the woods and looked around.

Cassy unsnapped her holster and rested a hand on the Glock's butt. The shadows wavered as the breeze picked up and she felt as if the woods were full of eyes, all watching her.

She knelt next to the third mound, a collection of rough clumps of earth thrown together without care. The clay felt cold and lifeless as she rested a hand on the ground.

Paul called from behind. "So, what's up?"

She looked over her shoulder. "Keep it down. Might be someone else out here."

"Like who?" Paul stood, arms akimbo.

Cassy called back, trying to be as quiet as possible. "Look, there's three holes and three missing boys. Tell me these aren't about the size of a kid. Three kids."

"That one's empty." Paul crossed his arms and surveyed the woods. She knew the look. He'd finally become uneasy.

She turned back to her work. Paul would have to sort it out for himself. She had to know for sure. She had to dig. So, she pulled at the dirt, doing her best not to disturb too much, until her fingers brushed something other than jagged clay. Oily ash coated her fingers as she continued to clear the dirt from what she hoped was a piece of charcoal.

Then earth surrendered a slightly parted mouth and sooty teeth, the remaining features of a face. "We got a body." She struggled to get the words out through the seething bile rising in her throat.

Paul scurried through the woods to her. "Jesus." He dropped the flashlight and pulled his gun. "Well don't touch it. Get away from it, we'll call it in."

The initial shock gone, she scratched the ground away and cleared dirt from the face. "Do you recognize him? Is it one of those kids?"

"I said leave it alone. I'm gonna radio Monterey, let's get to the car." Paul backed away then stopped. "You hear something?"

She didn't have to. The feeling of being watched returned one-hundred-fold. She froze and listened.

A twig snapped somewhere off to their right, and before she could react Paul fired two shots off.

Her partner stood motionless, pistol still held in offense. She reached out and lowered his arms then put a finger to her lips and signaled for him to circle around from the right. Cassy moved with Indian stealth around to the left. Moments later, they met by the body of a groundhog with a fresh bullet hole in its side.

"Nice shot." She meant it to break the tension. She failed. The overwhelming uneasiness enveloping them remained undented.

"Well goddamn it, how was I supposed to know?"

"And you made fun of me for checking my gun. Let's go see if you recognize the boy. I'll clear the other, and if there's another body, you'll look. Then, and only then, we will radio Monterey. Got it?"

Paul nodded and returned to the open grave while she cleared the other mound. It contained another body, and though Paul looked at both, the charred remains were too distorted for him to tell for sure if they were the Hanlon boys.

"Shit, we're gonna get an ass-chewing for this, you know? Monterey's all about protocol."

Paul's radio squawked before she could get a word out.

"Speak of the devil. Tell him I said 'hi'."

Paul answered. "Carson here, Sherriff. We got a real problem out here."

"It'll have to wait. Fielding with you?"

"She's here. I don't think this'll wait, boss. We have three graves and two bodies out here. Burned up real bad."

The radio was silent for a moment, then the Sheriff spoke. "I got a situation myself at the library. Five bodies. Jesus." His voice faded out.

"Monterey? Did you say five?" Paul paled.

Cassy stepped closer. The woods pressed in on her from all sides.

"Five bodies. Crandall's boy is here with the wagon. How soon can you get back?"

Every ounce of warmth drained from her. Five bodies. Two more right here. This was Washington Heights, not New York City. Oh, and she couldn't forget the suicide. An image of Lewis slumped on the ground, a blossom of crimson and gray on the barn wall behind him, jumped to mind before she could stave it off. What the fuck was going on? Nothing like this happened out here. Nothing.

"We can be back in twenty or so if we hustle. What the hell do we do about the graves? What's going on?"

Silence spilled from the radio as the deputies waited for an answer. The sheriff was probably as much at a loss as they were.

Cassy grabbed the radio. "Sheriff, here's what we'll do, if you don't mind. Paul and I will mark the graves and come back. When Davie's done, he can come out and take care of these. Sound good?"

"Sure, come on in." Monterey sounded defeated. Underneath the exhaustion was something Cassy never thought she'd hear from their boss. Fear. "Mark those graves and come back. We'll think this through. Monterey out."

"You heard the man, get to it." They staked out the head of each grave then made straight for the road and marked their exit. They sprinted back to the cruiser, and minutes later were barreling down route 56, sirens blaring.

CHARLIE

Two ham steaks sizzled on the flattop. A basket of fries bubbled in the deep fryer. Charlie slapped corned beef, Swiss cheese, sauerkraut, and Thousand Island dressing between two slices of rye, and tossed the sandwich down next to the ham.

It wasn't enough.

He looked out the serving window at Debbie chatting with Johnny Belfry, not quite able to hear their conversation. Had she told him? Charlie didn't think so. She looked so much like her mother as she brushed away a lock of blond hair, smiled, and laughed. And now he was losing her too.

No signs of a belly showed yet even in her tight uniform. Doc Crandall said she was six weeks along—breaking his promise not to tell—and they would have to do something soon. If Charlie wanted.

Was it up to him? Could he make such a life-changing decision for his daughter? Should he?

He didn't know. Even without the baby growing in her, Charlie would lose his little girl soon enough. College was around the corner, the lurking stranger of the world enticing his baby away.

A tinge of smoke struck his nose, and he looked down at the grill. "Damn," he muttered and flipped the steaks. Even though they were a little darker than usual, no one would complain. No one ever did.

It would never be enough, though. This diner supported him and Debbie okay. He could scrape together enough for an abortion if necessary. He could not afford to help with her school.

Maybe her mother would. Even though Charlie hadn't spoken with her in years, he was pretty sure Debbie still did. Maybe tonight he would make the call he should have made months ago, maybe tonight he could swallow his pride enough to ask for the help his daughter so needed. Maybe tonight he and Debbie could ask her together.

Charlie flipped the Reuben and pulled the fry basket out of the oil. The few voices in the diner seemed to grow louder and less clear, almost like the soft buzz of insects.

The ham-steaks went onto plates, and Charlie plopped a scoop of mashed potatoes on each, finishing them with gravy and green beans. He set them in the serving window and called for a pickup.

Debbie looked up from Johnny and smiled. God how he wanted her to stay.

So many years ago, her mother called this place the ass-end of the earth, said nothing here grew right. He didn't understand then. Things were different now. He spent his life in this belch of a town, and here he was—a diner cook. Sure, it was his diner, but in this little town owning your own diner felt like owning your own grave. Debbie deserved much more. The folds of his heart clung to her, making it hard to let her go. It was one thing to waste his life. It was another entirely to watch his daughter waste hers. She had to get out of this little stagnant pool and find a better place, a better life.

"Dad? Is something wrong?" Debbie took the plates. Her smile wavered as she stopped to look him over. "You look tired. Maybe you need to take a break. Are you getting another headache?"

As he forced a smile in return, he felt the tremor of his lips and the sag of his eyes. "I'm fine. No headache, I just miss you."

Debbie slumped and tilted her head. "I'm not gone yet. We got all summer, and you know I'll come home to visit all the time."

No, she wouldn't, and Charlie would never hold it against her. "Things won't be the same." He glanced behind her. "Has Johnny figured out what he's doing yet?" He tried to sound pleasant and interested. Debbie's frown told him he failed.

"No, not that you care. Really, daddy, he's a nice boy. He'll probably never come here again if you don't pull his Reuben off the grill." She winked and carried the ham-steaks away.

Charlie spun around. The dressing and cheese seeped out the edges and slowly blackened on the grill, puffing out soft tendrils of smoke. He rescued the sandwich, put it on a plate, cut it in half, and added a pile of fries. It was good enough for Johnny. Damned if he would make another.

The diner buzzed, and a sharp pain shot through his temples, so he left the plate on the counter, sat down on an old milk crate and rifled through his pockets. "Damn, where are those things?" His pockets turned up empty. "Debbie, you seen my pills?"

She popped her head through the window. "Top of the sink, Daddy. Need some water?"

"I got a drink here, thanks. I feel a bad one coming on." He got his pills and swallowed one, washing it down with diet cola and getting some temporary relief. He took the Reuben to the serving window where Debbie waited.

"You need to see the doc again?"

Charlie shook his head and shooed her away. "Get the sandwich out to your boyfriend before I decide he doesn't deserve it."

Debbie scurried off. Charlie watched her go then took a quick look around the dining room.

Jess Dawson, who sat with her husband Teddy, looked up from her ham-steak, raised a hand, and croaked. "Great as usual, Charlie."

"Thanks, Jess."

Teddy looked up as well, lips peeled back, nose scrunched. "Tastes like shit, Charlie. You shit on my steak, Charlie? Did you?"

Charlie rubbed his eyes and when he opened them again, Jess and Teddy were simply smiling at him. "What'd you say, Teddy?"

Something was wrong. The air above them darkened. Shadows drew themselves from nowhere and coalesced, like a swarm of wasps, into teardrops. The forms descended and licked at the tops of their heads. Teddy spoke again. This time the words came out as random syllables, a congestion of sounds tumbling over one another in a fight to make sense.

Charlie shook his head against the fresh pain in his temples. "I'm sorry, Teddy, once more?"

Teddy's smile crumbled, and he repeated the mishmash of sounds. Jess started to speak as well. Charlie cut her short.

"There's something over your head."

The couple looked up, then reached across the table, and bound their hands together. Teddy sucked in air, and Jess pursed her lips. They both turned toward Charlie, each trying to speak, neither able to utter a word, their mouths working like suffocating fish.

Debbie came to the serving window and put a hand on his. Her touch was so warm. She put a hand to his cheek and drew his attention. "Dad? What's going on?"

More darkness seeped from the ceiling, dripping down over the heads of everyone in the diner.

Charlie withdrew from the window as cold tendrils of fear slithered through every nerve, helpless against the slow cloud forming over Debbie's head. No way was this a migraine. "Everyone, get out! Don't you see them?"

Most of the people were on their feet by now, including Jess and Teddy. Johnny rose and hurried to Debbie, a tongue of darkness flickering over his mess of jet-black hair. Harsh consonants trickled out as he spoke to her. She answered. Charlie no longer understood her either. Was it just him? Did no one else hear the nonsense?

He stepped back and grabbed the spatula from the grill. "Get away from her!"

Voices swirled and jabbed at him. He saw looks of concern and confusion plastered on all their faces as they streamed toward the exit, their words lost on him. The harsh buzz of angry wasps mixed with the tremors of gibberish and enfolded him.

He moved as fast as his weight would allow, pressing against the slow spread of pain from temples to neck and down into the rest of his body. He sensed the dense cloud above his head and tried to stay ahead of the darkness, using the spatula to break it up.

The remaining few people congregated around the door to the kitchen, and as he burst through, all except Debbie and Johnny stumbled back, gibbering and squawking, exchanging looks and keeping their distance from one another.

"What are you saying? Why can't I understand? Would

you all stop?"

Johnny reached out as Charlie swung the heavy spatula. He aimed for the dark cloud of flame above the kid. His swing was too low and the flat side swiped across the boy's face with a dull thwack, sending Johnny to the ground. The teardrop shadow clung to the boy's scalp.

Johnny tried to scramble back. Charlie was too quick. He brought the spatula around again, this time with the sharp side. It sliced across the bridge of the boy's nose leaving a bright red line in its wake.

Debbie grabbed him by the arm, spewing nonsense. He shook her loose. "Don't touch me. What the hell is that? Don't you see it? Are you all fucking crazy? Am I fucking crazy?" She broke into tears and ran off toward the bathrooms.

Three more people ran out the door and pressed against the diner window to watch, leaving only Jess, Teddy, Johnny, and him inside. Jess and Teddy clung to each other like lost children as Johnny stuffed himself under a table and cowered, blood-soaked napkin pressed to the bridge of his nose.

He looked up in time to see the shadows regrouping inches from him. He swung the spatula back and forth, breaking the darkness up only to have it reform.

Bright flashes of blinding light stole his vision, numbness overtook his face and hands. All he could do was stumble to the counter, sit on a stool, and wait for the whole ordeal to end. Feet scuffled and the door slammed, leaving only Charlie.

Blind. Scared. Alone.

CASSY

assy cut the sirens and pulled into the library parking lot. The town's only ambulance sat at an angle by the front, backed in, bay doors open. Davie and Jake were here, and Cassy was in no mood for either of them.

As she got out, the EMTs bustled through the front doors with a body bag on a gurney. They stopped to rest, both men sweaty and out of breath, Jake looking a little white as he wiped his brow and leaned over.

Paul reached them first. "That bad?"

Davie nodded. "You want to look?"

"I don't think so." Paul turned to her. "Do you?"

"Nope, not unless I have to." She patted Jake's back. "You gonna be okay? Need some water or something?"

Jake shook his head and waved her off. "Need a minute to catch my breath."

She didn't want to talk to Davie. Talking to poor Jake didn't seem promising either. "So, who's the poor soul?"

Davie gave her a blank stare then addressed Paul. "It's the Clark boy. Looks like old Ms. Lyons finally lost her shit. She cut it off."

She moved between them. "Cut what off?"

Paul stepped aside. "Jesus. Who does that?"

Maybe she could get a straight answer from Paul. "What? Cut what off?"

"You know." Paul pointed down. "It."

"His cock, Cassy. Now if you'll excuse us." Davie jiggled the gurney then slapped Jake on the back. "Get up here and help me. We got a full bus, and two more trips to make."

Cassy sneered. "Thanks, I got it." Why did he have to be such an asshole?

Cassy and Paul parted to let the EMTs through. "Just making sure," Davie said as he passed. "I figured since you've never seen one—"

"Watch your mouth. I may be a woman but I'm still an officer of the law. You know what your problem is? You have no respect for anyone. And you wonder why we didn't work out."

"Okay, easy." Paul joined her as Davie and Jake pushed the gurney into the ambulance. "Things are crazy here. Let it go."

She curled one hand to a fist, resisting the urge to smack the asshole in the head. Things were crazy today, and she knew better than to get into it with Davie in the middle of it all. Still, she couldn't stop from getting the last word. "Just watch your mouth."

The gurney slid in and Davie went around to the driver's side without replying. Jake leaned against the bay doors and mopped his forehead again.

Cassy saw two other body bags in the back. "Who are they?"

Jake looked into the back as he caught his breath. "Well, one's Nigel Waterson's boy, and the other's Mia Johnson. You don't want to know what Ms. Lyons did to her."

From the driver's seat, Davie called out, "Talk about your backseat abortions."

Jesus, would the guy ever get a sense of decency? She

started to reply. Paul laid a hand on her shoulder.

"Let it go, deputy."

"He's such an asshole."

"I know. Let it go."

Jake looked at her and bit his lower lip. "Sorry. Tough day, you know."

"For all of us." She spoke harsher than she meant to, and added, "Thanks for your help."

Jake nodded. "Well, we best get moving. We'll be back for them other three, then I suppose one of you will have to take us out to the flats." He tucked the handkerchief in his back pocket. "Take care." He closed the bay and struggled into the passenger side. The ambulance pulled away as he swung his door shut.

Paul turned to face the library. "You ready?"

"As I'll ever be."

They went in and found Monterey by the entrance talking with Doc Crandall. The men exchanged grim words, both looking as if the world were ending.

"Glad you two made it. Here." Monterey held out two of his god-awful hand-rolled smokes.

Paul shook his head. "Had my limit today, right Doc?"

Doc Crandall gave a slight nod and pursed his bottom lip.

"You'll want it." The sheriff scratched his neck and waved the smokes.

Paul took one and slipped it into a breast pocket. "Maybe."

"Since when did we start smoking in public buildings?" Cassy took the other anyway and put it in her pocket. "And since when did you think I started smoking?"

Monterey waved them on. "Let's walk, deputies. You come too, Doc."

He led them through the library to the back study room,

explaining what little he knew along the way. The body at the front was Mandy Feins. Spinal cord severed, according to Doc. Garrett Turnstahl's daughter, Kathy, called the station earlier screaming something about the librarian. She was cut off. Monterey heard some commotion then Elana came on the phone and asked for an ambulance. He radioed Davie to meet him here, and they found the six bodies.

Cassy stopped. "I thought you said five on the radio?"

Monterey spun around. "Jesus, Cassy. Five, six, what's it matter? This is more bodies than we've seen in... well, ever."

"Just trying to be thorough. Sorry." She looked to Paul for help. He only shrugged and gave her another one of his "let it go" looks.

The sheriff pulled out a cigarette and lit it. "No, it's okay. You're right, I said five, meant six. Don't make anything of it, okay?"

She nodded, fighting the easy shot. More sloppy work. How did this guy ever get to be the sheriff?

"Good, follow me."

They reached the rear, and Monterey motioned for the deputies to look in one of the study rooms. "There isn't much to see at this point. Believe me—you didn't want to see what we found."

Paul glanced in first and turned around quickly.

Cassy peeked in next. The room looked like someone had let a monkey loose with an open can of red paint. A paper cutter lay on the floor, blood drying on the blade.

"Christ in heaven," Paul muttered. "She used it to...?"

"Cut his penis off?" Cassy finished for him.

Doc nodded. "Emasculated, if you want to get technical."

"What about the girl?" Cassy had to ask even though she had a pretty good idea at this point.

"Looks like the librarian jammed something in her vagina and pureed the insides. We found Elana up front clutching a brass crucifix."

"Dear lord. You can't be serious." She didn't smoke. This made her consider starting. What an absolute cluster fuck.

"I think they were unconscious, had some pretty bad head trauma," Doc added, as if being knocked out made getting slaughtered any better.

"This way." Monterey led them to Elana's office. Inside, he pointed out the collage on the bulletin board.

"Is that what I think it is?" Cassy stepped up to get a closer look at the photograph in the center.

"Depends. What do you think it is?"

Cassy rolled her eyes. What a time for one of the sheriff's stupid little tests. "Well, I think it's the stone we found—I found—at Lewis Burton's suicide. The one you had me cart over to his funeral for Tom. A fool's errand if you ask me."

"What's a rock have to do with any of this?" Paul joined her for a closer look.

Monterey remained silent until she and Paul turned to face him. "It looks like Elana Lyons was a little obsessed, don't you think?"

Doc Crandall picked over some items on the filing cabinet.

"Can you not touch stuff please?" She stared at the doctor until he put a votive candle back in place, then continued with the sheriff. "So what? She was an old, god-fearing woman who liked her privacy and liked to study old artifacts. How do any of those make her obsessed? A woman can't have a hobby?"

Monterey dropped his smoke, crushed it out, and crossed his arms. "You call killing kids a hobby? You got a funny way of thinking."

She shook her head, doing her best to ignore Monterey's

lack of respect for the crime scene. Maybe Paul could put it in better terms. "You know what I mean, right? Help me out here."

"She means it's not fair to take Elana's single act—however gory, crazy, or suicidal—and make her into some obsessed old woman." Paul raised an eyebrow. "Am I right?"

"Yes. Thank you. I mean, maybe she was on medication or something. She's been part of this town for how long, and now you want to make her into some crazy obsessed killer? You have no idea what was going through her head. Come on. Think about it. Something is wrong here. Very wrong." She tossed her hands up. If the sheriff couldn't see it now, he probably never would. Everything was cut-and-dry with him, distillable down to the simplest answer. Sometimes the simple answers were wrong. Sometimes things were too complex.

"Okay, okay. You might be right. Let's move on." Monterey ushered Doc and Paul from the room, leaving her to follow last.

The sheriff led the group to the checkout desk. Cassy and Paul walked around the counter to where two bodies lay uncovered on the floor. The young girl's face had been bashed in and someone had done a sloppy job of gutting her. Then there was the old librarian, a ragged gash drawn across her throat like an angry mouth, a blood-caked crucifix clutched in one hand.

She turned to ask why the bodies weren't covered, but the sheriff's phone buzzed and he held up a hand.

"Be right back." The sheriff moved a few feet away and answered the phone.

Doc came around the counter. "It's a shame. Never seen anything like it. Sorry you had to see them like this. I haven't had a chance to look them over yet." He tapped a finger against his lips. "So, you got two more in the woods?"

"Yes, two children in shallow graves. Two of the Hanlon boys we think. The third is still missing."

"There was a third grave, empty," Paul added. "Damnedest thing. I'd say maybe the kid got up and walked away, but they didn't bury themselves, and the other two were burned up pretty badly."

"Graves?" Doc eyed Paul. "How'd you know they were burned? How'd you know who it was?"

Paul shifted from one foot to the other. "Well—"

"I uncovered the faces." Cassy didn't need Paul sticking up for her. "We had to find out. They could have been alive still."

Doc nodded. "Fair enough."

Monterey returned, finishing his call. "Deputy Carson will be right there. Try to calm down." He snapped the phone shut.

"Damn. Debbie Ornthal just called. Paul, get over to the diner, some big fight or something. Cassy, wait for the EMTs to get back and take them out to the other bodies. I'm heading to the office."

As the sheriff turned to leave, she spoke up. No way was she going to take a ride with the leader of the asshole squad. "I'd rather deal with the diner. If you don't object."

Monterey continued toward the door. "Don't care, you two sort it out. Be empowered. You know where I'll be."

The ambulance rumbled up outside, and she thanked God for small favors. "We'll take care of it."

CASSY

Cassy approached the small crowd gathered in front of the diner. Their whispers subsided as she arrived, their faces turning in unison to the deputy, some ashen and drawn, others tight and red.

Jess stepped up to meet her. "He's gone crazy. He started swinging his spatula. Hit poor Johnny Belfry twice and scared us all to death."

Cassy studied Jess's face, then, finding nothing more, looked through the windows. Charlie sat at the counter, back to the crowd, frozen in space and time. Even from a distance, the muscles of his neck and back strained visibly to hard knots. Cassy faced the crowd again. "Anyone still inside?"

Jess clutched Teddy's hand. "Well, Debbie ran to the bathroom, and I think the boy is still in there." She surveyed through the crowd. "Otherwise, I think we're all out."

"Did he say anything?"

They were keeping something back, and Cassy was fresh out of patience. "Out with it. I need to know what I'm walking into."

Jess peered at Teddy, shook her head, then continued, avoiding direct eye contact with Cassy. "Well... There were these dark patches, like swarms of bees, only there weren't any bees. And they hung over our heads, angry and flowing. They didn't make a sound, but there was something, some sound, like a choir of furious angels shouting in my head..."

"Like God talking," someone from the crowd chimed in. A few folks laughed. Most lingered in uneasy silence.

"I didn't hear shit." Burke Dawson, chief of the volunteer fire department, came forward. "This is ridiculous. The man's bonkers. You're all bonkers."

Jess turned around. "Well, if it was the word of God, then I'm not surprised you didn't hear it. We haven't seen you in church for a while."

Cassy touched Jess's shoulder. "Focus. Did he say anything?"

"Well... Yes. And no."

Cassy rubbed her forehead. Why did this have to be difficult? "Okay. Either he did or didn't. Which is it?"

Teddy put an arm around Jess and spoke before she could. "It's like this. He sure shouted a lot, but the words... they didn't make any sense. Fact is... for a time there, none of us were making sense."

This was getting Cassy nowhere fast. "Don't take this the wrong way. You aren't making much sense now either."

Jess clutched Teddy's waist and leaned into him. "Well, go in there and see for yourself. It all happened so fast."

Cassy scrutinized Jess's face and found the frightened little girl behind an old woman's eyes. Go in there? Did she have a choice? This whole thing was probably some weird misunderstanding—stress, a hot day, an overworked man worried about his daughter. Probably.

After the scene at the library, she could not easily discount the weird. She surrendered to the situation, lifted her head, and spoke so everyone could hear. "I would appreciate it if anyone who was inside could stop down to the station later and help me fill in the facts." The crowd murmured. "You too, Burke, no matter how stupid you think this is." Before anyone could reply, she turned and entered the diner.

Charlie still sat at the counter, back to the door, hands at the sides of his head. She walked to the other side, and Charlie continued to rub his temples.

Something moved behind him. Cassy's hand dropped to her pistol as she looked over his shoulder. Shadows twisted beneath a table. She gripped the butt of her gun and slid it from the holster.

Johnny unfolded from beneath the table. She relaxed, holstered her weapon, and gave the boy a questioning look, not yet ready to disturb Charlie. Johnny lifted the napkin from the bridge of his nose and nodded in return. She signaled for him to leave, and he wasted no time. Johnny dashed out the door and the puddle of onlookers engulfed him.

Soft weeping drifted from the bathroom. Charlie's head still hung down. He wasn't any immediate threat.

The coffee behind her smelled fresh, so she took a couple of mugs, filled them up, and set one on the counter near him. She took the other to the alcove at the far end of the diner, where bathroom doors flanked a pay phone, and listened.

"Debbie?" she whispered, then tapped a knuckle on the door. "I'm coming in. It's going to be okay. Can I come in?"

"No." A single word heavy with shame and fear.

"I have to come in, kiddo. I need to know if you're all right. Are you all right?" She didn't want to scare the poor girl. What the hell happened, anyhow? Shadows and bees and choirs of angels? Maybe these people were a little touched in the head.

Debbie offered only more sobs.

Cassy tapped again. "I'm coming in. I brought you some coffee." She pushed the door open and stepped in. Debbie sat on the floor next to the sink, legs drawn tight against her chest. Thick lines of mascara trailed down from her closed eyes, her body hitching in a broken rhythm.

"It's okay. Your dad has calmed down. We'll get you out of here." Cassy crossed the bathroom, knelt, and held the cup out. "Here. This will help."

Debbie opened her eyes and looked from the deputy to the mug. She accepted the coffee, took a sip, and winced. She set it aside and stared at her knees. "I... he's gone."

"Who's gone?" Cassy set the coffee aside.

Debbie collapsed into another fit of tears and slid her legs out for Cassy to see. A large patch of blood tainted the crotch of her uniform. The girl tossed back her head, slammed both fists into her lap, and let out an awful howl.

Cassy fought against conflicting emotions—the urge to pluck the girl from the floor and hold her tight, the urge to return to the counter and pound the cook to a pulp, and the urge to flee the diner and run as far as she could. She wiped the sweat from her palms and focused on getting the facts first. She could deal with the emotions later. Or never.

"What happened? Did your father do this?" She took Debbie by both shoulders, trying to offer some sort of comfort. Debbie whipped her head back and forth, tears and spittle peppering Cassy's face.

"Debbie." Cassy shook her, a little at first, then harder. Maybe too hard, but damn it, she needed answers. "Debbie!" Her voice cracked against the bathroom tile like thunder in a bottle.

Debbie froze, sniffling as she stared back, more frightened than ever.

"I'm sorry, kiddo. I need you to calm down and talk to me. Did your father do this?"

Debbie wiped away a thick strand of mucus with her fist, mixing snot with faint streaks of blood. Her head shook a little, not enough to be a clear answer.

"Did he?"

"No. He never touched me. It just... happened."

Cassy looked down again. What did she mean? Maybe Debbie started her period. Why would she be so upset, then? And why was there so much...

Debbie confirmed what Cassy realized.

"I lost my baby."

Cassy grew hot as a mixture of embarrassment and sadness washed out her anger. This poor girl had too much ahead of her to deal with losing a baby. "Okay. We'll get you through this. The bleeding doesn't look too heavy. Do you have a pad?"

Debbie nodded. "My purse is behind the counter."

She handed Debbie the mug of coffee again and brushed the sticky strands of hair from her face. "Here, it should be cool by now. You stay here. I'll be right back."

Debbie's tried to smile. "Thank you."

Cassy considered the girl. No matter how bad this might be, Debbie would be okay for the moment, at least until the shock wore off. Maybe she could find a blanket or something to cover the mess.

She returned to the dining room and found Charlie standing at the counter sipping his own cup of coffee. The man looked a hundred and twenty if he looked a day. His jowls hung lower than usual; his eyes sat back, shaded by a deep knit brow; his skin looked pasty and slick. If he noticed her, he gave no sign.

He didn't look dangerous. Regardless, she kept a close eye on him as she slipped behind the counter. "You okay?" She spotted Debbie's purse on a shelf by a box of napkins.

Charlie hummed as he gazed deep into his coffee mug, as if an answer floated right under the surface. He stopped and looked up. "Was blind, but now I see. Do you believe in God?"

Cassy slipped the purse from the shelf and paused. What on earth did God have to do with any of this? Would God steal a poor family's children or make an old woman massacre her patrons? Would God induce a miscarriage? Was it God who whisked away her cousin from the face of the earth forever?

No, God had no business in this town.

"I can see by the look on your face you don't." Charlie pushed his mug away and rested his head on the counter. "You know, I couldn't understand a word anyone said. I felt like a stranger in here."

Cassy backed away a step and rested the purse on the counter. Her other hand fell to her hip, just above the gun.

Bruised bags anchored his eyes. "Don't worry, I didn't mean to hurt the boy. I was only trying to help. They all had the shadows on them. I didn't understand, not at first. I do now. The shadows were trying to tell us something wonderful is coming. Something magnificent..." Charlie's gaze shifted to a point beyond her.

The bathroom door snapped shut and Cassy turned. Debbie stood in the alcove, arms stiff and hung at both sides ending in tight fists. The bright stain on the uniform glared in the diner's fluorescent lights.

Charlie stood and took a step toward her. "Oh. Oh no. Not like this."

Cassy moved into his path. "I think it best you stay right

there. You know I have to take you in, at least until I figure out what to do with you.”

He looked at the deputy and nodded, eyes void of intention. Immeasurable sadness drew his features down even farther as tears trickled down his cheeks.

“You have a blanket or something?”

Charlie pointed toward the back room.

Cassy looked over her shoulder at Debbie, the poor girl standing rigid as ever. “You okay? I got your purse.”

Debbie nodded. She took a few stiff steps to the nearest table and sat down as Cassy brought her the purse.

“Go back in there and get a pad on.” Cassy stroked Debbie’s hair. “You’ll be okay. We’ll get you to the doctor soon.”

Debbie pulled a pad from her purse and went to the bathroom as Cassy made her way through the kitchen.

In the storage room, Cassy found an old blanket covering an open box of potatoes. The cloth smelled musty and earthy. It would have to do. A few shakes got most of the dust and dirt off it.

When Cassy returned, father and daughter sat at the table, his arm around her shoulders. “I thought I told you to stay put.” She stood over the two, ready to use force if needed. Then he looked up, and she could tell there would be no trouble.

“Sure.” Charlie got up and stepped aside.

Cassy helped Debbie up, draped the blanket around her, and walked her out. Only Jess, Teddy, and Johnny remained.

“Poor dear. Are you okay?” Jess moved in to take Cassy’s place and bunched an arm around Debbie. “Here, let me help you.”

“Is she going to be okay?” Teddy asked as Johnny moved

to Debbie's other side.

Cassy pulled Teddy aside, filled him in, and asked him to take Debbie to see Doc Crandall. "Don't say anything to anyone. This is private business, so be sensitive. Probably the boy doesn't even know."

Teddy nodded and returned to the small group.

"Johnny," Cassy called, "can I talk to you?"

He looked reluctant to leave Debbie, which she understood, but business came first.

"It's okay. This will only take a minute. Jess and Teddy will take good care of her. I need to know what happened."

Johnny let Debbie go and filled Cassy in on the details. None of it made any sense. Everyone started talking nonsense, and the next thing he knew old Charlie was trying to beat him with his spatula. "Sure, the guy doesn't like me, but jeez." He put a finger to the blood clot on his nose and winced. "Not too bad, though. He nicked it. Man, any closer and my nose would be gone."

"You want to press charges?"

Johnny blushed. "Nah. I don't want any trouble. I mean, it wasn't just him. I think he was scared is all. Besides, I kinda like seeing his daughter. You know?"

"Well, go on home. Maybe have your mom take you to see Doc later if the swelling doesn't go down. I'm still going to take Charlie to the station to cool off. Maybe he'll make some sense after a rest. You get some rest, too. I suspect you all could use some sleep, seeing as how no one's story makes any sense. We got a mess over at the library..." Cassy bit her lip. What a stupid slip-up.

Johnny perked up a little. "Yeah, we heard. Davie called Mr. Dawson while we were waiting for you to come out. Said there was a massacre over there. Mr. Dawson took off, suggested everyone else do the same."

Cassy had half a mind to hunt Davie down and lay him flat on his back—and not in a nice way. The asshole had the biggest mouth of anyone around, and one day it would get him in too deep. She looked over at Debbie. Maybe it was for the best in this case, though. The poor girl didn't need an audience, and neither did her father. "Looks like they listened."

"Uh, huh. I never seen people around here move so fast. I bet most of them locked themselves in, what with a killer on the loose."

She would never understand why people always turned bad news worse. "Listen, there isn't a killer on the loose. We don't know what happened. It's none of your concern anyhow. You get going."

Johnny rejoined the group, and the three of them led Debbie toward Teddy's old station wagon, parked by the curb in front of the swap shop.

Cassy went back into the diner where Charlie sat alone, his face vacant and pallid. He gave no resistance as she walked him out.

TOM

Tom returned to the cold, unwelcoming farmhouse. He climbed the steps, duffel bag slung over a shoulder, and slid the key in the lock. Instead of unlocking the door and going in, he glanced over toward the pole barn. What darkness lay inside, in the back, where his father pulled the trigger? What secrets huddled there, tucked away among the dust and blood?

No. He couldn't look, not yet.

Tom unlocked the door and went in.

The house was the same as always, clean and tidy, but without the stale funk of cigarettes. Maybe Pop gave up smoking along with the booze.

He climbed the stairs, pausing third from the top as it squeaked under foot. He and Kyle would skip it when sneaking out at night, or early Saturday mornings when racing down to watch cartoons. Pop slept light, and to hit the noisy step at the wrong time always evoked a round of curses.

His room looked untouched and faded, like so many washed out childhood memories. He unpacked, cramming everything in the old dresser, everything except the journal and the stone, which he toted back downstairs and set aside on the coffee table as he explored the rest of the house.

Every room was pristine, infected with the antiseptic aura of a hospital. Not a book out of place on the shelves, not an ash in the fireplace, not a dish in the sink. Had someone been here to clean since Pop...

A knock at the door. Tom's heart skipped a beat.

A second knock came, and Tom realized he still stood in the living room staring at the bookshelf. He hurried through the house and opened the front door.

Frederick Dunne, another local sheep farmer, stood on the porch looking like sculpted dust. He plucked a leather glove from one hand and held it out. "Well now. Didn't really expect you here. Got a call from your brother to come pick up the sheep. Sorry for your loss, by the way."

"Sheep?" Tom shook Frederick's hand. For the first time since returning to the house, he recognized the bleating and lowing in the field, the simple background music of his childhood.

"Yeah. You know, your father's sheep. I been watching after them since Lewis... passed on. Kyle said I can finally take 'em off your hands." Something on Tom's face must have thrown the man. "Of course, if you changed your mind—"

"No, it's fine. Take them, they're all yours." He took a step back into the house, feeling drawn in, wanting to return to the search for a shred of the Pop he once knew. "Whatever deal you have with Kyle is good."

Frederick studied him with thin eyes. "You okay, son? I mean, is there anything I can do for you? If it's not a good time—"

"Like I said, it's fine."

Frederick continued to stare, as if looking for some fracture or stain. Just as Tom thought he might have to close the door in the man's face, Frederick slapped a glove on his thigh, sending a puff of dust into the air, and slipped it back on. "Well, I'll get them loaded up."

At the bottom step, Frederick stopped and turned his head enough to show his profile. "I'm sorry about your Pop. He was a... a decent man."

Tom nodded and closed the door before Frederick could say anything more.

The journal sat on the coffee table like a cheap paperback. He reached to pick it up then paused. Everything in the house was the same. Then something the preacher said troubled him. He returned to the kitchen, and there on the shelf were three bottles of Maker's Mark, one of them half-empty. Pop quit drinking three years ago? Well, if he had, it looked like he failed there too.

Open bottle in hand, Tom went back to the living room. Maybe he couldn't bring himself to go into the barn yet, but he could tackle the journal. It was only words, after all—sticks and stones and all that.

It read like the fractured diary of a man edging too close to senility. Tom drank as he read about Lewis finding a stone, about honest-to-God brawls in the lodge, about a bachelor party, and about free-form rituals. Nothing in there showed anything to lead a man to suicide, nothing going beyond shameful and into the obscene or illegal, just men acting primal and dumb as men will do when left alone too long.

Pop never was one for being direct. Even though he never told the boys he loved them, never cried in front of them, Tom always sensed there was something more to the man, an unspoken depth of character. The diary read like the father he remembered, giving only a faint sketch of what might have really happened, as if Pop couldn't bear to put the truth down on paper even in his last moments.

Had he hoped to find a confession in those pages or some deep secret? Probably. But when he finished, halfway to a good drunk, the clouds around Pop's death only thickened, like an angry swarm on the western wind.

Tom took the bottle, now down to a few good swallows, and went outside. Driven by deep sadness and liquid courage, he walked to the pole barn, went inside, and meandered to the workshop at the back. He expected a sea of crusted blood and brains and maybe a strand of police tape flapping in the breeze. Instead, he found only the dusty remnants of Pop's life scattered across the tool bench, a clean spot on the wall, and one to match on the dirt floor. Like more childhood memories, washed out in spots, forever gone without a trace.

Tom collapsed to his knees, drew up a handful of dust, and blew it out across the barn. The particles fogged his view and settled back to earth. The whiskey burned as he chugged the rest and tossed the bottle against the far wall, where it shattered. Broken glass sprinkled the floor and caught bits of sunlight like bright chunks of fire. The dust called to him, and he drew more handfuls up, dumping them over his head as he cried until exhaustion overtook him. He stretched out in the dirt and stared at the clean spot on the wall. Welcome home.

CASSY

Cassy escorted Charlie to a basement cell and locked him in. He sat down on the cot, pathetic and lost, and some small part of her wanted to let him go so he could be with his daughter. She unlocked the door again, a small compromise for her conscience.

She returned to the office and found Monterey right where she left him—at his desk, shuffling papers, a man expecting bad news at any moment. No matter how uneasy she felt, the sheriff needed to hear what she had to say. "You know, Davie called his buddy Burke while I was in the diner, and he spilled the news about the library to the crowd. I'm surprised your phone's not going crazy. People think—"

"Don't care what people think right now." He pulled a fresh notepad out and centered it on the desk. "We'll plan out a course of action when Paul gets back. These murders are sad and tragic, but they're over. There's no real threat anymore."

"Over? What about the bodies in the flats? You think old Elana slipped down there before her bit at the library? You already think the poor old woman was crazy. Was she crazy enough to make that hike and kill those boys, too?" Cassy was unable to stop herself. There was a time for thought and a time for action. This wasn't the time to sit and work out some detailed plan. They had to do something, and they had to do it now.

Monterey looked up from the mess of paperwork generated by the events of the morning, one eye twitching. "You have to calm down. We have to stay in control, because no one else will be."

"At least we can call for help, right? Maybe we should get the State guys involved." Wasn't it about time the sheriff realized this was more than he could handle? Five murders—maybe seven or eight—were more than any of them could handle.

Monterey rubbed his eye, soothing away the small spasms. "I said no. This is my town, and this is my show. We do this my way. We may not see stuff like this every day—hell, the last time we had a mess like this was when your cousin disappeared, and there was no body then—but we are the law here and we will deal with our own problems, damn it." He swept papers from his desk and glared.

She backed away. She had never seen the sheriff act this way before. Was he catching crazy too? Was there something drifting through the town, some invisible malignancy touching people? Or something in the water? Maybe she should go home and curl up, hide out like the rest of the town, and wait for whatever storm brewed on the horizon to blow over.

Monterey must have seen the fear on her face. He pushed back from the desk and rubbed his neck. "Oh hell, I'm sorry. Look, we need to think of this as a challenge, not as a problem. Let's wait for Paul and we'll sort this out, okay? Why don't you get started on your reports."

Cassy nodded and sat down at her desk. She pulled out her pad and began scribbling, the words turning to doodles. She couldn't focus on getting the facts out. Monterey had returned to his paperwork, eye twitching again. She wanted very much to be somewhere else. "I'm going to go take Charlie some lunch."

He grunted and continued to scratch away at some form.

She pieced together a sandwich from leftovers in the little fridge and took it and a soda down to the basement. Charlie probably wasn't hungry, but sitting around on her ass waiting for someone else wasn't her thing.

The holding cells and processing station were kept clean, an easy thing to do since they were rarely used. The quiet concrete block pressed in on all sides, wrapping Cassy with claustrophobia as she walked down the hallway toward the cell at the end.

Ferguson pounded the bars with his fists as Cassy walked by. "Hey, bitch. You ready to let me out yet?" Before she could get by, he flopped out his dick and waved it around. "Here you go, you like what I got? Yeah, you like the goods."

She kept walking. "I've seen better."

Ferguson continued taunting her until she reached the last cell. Charlie's butt was still planted on the cot, and he was engrossed in his shoes. She tapped the little window and opened the door. "Are you doing any better?"

Charlie looked at her, then back at the gray floor. "A little."

She slipped into the cell and sat next to him. She offered the sandwich and soda. When Charlie made no move to take either one, she set them on the floor.

It didn't make any sense. She had known this man for years, and though he might be grumpy most of the time, he was sane as the daylight. Of course, she had thought the same of the librarian. And the other people at the diner weren't exactly on the level either. Was everyone in this town catching the crazies?

Charlie scratched his neck. "He's a good kid."

"Johnny?"

"I know he would have done right by her." He looked at her again, almost pleading. "He's going to be okay, right? You have to believe me. I wasn't trying to hurt anyone."

She patted his back. "I know. I think you maybe got stressed out. I don't think you're any danger. Why do you think I left the door unlocked?"

Charlie shrugged. "Fire hazard? Or maybe you're lazy."

There was the Charlie she knew. She snickered and got up. "Let's go with the fire hazard theory. Look, I can let you go at any time. Johnny's not pressing charges, and though part of me thinks you are somewhat responsible for Debbie's miscarriage, I can't exactly hold you on it. You seem calm again. You tell me. Are you ready to leave, or would you rather chill in here for a bit?"

Charlie dragged a hand down his face as he thought, then nodded. His pleading look returned. "I'm not ready to face Debbie yet. What do I say? What do I do?"

Cassy touched his shoulder. "I wish I could help you. I can't. This is way out of my area." She offered a smile and turned to leave. "Use the bathroom upstairs if you have to go. These probably don't work so well."

Ferguson remained silent as she passed this time, pants zipped up, glaring like a hungry rat. She reached the stairs and stopped. What was it Charlie had said at the diner? Something he was going to say before Debbie interrupted. She turned around and went back.

"What did you mean by 'something wonderful'?"

Charlie turned the soda can over in his hands, brow furrowing into deep wrinkles. "I thought it was about Debbie. I know now it couldn't have been."

"You thought what was about Debbie?" Cassy stepped into the cell. She remained standing.

Charlie stopped fidgeting with the can, popped the top, and took a drink. He wiped a dribble of soda from the corner of his mouth then faced her. "There's a baby coming. A very special baby."

Cassy raised an eyebrow. "And the shadows told you this?"

He nodded, but said, "Not really. I mean yes, but not with words or pictures. I know, but I don't know how I know. You know?"

This was getting weird again, and she didn't like weird. Even so, she had to ask the next question or it would bug her forever.

"Okay, so a baby is coming—a special baby. Special how?"

Charlie laughed and took another sip of soda. He lowered the can and traced the rim with his finger. "You'll think I'm nuts."

It was her turn to laugh. "Well, I already think you're a little unscrewed, so spill it."

His finger continued to circle the can's lip. "Special—like a-bright-star-in-the-sky special. But it's all wrong somehow. Like looking in a fun-house mirror."

She backed out of the cell. This guy had read too many bible stories. "You're right. I think you're nuts."

"Told you." He returned to his soda and said nothing more.

His words clung to her as she left the basement and returned to the office to wait for Paul.

TOM

Tom was eighteen again. The summer sun beat the afternoon dry as the desert. Dirt crusted his nostrils and mixed with the sweat on his face as he fought for breath, struggling against Alissa's dead weight. "Press tighter. She'll bleed out."

Kyle ran beside him, hand clamped down on her neck. Blood spurted out from between his fingers. "I'm trying. I'll choke her if I press too hard."

"Press. She'll die if you don't."

Kyle's foot caught on a rock, as if the earth conspired against them. His hand slipped from the wound, and he toppled to the ground.

Tom stopped, shifted Alissa, and tried to clamp the wound with one hand. Sweat stung his eyes. "Get up, I can't do this alone."

Crimson blood, too bright, washed down over her pale skin. Christ, she looked dead already.

The house stood a hundred yards away, white clapboard glowing in the sun, their one safe place. Kyle scrambled to his feet, tore off his shirt, and wrapped it around her neck.

Tom yanked his hand out from the fresh tourniquet. "Not too tight. You'll choke her." He moved without waiting for a response, and Kyle came with him. Seconds stretched to minutes as their feet pounded at the hardened field.

Kyle wept. Tom was too frightened for tears.

At last, they reached the front yard. Tom called for Pop as he lowered Alissa to the ground. The front door stood open. Where was Pop? He should have been in for lunch. Why didn't he come out? Didn't he see them?

Kyle called as well. There was still no response.

Tom pulled his brother close. "Here. Take her, hold her head and keep pressure on her—not too much. I'll find him." He moved aside as Kyle knelt, took Alissa, and cradled her head in his arms.

Kyle looked up, fat tears streaming down his cheeks. Tom's heart hurt when he saw those sorrow-filled drops.

She couldn't die. Not again.

"What are you waiting for?" Kyle's words stumbled over each other.

Tom turned and ran for the porch. Something wasn't right. The house yawned, a gaping black hole in place of the door.

It wasn't open before.

He jumped up the steps and stopped on the porch, still unable to see into the house even though he stood a few feet from the open door.

He couldn't go in there. Pop was in there, drunk. Pop would kill her.

Kyle shouted again from behind. "She's dying. Go get Pop!"

Tom turned around. Kyle rocked Alissa back and forth. He couldn't go in the house. He couldn't let her die either. He froze, uncertain of his next move. The world around him became spongy, and even though he was dimly aware of the dream, he still dreaded the outcome of any choice he made.

He reached up and touched the string of beads at his neck, beads he didn't have back then, beads he would receive many years later from a man he had yet to meet.

Tom faced the door once again and stepped through. The darkness dissipated like smoke in the wind and he stood in the entryway. Home, just as he remembered. Pop stood at the far end of the hall, half-empty bottle of whiskey in one hand.

Tom's mouth no longer worked and every word he tried to form got lost on its way out. Pop stared, eyebrows angled above his nose.

The world fell silent. Pop nodded as if he understood, then ducked into the kitchen. Tom's legs mutinied and left him unable to move.

Pop returned. He was no longer Lewis Burton. In his place was an old man, the dirt of millennium smeared across his white t-shirt and olive-green khakis.

"You have something of mine, I want it back." The words swept down the hall like an arctic wind.

Tom looked down. One hand clutched the Ruger so hard his knuckles turned as white as Alissa's skin. The other clutched the stone, oscillating greens and blazing reds.

The old man came to him, took his arm, and led him outside.

Kyle sat cross-legged, Alissa's head in his lap, stroking her hair and weeping. He looked up—didn't he see this wasn't Pop?—and a shadow of hope crossed his face. "You'll help her, right? It was an accident. We were just—"

"Shut up." The old man spoke in Pop's voice. "Keep quiet, hear? I don't care how this happened. It's a big mess, and it's time to clean it up."

Please. Not again.

The old man spoke to Tom in a voice of crumbling leaves. "Yes. Again. We are at the center."

It didn't happen this way, not the first time, not in the other dreams, not ever. Who was this guy?

Tom moved—why couldn't he stop?—and found himself standing over Alissa, gun pointed at her forehead.

A single thread of sweat traced down his brow and into one eye. In the moment before he pulled the trigger on the God-forsaken gun, Alissa opened her eyes and whispered through blood and snot and vomit.

"He's coming."

CASSY

Cassy sat on the station steps, notepad in hand, free of the confining office. She sketched out a few notes, looking for some connection among the morning's events. She came up empty. The afternoon grew late, and shadows lengthened in the street. How quiet her world had become.

The ambulance rumbled from up the street and she stood, thankful for the distraction. She stepped down to the sidewalk as Davie pulled to a stop, keeping her distance from the driver's side. She didn't want the jackass behind the wheel getting any stupid ideas.

Paul climbed out and came around the front, looking worn out. "Anything more?"

"No. Nothing. The sheriff's inside filling out forms, for chrissakes, waiting for you to return so we can come up with a... a game plan of some sort." Cassy crossed her arms. "Game plan. What the hell."

Davie tapped the ambulance horn, the blare echoing off the surrounding buildings accenting the town's emptiness. "Hey deputy. Promise me if you find out who fucked with those kids, you call me. I want a shot at 'em, okay? I mean it. And when I'm done, you can have them."

There was deep hatred in her ex-boyfriend's eyes, a mixture of cruelty and vengeance she'd never seen before. He was a stupid man who let his emotions run the show, and whatever brewed in his heart could only lead to trouble.

Paul replied without turning around. "I'm not calling you or anyone else. Go home like everyone else. This day will end soon enough, and we'll get a new one tomorrow." He shook his head.

Davie grumbled, rolled the window up, and sped off.

Cassy punched Paul's arm. "I bet your drive was fun."

"You lost. Let's go in."

Monterey ignored them as they entered, scribbling away at a fresh form, and Cassy wasn't surprised. She and Paul stood by his desk for several seconds before she ventured to clear her throat. "Sheriff? Paul's back. Time to get our plan together?"

The sheriff turned his paper over and continued to write. She tried once more. "Sir? I said—"

Monterey swept out a final sentence, set down the pen, and laced his hands behind his neck. "I heard you deputy. I've been thinking—pull up a chair, both of you—thinking about our situation here. You see, we have a homicide at the library, and we know pretty much who did it. And that person—that woman—is dead, so we also have a suicide. So, there's not much to do there, no threat to the community. We leave it be for now, document the scene tomorrow, file our reports, and be done with it."

Cassy shot Paul a look. She didn't like where this was headed. She kept her mouth shut anyhow. She wanted to see if her partner felt the same way, but he wore his best poker face. She ventured on, with or without his support. "And what about the bodies at the flats?"

Monterey rubbed his eyes then looked at her with stale hope. "The bodies. Right. Well, we don't know what happened there. It's a totally different problem. The scene is a mess, and

I'm sure we won't find many answers poking around in the riverbanks, so we wait for Crandall's report on the two bodies and go from there."

Cassy's blood boiled. "What? Are you saying we wait?"

"Yes, exactly. We wait. Not enough information to do anything." He smiled slightly, a sad and weary grin of a man without options.

It was Cassy's turn. She leaned forward and bared her teeth. "What kind of plan is that? We can canvass the woods, we can talk to more people, we can look for the missing boy, we can do something, anything. What about the Hanlons? Who's going to tell them? I mean, you can't expect us to do nothing." Before she could stop herself, she struck the weakest point she could find. "Did you give up this easily when my cousin went missing?"

The room fell silent.

Monterey's smile dissipated.

Paul grabbed her shoulder and pulled her back. "I think you've said enough, Deputy. Maybe you should go home. What do you think, Sheriff, can she take the rest of the day off?"

An errant shadow crossed Monterey's eyes, blossoming from the pupils, waning at the edges. "I think a little time off sounds like a mighty fine idea, don't you think? And on your way, why don't you go talk to the Hanlons, tell them what we know, and share whatever crack-ass ideas you have, too. Now get out of my station."

Something dark brewed in this town, some unsettling unknown, and these men were content to sit here and wait for answers to fall into their laps. If they wanted to play stupid, then so be it. She was done.

Cassy rose, nothing more to say, and left. She climbed in her Hyundai and spun the tires as she drove from the lot, wishing haunted dreams on the useless man inside.

She arrived at the Hanlons' cabin only to find it deserted except for poor Zak, locked in the kennel, looking neglected. She knocked several times and circled the house, peering through windows. Only the woods offered a response, the constant chattering of insects and rodents.

The place felt thick and dense, as if it sat at the bottom of the ocean. She blew out of there as fast as she could and headed home. Her first instinct was to radio back to Paul. She fought it. At this point, neither he nor the sheriff cared what was going on. Her information would be lost on them.

Once home, she changed into a t-shirt and jeans, fed Herbie, and settled back in her bed. Maybe she did need a rest. Maybe the day had been too much for her.

Then Cassy found herself once again pulling Alissa's report from the nightstand drawer, spreading the pictures out, and sinking into the painful circumstances. She couldn't do anything to help the missing boy without getting in deep shit with Monterey. Maybe she could do something more about Alissa.

It was time to go talk to Tom again, time to ask the right questions.

LEWIS

February 6, 2008

ewis walked into the Lodge banquet hall and stopped at a serving station lined with bottles of liquor. Vodka, rum, gin, and his old standby—bourbon. A portable stereo blasted a heavy techno beat on another, and between the stands, a keg soaked in a bucket of ice, the floor around it turning dingy gray. Tables and chairs cluttered the room's perimeter. A ragged circle of men littered the center of the room, cheering and hollering, a few waving bills in the air.

Since its founding, the Lodge served with dignity and honor, dedicated to God, family, and the betterment of humanity. All those years of effort washed away by poor judgment.

The liquor bottles mesmerized him. A plastic cup, some ice, a big splash of bourbon and all could be right again. He didn't come here for a drink. He came out of concern for the building. But seeing these men here, and seeing the booze spread before him, made him feel little more than a glorified janitor.

The bottles stared back.

One drink would be okay, wouldn't it?

A shadow fell on the bottles as he thought he might actually pour one.

"C'mon, Lew. Drink up." John Spectre patted Lewis on the back, grabbed a cup, and poured himself a beer.

"No thanks." Lewis scratched his forearm and looked away from the booze. He scanned the room and turned full circle, facing John once more. "I see you put together a nice little party for your boy. Sending him off to marriage the right way."

John glanced at the circle of men, looking more self-satisfied than he should. "It's nothing. Come see the show. We got a brunette and a blond. Spirit and Sanctity. Great names, don't you think?"

"Sure. You think pretty highly of the boy, I take it. You must, seeing as how this all goes against Grand Lodge policy. Tell me, how did you get this approved? I don't recall a vote."

John looked again at the crowd, his smile faltering. "You serious?" When Lewis said nothing more, the smug grin faded away, replaced by a slight sneer. "Lighten up. Have a drink. It hasn't been that long, has it?"

Lewis wanted a cigarette. Even more, he wanted bourbon. He wouldn't give in, though, not after three years of hard-won sobriety. "Thanks, maybe later." He pulled away—God, it was difficult—and headed into the hall for a better look.

John followed along. "Hey, what's wrong? It's just a little fun, you know?"

Lewis stopped and turned, hot blood thumping through his skull. Jesus, what wasn't wrong with the situation. "I'm sure I got a long day ahead of me tomorrow cleaning this place up. I don't suppose you'd want to help."

John furled a lip. "Forget you, old man." He breached the circle and added a few of his own dollars to those flapping in the air.

The slathering pack throbbed, hands and cash waving in the air. Blond hair crested above them, then retreated. A brief surge of jet-black hair followed, and as Lewis reached the circle, the men—most of whom he didn't recognize—parted.

Two young women slithered in the center, glistening in oil, their hands exploring soft, curved surfaces from top to bottom. The blond—Sanctity, wasn't it?—slipped one hand down to her partner's crotch, and they groaned in unison. Their lips parted, their tongues flickered, and the men hooted.

What a disgrace. Lewis wanted to look away. He couldn't. How long since he'd seen a woman, let alone touched one? Too long. For the first time in what seemed forever, his equipment fired up.

The music faded, and the women stopped. Sanctity took a quick bow as Spirit snuggled up behind her, their skin rubbing together like vinyl on vinyl. "Thank you, boys, it's been a pleasure. I can see you all enjoyed yourselves tonight. We're gonna pack up now. We might stick around for a drink or two if you don't mind."

A few men laughed; others murmured approval. Then, a voice across from Lewis cut through the noise. "Toy show!"

A moment later, another shout. "Toy show!" Then another, and another, voices accumulating like snow in a blizzard until the room echoed with the slow chant.

The girls exchanged looks, and Spirit smiled, her heavy breasts pulsing as she shrugged.

Sanctity turned back to the pack. "Okay, okay. Settle down, boys. We'll do the show. You have to pass the hat, though. It'll cost..." She looked back at Spirit, who first held up two fingers, scanned the boys, then quickly added a third. Sanctity brightened and turned back to the hungry, howling crowd. "Three hundred, boys, and I guarantee you won't see anything like this again if you live to be a thousand."

Someone produced a Cincinnati Reds ball cap, tossed some cash in, and passed it on. The hat made its way around the circle until Spectre's son snatched it away and counted the money. "More," he shouted, and sent the hat around again.

The makeshift collection plate traveled from hand to hairy hand. The sanctity of the Lodge dribbled away with each bill dropped in. The hat reached Doc Crandall's son. Before he added to the kitty, he turned and whispered in his buddy Jake's ear. Lewis's gut grew fat and heavy, like climbing the first hill of a roller coaster. He really wanted a drink.

Jake split from the pack, and Lewis followed him to the door, stopping by the booze. The bourbon sure looked good. He would wait there, by the door, until Jake came back. That's all. Just wait.

And maybe have one little drink.

He should have a drink.

He looked suspicious standing there, right?

His forearm itched again, and he clawed at it. No one would know, and no one would care. Before he made up his mind, he found he'd already poured a small shot. Problem solved. The bourbon smelled like charred oak and alcohol as he held the cup to his lips. He tossed it back, bit against the old familiar burn, and enjoyed the warmth snaking through his body.

He wanted to go back, rejoin the mob, and rip off his clothes. He could show those little girls what a finely aged body could do. Hell, they looked like they would do anything for enough cash. He kept a wad of bills in his dresser—never did care much for banks. He could be there and back before...

What was he thinking? Did it take only one shot to get him this worked up, even after all these years? He came here out of duty to the Lodge, not to get laid. He cared for this place even if these guys didn't, and he needed to make sure nothing happened here to get the Lodge shut down. Or worse.

He waited for Jake to come back. Ice clattered into his plastic cup, and once again, without really realizing what he was doing, Lewis found himself with three fingers of bourbon pressed to his lips. He sipped at it and watched the circle.

The room quieted down. Some men pulled up chairs, others plopped down on the floor.

Sanctity counted the cash. Twice. "Alright, it's all here, boys, and then some. You ready for a treat?"

Spirit worked her way through the circle to a bag in the corner. She brought it back and held it out, a sultry smile splayed on her lips. Sanctity unzipped the bag and feigned surprise as she looked in. "You're such a naughty girl!"

Spirit blushed in places Lewis didn't know possible. "All for you, sweetheart."

Footsteps echoed in the foyer. Jake returned holding something close to his chest. Lewis followed him back to the circle and around to where Davie sat on the floor, never quite able to get a good look at what Jake cradled.

Spirit blew a stray black strand from her face. "Someone hit the music again."

A few guys sprang up at the same time. Monterey moved faster than the rest. He smacked the play button and returned to his seat.

Jake leaned over and showed Davie the secret object. Lewis still couldn't see it. He no longer needed to. He had a notion of how Davie's sick little mind worked. He leaned down. "Put that thing back where it came from. Haven't you seen about enough yet?"

Davie brushed him off, and as the girls began to pull toys from their bag of goodies, the crowd shifted, pushing Lewis away. He let it go. Those girls wouldn't be crazy enough to use some dirty rock. Besides, the bourbon tasted better with each sip, and the girls weren't anything to balk at either.

The things those girls pulled from their bag looked downright torturous. Who came up with such devices? Some had rubber spikes and wiggly bits. Others had sparkling chrome skins.

Spirit selected a hard, silvery thing and traced circles on her partner, doing things Lewis never imagined one woman doing to another, until finally the blond sat on the floor and spread her legs to let the other woman...

He looked away. He didn't want to—every part of him turned to granite as blood coursed through his veins. If he watched any more of this, he might jump right in there.

The pack continued to howl, voices ebbing and flowing like the waves of some primitive ocean, hurting his ears. He tossed back the rest of his drink, hoping to dull the pain.

He should have another. Why stop at two? Three was no worse, right? Yes, three was okay, then maybe he could watch a little more of the show. How would he know if things got out of hand if he didn't watch, right?

He returned to the serving table and poured a stiff one, filled almost to the top—and why not?—then returned to his place among the scraggly group. Just to watch. Just in case.

The air buzzed hard, fast, and rhythmic. He almost felt oil in his nostrils, almost tasted it, and he smelled the rawness of the women, their salty skin, their well-conditioned hair, their dusty makeup. And something else slithered beneath the almost unfamiliar sensations, an exciting and terrifying scent connected to some primal part of his memory.

Sanctity moaned in rhythm with Spirit's strokes. The pack circled tighter around the women.

Sanctity climaxed, and the whole room seemed to climax with her in shouts and laughs. She panted a little, opened her eyes, and smiled up at Spirit. "Okay, honey, it's your turn."

The satiated stripper rose and started to pick through the bag of toys. Davie put an arm out and stopped her. He reached between his legs and the room fell to silence as he pulled the stone out and held it up in offering. "Try this."

Everyone quieted as if hypnotized, an almost palpable anticipation spreading among them. Lewis should say something, but what words would put an end to the show with such a dark and appealing act about to reveal itself? And did he even want to stop them? He stepped back from the crowd and drained away the rest of his bourbon.

Sanctity took the rock, her delicate fingers straining to wrap around it. "I don't know..." Her eyes glimmered as she turned to Spirit and held out the stone. Their faces glowed and sparks seemed to pop in their eyes as they ran their hands over its surface.

Davie started to chant in a soft voice. "Cock rock. Cock Rock." The snowball of voices grew once more, the words spreading like a swift, infectious disease.

Spirit lay down and presented herself, oil pooling in the divot of her belly button.

Lewis found himself chanting as well, speaking the words as a solemn prayer. The world dimmed, and the air undulated with the soft intonation. The music stopped. No one bothered to start it again.

Sanctity held the stone high above her head, an offering to some unseen higher power, a being hungry for sex and savagery. Then she knelt between Spirit's parted, limp legs and plunged it in deep.

"It's fucking cold!" Spirit sucked in a breath so hard Lewis thought she might be hyperventilating. She writhed against the stone, looking caught between the need to get away and the desire to drive it deeper. As Sanctity withdrew the rock, Spirit's foot spasmed and sent the stone skittering across the floor.

Sanctity snatched the stone. "Hold her."

Men on either side reached out and clenched their victim's limbs. She writhed and struggled. They held her fast.

Sanctity rose and offered the stone again. *Cock Rock!* She dropped to her knees and plunged it in. *Cock Rock!* The room vibrated.

As the stone emerged again, its reds and greens glistened in the light. Did he see blood on the rock or was it a trick of the light? Lewis took another step back.

The ritual continued in short repetitions. Stand, offer, *Cock Rock!* Kneel, plunge, *Cock Rock!* Spirit twitched and jerked against the stone until she arched her back in a final release and fell limp.

Sanctity held the stone up one last time and transformed into a mass of trembling, pallid flesh. She looked at Spirit, laid out spread eagle, limbs held fast. The sparks in her eyes died out, and the stone slipped from her hands. It thumped on the floor, sending a dull echo through a room of men holding their collective breath.

Lewis dropped his plastic cup, a knotted sickness growing in his belly. No way was this happening. "Is she...?"

The men who held her recoiled.

No one moved.

At last, Sanctity whispered, "She's breathing." She fell to her knees next to the crumpled mess and cradled Spirit's head. She wept, running a hand through Spirit's dark locks. "Help her."

The crowd remained mute, unmoving.

Lewis thought of his field on a hot summer afternoon many, many years ago. He'd been drinking then, too.

"Goddamn it, help her, why won't you help her, please, please, please..."

Help her.

He saw Kyle as a teenager cradling another young woman, one who slipped beyond help a decade ago. A woman who still lingered in the corners of dreams.

The fog lifted from Lewis's head. Maybe this woman he could help. "Party's over. Everyone out. Now."

Most men turned and looked, frozen in the headlights of uncertainty. A few scuttled back and made for the door.

"I said now." He began to work around the circle pushing at those who still sat, corralling them out of the room.

Monterey lingered at the door and took Lewis by the arm as the last man left. "You need help?"

"Christ, I don't know. She's breathing and she doesn't look hurt." Lewis eyed the bottle of bourbon on the table.

Monterey noticed. "Tell me you didn't."

Lewis nodded. "Don't matter, though. Not right now. You get on out to the lot and make sure this place clears out. I'll stay here until she comes around and call you if I need you. Get Doc Crandall's boy to bring the ambulance too."

"Sure." Monterey moved to the door then stopped again. "You be strong, okay?" Then he left Lewis alone with the two strippers.

They were on the floor, still naked, one still cradling the other, and all the shame Lewis should have felt during the entire bastardized evening flooded in on him. He found some tablecloths under one of the serving tables and took a couple to where the women lay. He knelt and began to unfold one.

Sanctity looked up, eyes wild, her face streaked with tears and makeup. "Don't touch us! Don't you touch her!"

Lewis held his hands up. "I'm not going to hurt you. I want to cover her up, okay? What's your name?"

"Jessica."

"Well, Jessica, let's get you both covered and go from there."

Jessica nodded. "This is Dorthea."

"That's a pretty name. Yours, too." Lewis spread one tablecloth over Dorthea and draped another around Jessica's shoulders. "Let me see what we have here."

"You a doctor?" Jessica held Dorthea's head up a little.

"No. The EMT's on his way. I hope." Lewis bent down. A faint smile lingered on her pale lips and she took deep, steady breaths. "I don't think we need one. Look for yourself."

Jessica did, and she erupted in a mixture of tears and laughter as she hugged Dorthea tighter "Oh God. She's asleep."

DORTHEA

orthea surfaced from dreams of a stone, a wrinkled old man, a baby covered in blood, and black flames. The room was too dark. Had Jessica drawn the curtains before she left? Dorthea didn't think long on it. The question eroded in the presence of a raw smell, a wet and beckoning odor. Her belly roared with hunger. And the baby, he smelled it too, the way he rolled and kicked and played on her organs.

She clutched her belly and rolled to her side. What smelled so strange yet so wonderful? "Jessica? Are you home, baby? Did you bring me something to eat, something good?"

Shadows in the closet moved, and panic raced through every nerve. Her mouth dried, leaving her only a whisper. "Hello? Is someone there?"

Clothes rustled. Hangers clattered. A small form stepped from the gloom and stopped. The voice of a boy scurried to her. "Smells good, don't it."

"Oh my God, who are you? What do you want? Whatever you want, take it. Leave me alone. I won't be any trouble. Take what you want and leave!" She struggled to sit up, and the roar in her belly grew, filling her ears, deafening her briefly before settling back down.

Something was wrong with him, shadows clinging like camouflage. Then the dusk-covered child scampered across the room and out. Was she still asleep, dreaming in images controlled by the strain of pregnancy? Would she never wake up?

His voice skipped in from the other room. "I know you smell it. The old man tells me you gotta eat. Sheesh, you're probably starving by now. What you want, what you *need*, isn't on any menu around here. No way."

She swung her legs over the bed, listening to the boy rummage around in the kitchen. He pulled something heavy from a cabinet, getting something from the silverware drawer, dumping something thick, wet, and meaty into the sink.

"You got a blender?"

A blender? What kind of wicked, messed up dream was this? She pinched her arm, and it hurt. She still wasn't buying it. This had to be a dream. Okay, she would play. Why not? If she was stuck in this nightmare, she may as well follow it through. Maybe it would end... God please let it have an end. "I'm coming. I think it's under the sink."

Dorthea got up, balancing against the weight of her belly, and made it to the bedroom door before stopping to rest. The curtains in the living room were drawn as well, soaking the place in twilight. In the kitchen area, the shadow-clad boy dug around under the sink.

"Found it. Cool." He stood up, breaching the little stabs of sunlight streaming through the curtains. He was not wearing shadows.

This was one hell of a dream. Pregnancy sucked.

Flecks of skin and ash shook from him as he worked. On the counter sat an empty Costco bag and two plastic containers, the clear kind used for leftovers, filled with dark liquid. He pulled a lump of meat, a roundish shape the size of a fist, from the sink.

A dry-heave rippled through her, clenching the baby. But the smell was wonderful, and her unborn booted her spleen, urging her on like a jockey in second place.

"Come here. Cop a squat. This'll take a few minutes." The boy looked at her and grinned, his eyes like bright marbles nestled in black and red flesh. When she didn't move, his smile faded, replaced by an undecipherable mixture of emotions.

"I said sit. All I gotta do is help you eat and make sure you get to where you're supposed to be. But that's later. For now, it's about eating. Sit."

He sounded so mean and yet so sincere. How was that even possible? She moved as fast as she could and took a seat at the kitchen table. Even if she was dreaming, there was no sense in pissing off the monster.

He glared at her before turning around and hacking at a chunk of meat on the counter. He pulled a second lump from the sink, softer looking, brown, and shaped like a kidney. "I got a riddle for you. You like riddles?"

"I guess."

He whacked off more bits from the kidney and dumped them into the blender, then added some liquid from one of the containers. "Well, this one's pretty good. My brothers didn't get it, not at first." Another hunk of meat came from the sink— liver, maybe—and he sliced at it. More chunks went into the blender then he stopped the cleaver mid-swing. "Okay, so how do you make a cat sound like a dog?" The cleaver came down.

She mulled the question over as he continued to chop up different meats. No, not meat, organs. She was sure of it now. Whatever it was, the smell still made her stomach roil. Christ, she couldn't think. Why was he talking about cats and dogs?

Whack!

She was so hungry.

Whack!

The *baby* was so hungry.

Whack!

"Jesus, already." She couldn't take much more. She had to have whatever was in the God-forsaken mess of a blender.

He turned around. "Almost done. You like smoothies? Well, I got a hell of a smoothie for you here." He started the blender, whipping the mixture until it reached a uniform color.

"So, you get it yet?"

She stood up. Was it her who stood or had the baby commanded it? She didn't care. "If you don't give me a drink now, I'm going to rip your fucking head off."

"Whoa, sure. No sweat, lady. Don't get nasty, okay? I'm trying to help." He found a glass and filled it, the concoction sliding from the blender like half-melted ice cream.

She grabbed the drink and took a big gulp, fighting the urge to vomit, sucking down the pulpy, lumpy mixture. The baby in her belly quieted. The thick stuff hit her like a fifth of cheap gin.

"Good, lady. Real good. You sit there, drink, and this will all be over soon. I got enough for three or four batches easy, and tonight... well, tonight you're gonna have a baby."

His words only registered on the surface. She sat down at the table and drank as the boy returned to work. Sure, this kid was creepy, and telling her the baby was coming was pretty fucked up. She didn't give a shit. The food made the baby happy, and for the first time in months, she was happy.

DOC CRANDALL

Doc sat at a desk in the clinic's little morgue and chugged an energy drink, a risky thing for a man his age, but he needed it today. The clinic saw enough business in the morning to keep him hopping. Even though things thinned out after lunch, he still had the bodies to deal with. So many autopsies meant a very long afternoon.

Jake stood by the cooler looking bloated and worn. "Well, that's the last of them till Davie gets them other two back. Can't believe they all fit." He walked along the row of doors, touching each one as he went. "Mind if I, you know... watch?"

Most men might think Jake a little touched in the head, asking to help examine dead bodies and all. Doc saw the innocence in the request. Jake wanted to learn. "I suppose. Keep your hands in—"

Samantha, Doc's right hand at the clinic, popped in. "Got someone to see you. Pretty important. Looks like a miscarriage."

Doc rolled his head and pinched the bridge of his nose. Would the day never end? "Right. I'll be out. Put her in exam two in case we have to do a D&C."

Samantha disappeared.

He rose and headed for the door. "Well, these will have to wait. Can't say how long I'll be. You're welcome to stick around."

Jake frowned as Doc passed by. "What'll I tell Davie when he gets back?"

Good question. Davie would want to help, too, and Doc wasn't up for hours of his boy's wise-ass remarks. "You help him unload and tell him... tell him to take the rig and a radio, and go home. Tell him you're staying with me to do the heavy lifting. Samantha will call him if we need an ambulance."

Jake lit up and stuffed both hands into his pockets. "Sure, got it. And thanks, Doc."

"No problem. Now you go rest a little, drink some water. You really are gonna have to do some lifting here."

Doc found Debbie Ornthal waiting in exam two, sitting on the table in a loose gown. He did a cursory exam and checked her vitals—all normal. "You alone? No one with you?"

She shook her head, scared, eyes red from crying.

"You want to call your dad?"

Again, no.

"I see. Well... he knows. I had to tell him about—"

"He was there when it happened. Can we get this over with? I hurt all over." Debbie trembled from head to toe.

"Sure. Let's get you in the stirrups so I can see what's going on." He helped get her legs situated and started the exam. She was young and healthy, pregnant less than ten weeks. "Looks like you'll be fine. We'll do expectant management—let it run its course naturally—and I'll see you in a week. Wear a pad for the bleeding. Come back right away if you have to change it more than once an hour. Now go on out to Samantha, tell her what I said, and she'll tell you what to do from here."

Debbie nodded.

"If you'll excuse me, I have a ton of work stacked up in the back." He turned to leave and gave a sad chuckle at his unintentional joke.

"Do you think..."

Doc looked back at her. Fresh tears welled in her eyes, and he thought of his own secret loss from years ago. Guilt strung his heart up like a horse thief, and he wanted to tell the poor girl he understood. He wanted her to know she wasn't alone. He sure understood the loss even if he didn't know what it physically felt like.

"Do you think I can still have children?"

Behind the tears was a need for something to latch onto and carry her through the coming weeks. He understood her need for hope as well. "You'll be fine. Yes. You will still have children. Lots and lots of them, if you want. Don't worry about that right now. You need to take this one day at a time. And talk to your dad. He's there for you."

Debbie smiled even though tears trickled down her cheeks. He smiled with her, and he felt she knew she wasn't alone.

"I'll see you in a week."

He returned to the morgue and roused Jake from the couch to start the examinations with Elana's body. Before they got far, Davie returned from the flats with the remaining corpses.

As Jake and his son unloaded the ambulance, he continued to examine the old librarian, finding nothing to account for her behavior. The cause of death was obvious. But what made this woman take the life of five other people in her own library in such a cruel way? Whatever it was would stay hidden at least until a full autopsy, and even then, he doubted there was any medical explanation. Sometimes people just got mixed up.

As he covered her corpse and got ready for the next, Samantha poked her head in again. "You're not gonna believe this. We have another one."

He paused, one glove on, the other in hand. "Another one? Another what?"

Jake and Davie stopped as well, and all three men looked at the nurse who stood in the doorway.

"Another miscarriage."

MAC

Mac took off his pastoral gown and hung it in the shallow oak wardrobe. The christening was rough, a colicky baby made worse by a little water on the forehead. At the end, Mac felt as if he had christened the devil himself. One chaotic ordeal was behind him now. Another loomed ahead. He had put this off for far too long, and seeing the stone again made him believe he could put it off no longer. He settled into his chair and reached for the phone as Cynthia wandered in.

"Everything's put away. Ready to go home?" She took a seat and looked from him to the phone. "Who are you calling?"

Mac sat back, wondering how to make this work. "I have a few calls to make about tomorrow's bake sale. And I still haven't finished my sermon yet."

"Well, you give me some names and I'll make the calls while you write. I can run out to Ornthal's in a bit and pick up some dinner."

He tried to remember she just wanted to help. It didn't make the situation any easier. "It's only some business, and I'd rather take care of it myself."

She crossed her arms and pulled her head back. "Why can't I help? I mean, how late are you going to be, and what about dinner? We're a team. At least we were at one point."

He tingled all over. Why wouldn't she go? "Look, I don't need help, it's..." He searched for a better excuse. He found none. How could he be mad at her for wanting to help?

Maybe it was time to come clean. She probably knew the situation. It wasn't hard to see the signs when you lived in a town like Washington Heights. He should tell her everything—why he chose to work late, why he insisted on separate beds. Why he never gave her children.

Mac took her hand and knelt next to her, forcing the worn-out smile of a long marriage. As he opened his mouth to speak, gazing into eyes showing the first signs of cataracts, he recognized a fresh fear. She did know the truth. She did not want to hear him say it.

He would keep the charade going at least another day. "Dear, seriously, I'm okay. I'll be home in a little while."

She pulled away and scowled. "No. We work as a team. If you're staying late, then I'm staying with you. You're here alone too much, and it's as if I don't even know you. What have you been doing? What changed so much to give you all this extra work? You've acted strange ever since... well, you know." She reached out a hand and placed it on his side.

He winced at her touch, but let her hand stay. She looked him square in the eyes, and he saw the deep affection they shared in their younger days welling up.

The tenderness faded before he could respond. And why shouldn't it? He was unable to connect with her anymore, the veil of his life now thinned to near transparency. He wasn't Jesus. He was a simple pastor, and he could only deny himself so long.

She pulled back her hand and crossed her arms again. "And that was almost a year ago, I think. You never did tell me what happened. No one seems to know. You boys and your silly little Lodge games. It isn't right, I tell you." The tears started, and Mac sat helpless as she continued in little more than a whisper. "I just want you back."

He stood and brought his face within an inch of hers. The cloying scents of thick, powdery makeup and cheap perfume stung his nose.

"Go home. I'll be there later and we can talk. I need to do this. For me. I need to set things right." He tried to sound gentle, but he couldn't mask the anxiety in his voice.

Cynthia searched his eyes, sniffling, dabbing at tears with a handkerchief.

Mac knew people, he knew his wife, and he knew she wanted to believe him. Thank the Lord. Whatever she told herself worked.

Her lips curled up in a cluster of wrinkles. "You need to set things right for the bake sale tomorrow."

"Yes. For the bake sale tomorrow."

"And you'll wake me when you get home? If I fall asleep, I mean."

"I will."

"And we can talk then."

"Yes, my little lamb, we can talk then."

She took a deep breath and patted his arm. "Good. I will see you at home." She rose to leave, stopped at the door and turned back. "I love you."

Mac closed his eyes and tried his best to sound sincere. "I love you, too."

CASSY

The farmhouse looked awkward and alone as Cassy pulled up the gravel drive and parked by the pole barn. Her instincts thrummed as she climbed from the car, leaving the door open, wary of making too much noise. She rounded the corner of the house. The front door stood ajar.

She should have brought her gun.

The steps creaked, and once on the porch she paused, listened, sensed. The place was empty. Tom had to be here somewhere. His truck sat parked a few yards away.

Faint sounds of movement. From the pole barn.

Cassy stepped off the porch, careful to make as little noise as possible, and made her way to the barn. A soft rustle drifted from the building, movement in the dirt at the back.

She crept past the tractor until she saw Tom lying on the ground, hands clutched over his eyes.

She rushed in and knelt next to him. Sunlight glinted from broken glass scattered on the ground. "You okay? What happened?"

Tom lowered his hands. Dirt covered his face and hair, twin streams of mud smeared down from both eyes. He was crying.

Cassy brushed hair from his face. "It's okay. Shhh. Can you get up?"

Tom nodded.

She helped him to his feet and braced an arm around his waist. "Let's get you cleaned up, okay? Are you hurt?"

"No. Just... had a little too much to drink." He leaned against her and they made their way back out of the barn. "I came out here... I thought if I could see, I might understand."

"Uh, huh. I get it, I do. Believe me, this is no way to find answers." She helped him up the steps to the front door.

He nodded again and let go. He leaned against the side of the house and looked at her. "I wanted to know why. But you know what? There are no answers here."

In those eyes, she saw the same dark sense of loss she carried with her every day, the same angry questions her soul screamed out ever since Alissa's disappearance. He stood at the edge of the same well of obsession she fell into nearly a decade ago. "Tom, there may never be answers. Come on."

She took his hand and led him in. "You go on, get a shower and cleaned up."

He looked at her once again, and she could not resist. They needed each other, needed to have simple and innocent human contact, so she hugged him tight. He relaxed as he wrapped his arms around her and their mutual sense of loss intertwined—hers for Alissa, his for his father. For the first time in forever, Cassy felt as if she wasn't alone.

She backed off even though she could have remained embraced by him for hours. Tom needed to get out of there. She held both of his hands. "Go on. We'll talk when you come back down."

He climbed the steps and disappeared around the corner at the top. She listened to his footsteps for a few seconds then went into the living room to wait.

The journal and stone sat on the coffee table, tempting her like a broken Rubik's cube. Pipes clanged as Tom started his shower. Had he read it yet? It looked a little more ragged than before, leafed through at least. She should wait and ask him about it.

She couldn't wait. Curiosity got the better of her. Besides, maybe she would see something in there he didn't, and she could help. She picked it up and read.

She lost herself in the scattered entries, a stream-of-consciousness blending one event with the next.

"It's stupid." Tom stood at the door wearing clean cargo shorts and Hawaiian shirt, hair still damp.

She looked up from the journal and blushed. A page tore as she tried to close the journal and put it back. "I'm sorry. I thought—"

"It's okay. Did you finish it?"

"I got to the part about some ritual. They were scaring people with blanks."

"Yeah. Kyle's idea. Not much more after that. Says they only did it twice then stopped. It doesn't say why." He came and sat next to her on the couch, not quite touching. "Pop never was much for words."

She picked the journal back up and looked at it. What was Lewis trying to say? And why was she so fixated on the damned thing? She opened to read again. Before she found her page again, Tom slid it gently from her hands and tossed it aside.

"I think maybe you're looking for answers in there, too." He stared at her, his expression a wall. "Why'd you come here?"

He was right. She was looking for answers, and it might be time to follow her own advice. Try as she might, she couldn't let it go, not yet. Tom sat right in front of her, and she may not get another shot at this. She felt a little sick at the idea of exploiting him in a vulnerable moment. Not enough to stop herself, though. "I came because... this sounds stupid, I know. You see, part of me thinks your leaving had something to do with my cousin's disappearance."

Tom looked away and gave no answer.

She continued, uneasy in the silence. "I mean, you left so close to when it happened, and you changed. Before you ran off, I mean. Alissa disappeared, you withdrew, and I think you skipped out because you know more than you let on. "

Tom refused to face her again. "What did you say about there being no answers? Can't you let her go?"

She reached over and gently turned his head toward her. A tear trickled down her cheek, and she brushed it away. "I tried. Really, I did. You don't know how much trouble this has caused me. I mean look at me. I could have been anything. I could have left this little town. Like you did. I didn't. I stayed here, not because I love this place or because of strong ties, but because I couldn't let her go. I almost did, then... this place changed again. About a year ago. And the old obsession rose up so bad I saw her... calling to me, trying to talk to me. I don't know what she was saying. And I can't let her go." The words rushed out and more tears streamed down her cheeks. She wasn't telling him anything more than she already told Paul. Somehow, this was different. In Paul's eyes, she saw distant sympathy. With Tom, the empathy was almost tangible. She hugged him again. "What is it you can't let go of?"

He pushed her away. "I wish I could tell you. I can't. Maybe later. For now, I need to work this through." Stress etched his brow and the corners of his eyes.

Yeah, he wanted to talk. She watched him closely, waiting

for the seal to break. It never did. As she studied him, another emotion crept in on her, and before she knew what she was doing, she leaned in for a kiss. She met only empty space.

He was up before she got too close, and he hovered over her, blushing. "I like you. I always liked you. This isn't the right time."

She got up and made for the door. She felt like an idiot, couldn't get out of there fast enough. "I'm sorry. You're right. I'll leave you alone. If you're—"

Tom took her by the wrist. "No. Don't leave."

Cop instincts were a bitch. He was lucky she didn't throw a punch. She stared at his hand, then looked him in the eyes. "Let go."

He dropped her hand, turned red, and pocketed both hands. "Oh. No, it's not like that... I don't want to be alone. In this house. And I'm hungry."

Her anger bled out as he offered a sheepish grin. Who could stay mad at such a sad attempt to smile? "Okay. I'll let it pass this time. Let's go grab a bite. Not the diner, though. Remember Sticky's, out the highway?"

Tom brightened a little. "Sure. Twenty or so miles out, a hell of a drive for beer, unless you're underage. Sticky would sell to anyone. How's he doing?"

"Gone off a few years back. Florida, maybe. The bar's still there, though."

Tom was half-way to the door before she finished. "I'm game. You driving?"

Half an hour later, Cassy pulled her little green Hyundai into the lot and parked by the rear entrance. A young man in kitchen whites stood outside smoking. She and Tom walked around to the front, which overlooked the highway itself. The first drops of a cool summer rain kissed down on the world as late travelers trickled past.

They went straight to the bar where a young man in a Nine Inch Nails t-shirt washed glasses in a sink. Tom pulled out a seat for Cassy then took one himself. She never was one for those little acts of chivalry most men used to get in a woman's pants, but it seemed different with him, genuine.

The bartender stepped down. Tom ordered a Miller draft and a plate of chicken wings to share. She ordered a Heineken and two shots of Jägermeister. The bartender got their drinks and went back to idly scrubbing pint glasses.

Cassy slid one of the tiny glasses over.

Tom stared at the shot. "I shouldn't."

Cassy raised hers. "You should. It'll do you some good. Cheers. To kismet."

Tom smiled a little, and the weight on her heart lightened a hair as they clinked glasses and tossed their shots back. She sipped her beer to soothe the burn. "Where were you all these years?"

"Traveling, mostly. I don't know. It's all a little blended together." Tom took a drink as he thought. "Before I came back here, I was living in the Keys. I own a little fishing charter boat. I do okay—make enough to live on. Before, I spent about a year in Peru. And before Peru I spent a lot of time out west doing a little of everything."

"Peru? What on earth made you go there?"

"Don't know, really." He glanced at his beer, and she sensed his hesitation. It lasted only a moment before he relaxed and continued. "Okay, I do know. I did a lot of drugs. Not the hard-core designer shit, just enough to keep my mind fuzzy."

A swallow of beer caught in Cassy's throat. She gulped it down and coughed. "Drugs? I never figured you for—"

"I know. I grew up in a place where you can't spit without hitting someone's crop, and I never touched the stuff. Like you said. I changed." He stopped and took another drink, then stared into his glass.

Cassy touched his knee. "I didn't mean anything by it. I'm just surprised. Go on."

Tom continued staring into his glass. "So, I worked as a baggage handler at the Van Nuys airport, and there was this guy I used to trip with, mushrooms mostly. Anyhow, he told me this story—you know the kind, a friend of a friend told him—about this tribe in Peru called the Urarina. They brew this mean stuff, supposed to trip you out and clean you up at the same time. Send you on some kind of spiritual journey. Well, he would tell me this story every so often while tripping, and one night we made plans to go. Bought camping gear, plane tickets, everything we'd need."

The bartender stopped by and dropped off their wings. Tom scarfed down six before continuing.

"We get to the airport and he backs out. Scared, I guess, or maybe he didn't believe the story in the first place. Either way, it didn't matter to me. It was time for me to move on, and Peru seemed as good a place as any. So, I went." A middle-aged woman brushed by them, and Tom turned to watch. "Didn't expect the bar to be so busy."

Cassy looked toward the back. At least twenty or so people sat at tables drinking, most regulars, a few she didn't recognize. Everyone looked cheerless and scared, like rabbits hiding in a hole. "No busier than usual. Seems a little quiet." She tapped Tom on the shoulder and he turned around. "So? You went. What happened?"

"Well, the story turned out to be true, sort of. There is a tribe with a shaman named Hruesco, and they do this vision journey thing. Not as simple as it sounds, though. They don't just hand you the stuff. They're not drug dealers. Most people who go get turned down, but I had nowhere else. So, I stayed, and after a while, they got used to me being there.

"One night after maybe eight months of camping out and living with them, Hruesco wakes me and leads me deep into the woods. After walking for what felt like hours, we stop at a clearing where a few other tribesmen are sitting around a pot of boiling liquid. And the place was silent. I mean eerie silent, like the forest shut down.

"He points me to an open spot in the circle and he passes out cups of the awful stuff brewing in the pot. It hit me harder than anything I ever touched. I felt stripped to the bone, open to the universe, and I saw..."

Tom stopped there, and Cassy couldn't tell if he was reluctant or unsure, so she waited him out. She put a hand on his shoulder, and as she looked once more to the back of the bar, she saw Davie and Jake playing pool. They didn't see her. She ducked a little so Tom blocked her from view. "Shit."

Tom looked up. "What?"

"Nothing. Just someone I'd rather not see right now." Did it really matter, though? Maybe Davie should see her here with someone else, maybe then he would leave her alone. So, she straightened again. "It's nothing. What did you see?"

Thoughts creased Tom's face as he stared at her. "It's not so much what I saw as it is what I felt. It's like... The universe is a symphony, and for that one night I would swear I could hear it, could almost predict what notes would play next. Sometimes in my dreams, I hear the shaman speaking to me in his broken English, filling in the gaps, and he hums the same music I heard during my vision journey. By the time I wake up the tune is always gone and I'm left feeling deaf to what's really happening around me." He finished his beer, shook his head and laughed. "Crazy." Then his hand went to his necklace, and a smooth calmness return to him.

"Is that where you got those beads?"

He looked down and dropped his hand. "Yeah. I woke up back in my tent the next morning wearing it. I asked Hruesco about it, and he said I wove it from my dreams. It's made from Huayruro seeds."

Cassy reached out. "May I?"

"Sure. No one's asked before. I don't see why not."

She touched the smooth red and black seeds, and the din of the bar gave way to music, a complex mixture of instruments, so quiet, like a distant radio playing a forgotten song.

Tom slid her fingers from the necklace and held her hand between his. "You okay?"

She looked from the necklace to him and a deep connection overwhelmed her. She knew what she was doing as she took his other hand, held tight. She tried to stop herself as she closed her eyes and leaned in once again. This time he did not resist, and when their lips met, the complex music played once more, her body vibrating with an alien frequency.

She withdrew after several long heartbeats and tossed a twenty on the counter. She stood and glanced toward the back of the bar. Davie was watching. Good—maybe the jerk would finally get the message. "I think I'm ready to go. Why don't we go back to your house and have a few more drinks."

Tom nodded and touched his necklace again. "Okay."

Cassy nearly laughed at the stunned look on his face. She leaned in and whispered in his ear. "Don't get your hopes up, okay? It's just drinks."

KYLE

yle watched Tom and Cassy from the shadowed corner behind the pool tables. No way would she kiss him if Tom had spilled his guts. That still didn't set things right or quell the notion to pound his brother into the floor. Why should Tom get any chance of happiness after skipping town to avoid sharing in the family guilt?

At the pool table, Davie scratched an easy eight-ball shot and stepped back, crossing Kyle's view to pass the bar's only cue stick to Jake. "Rack 'em and break 'em, asshole."

Across the room, Cassy dropped a bill on the bar and led Tom out, passing a young woman near the entrance who wore uncertainty like a lost child. Had she been standing there all along?

Her shoulder length hair spilled in loose curls. She wore cutoff jeans and a plain white tee. If ever a woman looked like Alissa, this was she. Was she an illusion, a sad trick of an overstretched mind? Maybe she was something snapped out of the subconscious as he tried to keep together the fragments of his life. Maybe she was an externalization, maybe she was the simple onset of madness. Or maybe she was another night of regret.

Davie nudged Kyle, apparently wanting to hide in the shadows as well. "Slow night, eh?"

Kyle smiled—the cheap version, not the one reserved for clients. The last thing he wanted was to talk.

Jake made a hard break, scattering the balls, sinking none. He held the stick out for Davie. "You're up."

Kyle exhaled as Davie stepped away, glad to have his cloak of gray all to himself again. He watched as the woman by the front door scoped out the room. Their eyes met, and his feet felt thick and cold as her lips rose at the ends.

Davie stepped back without taking his shot and leaned against the drink railing, blocking Kyle's view of the young woman. He downed the last swig of his beer and tossed the bottle into a nearby trashcan, where it shattered against others. "You know what? I don't think I want to play anymore."

Jake slouched and scuffled over to join them. "I got another round on the way. We got plenty of time." Then, to Kyle, "You wanna play? I hate to waste the quarters."

Kyle shook his head. Let them leave. The place would be a little less crowded without them.

"Shit, I hate wasting quarters."

Davie snaked an arm around Jake and waved at the bartender for his tab. "Well, you can play with yourself, or you can come with me. This place is a bone-yard. Full of regulars. What do you say we hit up Lucille's out route fifty? Ain't been there in a while. They got some pretty hot chicks, right?"

Only one woman interested Kyle, and she stood by the door, pallid skin and empty eyes, staring at him. "You two go on. I'm fine here." His skin began to itch under her gaze, his stomach began to complain, and the dull noises of the bar faded away.

From somewhere in the distance, Jake mumbled to Davie. "He's not interested. The guy's like a damned statue anymore. Or a robot. Or... I don't know. Empty."

"I can hear you. I'm standing right here." He managed to break away from the woman and look at Jake. "And you're right. I'm not interested. Lucille's is a dry well. This whole town and everything for miles around is like a worn-out welcome mat. Still useful in a way, but mostly just ignored." He gestured toward the door. "There's a fresh face for me. So, you two go on and look at the same old trash you been staring at for years."

The other two looked at the door then at each other. Jake shrugged and Davie said, "Sure, okay. We'll leave you to it." Jake gathered his quarters, Davie paid their tab, and they left the bar, walking right by the woman without as much as a glance.

Kyle finished his beer and set it on the table.

She ran a hand through her hair and smiled.

He went to the bar to pay.

She winked at him, motioned for him to come, then turned and left.

He followed.

She wasn't out front. He knew where she would be. He lit a cigarette and walked around back to the parking lot, taking his time, making her wait.

She stood next to his corvette with a hand on the roof, another pretty girl waiting for a ride.

He got in, and so did she. Neither spoke as he started the engine, pulled out of the lot, and got on the highway. Which direction didn't matter yet. He would get her home soon enough.

Her wonderful odor teased him, vaporous and faint, with traces of cheap perfume and skin lotion. The smell made him think of a late summer evening after a rain, and he felt seventeen again.

There wasn't another car in sight. Kyle shifted into high gear and floored it until the speedometer leveled out at seventy-five. He couldn't stop stealing glimpses at her. Why hadn't she said anything? "So, you talk much?"

Her smile faded as she gazed at the road.

He studied her face as best he could. One minute she was Alissa, the next she wasn't. Her features didn't change. Something about her faded in and out, like music from a weak radio station at the edge of reception.

She leaned forward. A surge of excitement rippled across her face as she pointed up the road. Then she looked at him— finally something—and nodded, jamming her finger against the windshield.

"What's the deal?" His skin felt thick and dry, like a wool blanket, as the itching returned. What was wrong with this woman?

She pointed again, tapping the windshield even harder.

Kyle turned in time to see the sign. The next exit would take them to Pop's old place.

His innards sank and a hot, heavy feeling overtook his bowels. As much as he wanted to resist, his body betrayed his will. The right foot let off the gas, the hands rotated the wheel, and to top off the coup, the left pinky flicked the turn signal.

"Why me, why now? Are you making me do this?" Despite his effort, he couldn't mask the panic in his voice. He no longer believed he drove the car.

She remained silent for the rest of the drive. He did not. His words spilled out, one atop the other, asking her for an explanation, begging her for control, shouting at the car that sped on without any concern for the wishes of the driver. In the end, he got no answers, only a hazy finger pressed against the windshield, pointing the way.

They arrived at last, and a mixture of relief and renewed fear washed over him. They sat before the old Lodge building instead of the farmhouse. The brick building rose in the gloom of the night, its darkened windows and stark angles casting black upon gray. The headlights streamed past the building and gave only dim light to the front porch.

If this doppelgänger were some part of his exhausted imagination, then going to Pop's would have made sense. This place? No, what happened in the Lodge had nothing to do with Alissa by any stretch of a twisted imagination. What happened there was, for him, much worse.

"I don't want to go in there, I don't want to go, I don't want to go—"

She reached over and rested a steady hand on his forearm. His skin cooled where her flesh met his, and as he started to think the temperature where they touched would continue to drop well below freezing, she withdrew.

His words dried up.

He was alone in the car. A bead of sweat broke on his forehead.

The woman stood in front of the car, paler and more waxen than before. There was something new as well, he sensed it.

She motioned to him, and he got out of the car.

She wasn't real, couldn't be real. She looked so much like Alissa, but Alissa was dead long ago, taking his heart and soul with her, never to come back.

Kyle clenched his hands so tight his fingernails drew blood. His teeth ground against one another. It helped. A little.

"I'm not going in." Not as firm as he hoped. Even so, he made progress as his muscles began to obey him again, and his breathing slowed. The sweat dried up, leaving his skin cool.

"I'm not going in there." Louder this time, his words

severing the last puppet string. He would not move. He was in control.

Alissa shook her head. She pointed behind the old Lodge, to the line of trees beyond marking the edge of the ravine.

Why would she bring him here? What did this place have to do with her? He was in control again. He was also now inclined to follow this girl. Behind the Lodge festered something only he and Pop knew about. "Where are you taking me?"

She turned, walked away, and disappeared around the side of the building.

Beyond the Lodge, down the ravine, was something tucked away in the opening of a cave unrelated to her. Or was it? Maybe Pop told someone, or maybe... Jake. Jesus H. Christ, that was it. The freak wasn't as dumb as he looked. He put her up to this. She was here for money. Following her now seemed like a smart thing to do.

"Get back here you bitch! You think you can fuck with me? You think I—" He rounded the corner of the Lodge. She glided across the short stretch of grass toward the tree line. It had to be some kind of trick.

He plodded along behind her, each step bringing him closer to the fractured and tilted gloom of the woods, crosscut by branches and leaves, broken only by the dim reflected moonlight on the woman's skin and clothes.

She stopped at the tree line, and as he neared, she rotated in one smooth movement.

Now he saw what was different about her, the nagging change from when she stood in front of the car. A tiny black smudge marred her forehead above the left eye. He continued toward her, and the mark coalesced into something much cleaner, more defined. The hole in her head, slightly stippled and blackened around the edges, started to ooze. Another mark appeared on her neck, a slashed opening seeping crimson.

"Alissa," he whispered to the indifferent night. He dropped to his knees and began to cry. He wanted to run to her, hold her close and never let go, and at the same time, he wanted to run far away. For the moment, he was unable to do either, and simply knelt in the grass crying as his heart's first desire faded away, taking with it once again all hope of redemption.

As the last traces of her disappeared, he thought he heard three words carried to him on the evening breeze.

He howled against those words and the confusion they carried, fleeing back to the Corvette and racing away from the horrible place. He arrived home coated in a greasy sweat, a full bottle of bourbon waiting on the counter. He snatched it up, turned on all the lights, and sat with his back against the great-room wall hoping there was enough bourbon left to wash away those last three words.

He's almost here.

MAC

Mac hauled the last table from the dolly and set it up. The legs screeched against the hard linoleum as he pushed it into place, lining it up with the others in perfect formation. He looked around the room. He should feel excited for the bake sale tomorrow, happy to have his congregation around him enjoying a little Christian fellowship. Instead, he felt only cold knots in his belly.

He was out of things to keep himself busy, out of distractions from the underlying wrongness he'd felt ever since Tom brought the stone into the church. The first time he saw it in the Lodge he felt only a mild disgust, thinking it verged on the obscene. Today the stone seemed different, almost threatening, as if it dragged behind it a blinding darkness.

With nothing left to do in the basement, Mac returned to his little office upstairs to wait. His call with Victor had been short and awkward. In the end, Victor agreed to meet him here. So, Mac sat in his office, caught between an unfamiliar fear and an inescapable anxiety, trying to find the right words for Sunday's sermon.

"Knock, knock." Victor stood in the doorway.

Mac put down his pencil and smiled. "Thanks for coming. Sit. I can make some tea if you'd like."

Victor walked into the room and stood near the doorway,

arms wrapped across his chest. "No thanks. I don't think I'll be staying long. I said I would come, so here I am. What's so important it takes you the better part of a year to call?"

What was so important? And why was Victor so upset? Who stabbed who here?

Mac tried to let it go, to be the pastor he wanted to be. This loose end needed tying up, and soon. Something waited on the horizon, some bright, black, terrible thing. Where to begin? Victor would think him crazy if he came right out with it. No, he needed to take this one step at a time. "I've been working on my sermon for Sunday. Please, have a seat. I could use your help. You used to help me, remember? You've always had a good sense of the spirit."

Victor looked frustrated and opened his mouth to speak, then shut it again. Instead of launching a snappy comeback, he simply sat down. "Okay. Let's hear it."

"Well..." Mac looked at the page on his desk, blank except for a couple of verses from the I Corinthians. He folded the paper in half. This was crazy. "I've had this verse stuck in my head all day, since... let me read it to you first:

"Listen, I tell you a mystery: We will not all sleep, but we will all be changed—in a flash, in the twinkling of an eye, at the last trumpet. For the trumpet will sound, the dead will be raised imperishable, and we will be changed."

Mac looked up from the desk, the folded paper still in his hands, the verse so ingrained in his head he'd not needed to read.

Victor smirked. "You can do better. I mean, what's it even mean?"

Mac bowed his head. This was too rough. "I don't know. It's not for my sermon. I'm scared, and I don't know why. Those damned words have been stuck in my head ever since

Lewis's boy stopped by today. He had the stone from Lodge. And I don't know what's happening here, I don't know why it bothers me so much, and I can't bear not talking to you anymore. I should be pissed, furious with you for sticking me. I'm not. I wanted you here again. I wanted to know you're okay, and maybe I hoped you missed me a little too." The tears came, not in great gushes but in trickles. He hadn't cried in ages, and it felt good. All the responsibility for the souls of Washington Heights slipped from his shoulders as the tears rolled.

Victor got up and came around the desk. "It's okay." He knelt and rubbed Mac's back. "And I have missed you, at least a little." His voice cracked and Mac looked up to see tears at the edges of the younger man's eyes. "And I'm sorry. You said you would leave her, you said we could make this work. In the Lodge on the day you told me it was over, I went blank. I hated you more than I've ever hated anyone, and I wanted you dead. And do you know what the shit of this is? I wanted everyone else in the room dead as well."

Mac took Victor in his arms. "I'm sorry too. I won't lie to you; I don't think I can make it work. I also don't think it matters much after tonight."

Victor wiped the tears away and withdrew. "Why?"

Mac's tears dried as well, and he returned his attention to the folded paper on his desk. He didn't know why. He didn't have to. "You must feel it too. You came to see me. You didn't even have to take my call, yet here you are."

Victor said nothing. When Mac turned back, there was recognition on his face. Victor felt it.

Mac stood and pulled a key from his pocket. "Come on. I cleaned the little room in the basement and put fresh sheets on the bed. Let's watch a DVD and spend some time together.

Maybe after a while we'll both think this is stupid and you can go home and I can go home and Washington Heights will start the day tomorrow the same as it does every day."

Victor tried to smile, a tense and unhappy expression. "Or maybe not."

"Or maybe not. What do you say?"

"Okay."

They retreated to the makeshift bedroom and embraced in quiet communion, Victor slipping off to sleep first as the movie ended. Mac muted the television and watched the static until his eyes grew too heavy. He drifted between dreams and reality, clutching Victor, until sometime later fresh light streamed in from the activities room. He rolled over and opened his crusty eyes. The door swung open, and a shadow stood watching.

"I was afraid." A whisper. Cynthia. "I walked home, and the town... it's like everyone's disappeared. I waited for you."

Was he dreaming? Was she really here? Mac rubbed his eyes and blinked. "My little lamb?"

Victor rolled over and groaned.

The shadow moved into the room and stood over him, backlit by the television, and yes, it was her. "Oh dear. I'm so sorry. I—"

"Shhhhh." Cynthia placed a hand on his forehead. "It's okay."

She began to undress and, for the first time in forever, the thought of her naked aroused him.

Cynthia pushed the men apart and crawled in bed, groping at both, waking Victor from sleep, exchanging kisses with each, encouraging kisses between them.

Mac's heart beat hard in his head as blood rushed through his veins, driven by sensory overload—muscles, skin, heat, saliva, hair, sweat. But what drove it most was the fear hanging above them like thick, greasy smoke from a funeral pyre.

JAKE

Jake sat at the bar nursing his beer, a twelve-pack to-go sitting next to him. Closing time drew near. The club was still a scattering of men lingering for the last show. They were permanent fixtures, pasty-skinned and sunken-eyed from a life in shadows, wearing different clothes, sipping different drinks, somehow all alike, each looking for some distraction from his crappy little life.

Davie sat down next to him. "You ready? I got a couple of the girls from the early show lined up. Grab those beers and let's hit it." He slapped Jake's shoulder, gave a wink, then headed for the door.

Jake rubbed his shoulder and watched his jerk of a friend leave. One day, he might hit back, and Davie would respect him. Hell, maybe next time they came he would refuse to pay. Why did he always pay? For that matter, why did he even hang out with Davie?

Jake waved at the bartender for his tab and slumped. He knew why. There wasn't anywhere else to go. And even if there were, he had no one else to go there with.

He made his way to the Wrangler, where he found his friend with a brunette and a redhead. Davie had the brunette pinned against the jeep, trying to get a little action, while the other woman stood in awkward silence.

"Hi. I'm Jake." He held out a hand.

The redhead looked him over, then took his hand loosely. "Amber. She's Chastity. I'll take one of those."

"Sure." Jake popped one out of the pack, handed it to her, then tapped the hood to get Davie's attention. "I'm here. You ready to go?"

Davie sighed and looked up. "You got great timing. Let's roll."

The girls climbed in the back, Davie drove, and Jake rode shotgun. He pulled out more beers and passed them around.

Davie and the girls chattered on about some shit or other, small talk to pass the time. Jake was in no mood for conversation. Something bugged him about the night—maybe it was too dark, or maybe it was the strange shimmer of the stars. He watched the night undulate across the fields as they drove, letting the chatter fade into the background, concentrating on the white noise of the jeep's engine.

They rounded a bend, and the flats drew out alongside the road. Jake lost himself in the crosshatched shadows of the trees. Soon they would pass a thick branch stuck deep in the earth—the one Davie told him about—with others out of sight deep in the woods marking three empty graves. What were they doing, picking up women on a night like this? They should be home, praying for the souls stripped from the town today like so much loose bark.

They almost passed the dim firelight before Jake noticed it. Even though he wasn't sure if they had passed the graves yet, he was sure nobody had any business being out here at this hour. Maybe it was some freak who heard about the graves, or maybe a couple of Goth kids looking for a thrill. Didn't matter. Whoever it was, they had no right.

"Slow down." He put a hand on Davie's arm. His spine felt cold and electrified, and his chest felt compressed.

Maybe it wasn't some kids.

Davie glanced over. "What the fuck? Why?"

"Slow down, okay? Please? We need to slow down." His voice cracked as he spoke. There was someone in those woods. Someone who had no business being there.

Davie slowed down. The girls stopped talking.

Jake looked back. The two women had moved to the opposite side of the Wrangler, as far from Jake as they could be in such tight quarters. Great. They both had the look he knew so well. What's with the idiot? He hated how he could not control his voice when he got worked up. He took a deep breath and turned back to Davie, speaking as calmly as he could.

"There's someone in the woods."

Davie raised an eyebrow and sneered. "What—"

"Stop the car. Whoever did that thing today, well, maybe they're back. For another look. You wanted a shot, right?"

The Jeep canted forward as Davie hit the brakes and pulled to the side of the road. Something behind his eyes turned in fits, a loose gathering of gears spinning slowly at first, then falling into a neat rhythm as his expression iced-over.

Jake rubbed his shoulder again. Maybe this wasn't such a good idea. What would they do if there were someone back there? Or even worse, what would Davie do if there weren't anyone there? Jake would never hear the end of it. He should have ignored the damned fire.

The two looked at each other. There was no taking it back. Whoever was in those woods was in for a treat, and it probably wouldn't matter who it was. Davie looked ready to do his worst.

No one dared speak as Davie glanced at the women in the back. He turned back to Jake, his eyes pale and hollow.

"What are you going to do?" Jake felt stupid again, unable to stop himself from asking. He knew what Davie would do.

The Wrangler moved as Davie pulled out, swung it wide across the road, and headed back toward the fire. "You tell me where."

"Well... maybe it was nothing at—"

Davie slapped the back of Jake's head. Hard. "Tell me, you moron."

This wasn't what Jake wanted, was it? If he didn't tell Davie now... "A bit up the road."

Chastity popped her head between the seats. "Where are we going? What's the idiot talking about? Who came back for another look?"

Jake pointed across the road. "Through those trees. You can barely see it. It's nothing." He didn't believe his own words. It was something. A fire burned back in the woods.

The Wrangler slowed, and Davie pulled across the road again. He cut the engine and let the jeep drift to a stop in the breakdown lane.

Amber joined Chastity, their heads side-by-side like two kids on a trip to Disneyland. "This is about those murders, isn't it?"

"It is." Davie killed the headlights.

"Sure. I heard about it—"

"Be quiet. I need to think."

The four sat in silence for several moments, and as Jake began to think they'd sit in the Wrangler forever, Davie got out of the car.

"Come on, moron. You two stay put."

Jake reached for the door then hesitated. He glanced out the window to the woven shadows and dithering grays of the trees. The soft firelight stirred the darkness, making him a little sick to his stomach. Whatever Davie thought they might do here couldn't be the right thing.

"You coming?" Davie's voice pulled him from his thoughts. He got out and looked at the women in the car, a blush covering his cheeks as they traded a look once again.

Amber cocked her head. "You expect us to sit here?"

Chastity pushed the driver's seat forward and wiggled out. "I'm not. You boys do what you want. I'm out of here." She held the door for Amber. "Why don't you come with me, girl? These pricks aren't interested in us."

She was right. Jake wanted to tell them to stay. This was all a mistake, and hey—Davie was a little ticked off. No problem. He would get over it.

Jake knew it wasn't a mistake, and Davie wouldn't let it go. He and Davie had lost interest, and despite his fear, something drew him toward the woods.

Amber scrambled out and the two women started to walk south.

Jake stepped to the rear of the Wrangler and watched as the women began to fade into the night. "You might want to head—"

Chastity raised a cell phone. "We got it. Not the first time I had to walk away. Won't be the last. You might try it sometime." She called someone. Her voice faded as the distance between them grew.

Davie grabbed Jake's shoulder—the one he punched earlier—and squeezed, speaking in little more than a whisper. "Forget them. Let's go."

The woods parted as Jake followed Davie in, the soft rhythm of the wetlands at night swelling as he entered. The wavering shadows of elms and maples closed the Wrangler off from view. Would they find it again when they came back? Jake did his best to remember where they had parked the Jeep. The woods at night smoothed everything together, making it difficult to pick out any landmarks. Isolation wrapped its cold arms around him as the Wrangler became little more than a shadow behind him.

The firelight was farther away than Jake thought at first. They were going in circles, no doubt about it. As they would close in on it, Davie would turn one way or the other to avoid a mass of impassable deadfall, and the firelight would fade off to one side.

The night air cooled Jake's sweat, sending tiny slivers of ice across his skin. "Do you know where we are? Let's head back, okay? We'll call Monterey and let him know someone's out here. This isn't for us to deal with."

Davie ignored the pleas and continued to work his way through the matted undergrowth and pockets of muck.

"Hey," Jake whispered again, "I said—"

Davie stopped and turned, a strange pattern of grays accenting the contours of his face. "You think we should go back? Call Monterey? He won't do anything. He'll want to sit and think things through, and we'll be lucky if he decides anything before the sun comes up. By the time the sheriff gets his balls on, this guy's gone." The shrill cry of a lone whip-poor-will pierced the night, joined by a second. Davie resumed his pace, turning south.

Jake followed. The firelight faded once again, but he didn't dare say anything more.

They arrived at a small clearing some time later, and Jake realized why his friend had changed directions. In the shifting night, he saw three empty holes, like gaping mouths of sorrow.

"We didn't need to come here." Jake didn't want to see those graves, crumbled and tattered around the edges like chapped lips. Even if two boys were murdered—maybe three—their deaths didn't give him and Davie the right to go blustering through the woods and hijack some lone camper, did they? The fire was probably surrounded by a bunch of sleeping kids, either stoned or drunk or both, hurting only themselves.

The crushing gray gloom said otherwise. There was no soft chatter, no drunken laughter. There were only the constant night voices.

Davie nudged Jake's shoulder. "Have you seen enough, or do you want to get in one, feel what it must have been like for those poor kids?"

"I've seen enough." But he hadn't, not really. He squatted next to a hole and grabbed a handful of caked dirt. He rose again, letting the chunks of earth slip from his hand back to the ground. Two boys were dead. Right or wrong, he would follow his friend to the end. "Let's go."

The path to the firelight seemed straighter from there, as if the graves were always meant to be their starting point, and it wasn't long before they reached their goal. They approached a u-shape of deadfall piled several feet high blocking the fire on three sides. The open end faced the river, and they had to step around to see what was inside.

A small fire burned. On the far side, nestled in a crook of deadfall, an old man dressed in a cargo pants and a dirty tank-top sat legs crossed, his eyes closed. Even though the flames chased dark shadows across him, the old man's face seemed clear of all gloom—not quite glowing, just absent of shadow.

Davie took a careful step into the deadfall and stopped. Jake withdrew around the edge, keeping his friend in sight, unable to look upon the old man any longer. The swirling light and shadow surrounding the placid pool of the man's face twisted his stomach like a rubber band. As he rested against the mass of branches, he listened to the old man's labored breathing. Did Davie really think this guy killed those boys? He risked another look at his friend and found nothing had softened in Davie's features.

"What are you doing here?" Each word tumbled from Davie's lips like a stone.

Jake rose and joined his friend, wanting to be something more than a weak sidekick. He could help here, and do something to get some respect from Davie.

The old man breathed in a slow, steady rhythm. He gave no response, a soft smile lingering on his lips.

Davie moved around the side of the fire. Jake put out a hand to stop him. "Wait, a minute." He searched for the right words, ones that wouldn't anger his friend. He found nothing certain and resigned to say what he had to say. He leaned in and whispered, "It's not too late to turn around and leave. This man has no place else to go. Maybe Monterey won't come out here, but we could call one of the deputies. Paul would probably come, and Cassy would be here in a flash—"

"Stop it." Davie shrugged the hand off and stepped toward the old man.

Jake should have quit talking at Paul. There would be no stopping his friend at this point. He backed up a pace. If only the old man would open his eyes, he would see how sorry Jake was for all of this. The guy made no move.

Davie nudged the man in the ribs as if waking a sleeping dog. "Hey, I'm talking to you."

The old man coughed and opened his eyes.

Jake could deal with the look of disgust he often got. Even though this old man may not be responsible for the deaths of those boys, he had no right to look at them as if they didn't know any better. Jake was a decent man, worked hard, and did his best every day. It wasn't his fault he had nowhere else to go, or that his only friend wasn't such a great guy. No, Jake was all right, and he did know better. God just didn't see fit to give him the equipment to do anything about it. No one pitied him, least of all some dirty drifter camped out in the woods.

Davie—did he see the look too?—stooped down, grabbed both of the old man's arms, and yanked. "Stand up. We got something to talk about."

The old man steadied himself as Davie let go, then smoothed his wrinkled clothes. "I don't think you're interested in talking." He turned his gray eyes to Jake. "Are you?"

There was the damnable look again. Jake sprang around the fire and threw a fist into the old man's gut. The muscle was firm and resistant. Dull vibrations ran through Jake's hand and arm as the old man buckled. He raised a fist to strike again.

Davie caught it up. "Not here. I have a better idea." Then he turned to the old man who still held his gut. "You're coming with us."

The old man stood and nodded, eyes still filled with awful pity. "I'm tired of walking. I could use a ride." He let Davie take an arm to lead him back to the Wrangler.

Jake kicked dirt over the fire until it dwindled to coals then followed the other two back through the woods. He and Davie were doing the right thing. Two boys dead, and this guy happens to be out here. Sure, some coincidence. They'd take this guy back to the sheriff and be heroes. Maybe then those shitty looks would stop and Jake would finally get a little respect around here.

The three of them reached the Wrangler, and the old man climbed in back without being told. Jake and Davie climbed in and exchanged looks. They had gone too far to back out now.

"So, do you want me to call Monterey now? I mean—"

"No." Davie started the Wrangler and pulled out, his eyes fixed on the road ahead. "You still got a key, right?"

Jake twisted the ring on his finger, the raised square and compasses digging into his thumb with each turn. "Yeah..."

Maybe they wouldn't be heroes after all.

DOC CRANDALL

Doc sat in his shadowed booth at the back of Lucille's as his son and Jake spoke at the bar. His son. His only son.

Davie left, and Doc turned his attention back to the stage where Stacy finished her last dance with a twirl on the pole. She looked good—too good, all things considered—and he wondered how she managed to stay in such shape.

A hulking man stepped into view, bald, with more tattoos than skin. Lucille, the club owner. "Last call, Doc. You okay to drive?"

Doc took a final swig of beer and tossed a fifty on the table. "How's the summer treating you? Been out to ride much? If you're okay with it, I'll take a shot of the usual. Thinking about going back for a little visit, too."

Lucille shook his head. "I'll get you the shot, but man, I don't think she'll talk to you." He scooped the fifty from the table, disappeared, then returned with Doc's Cuervo, sans lime and salt. "Here. If you need a lift, let me know. I got the sidecar on the Indian and a spare helmet." Lucille hovered a little longer and added in a quiet voice. "You know if you mess with her again, I'm going to have to do something about it."

Doc downed his shot and looked up. "I think I finally got it in me to atone. That okay with you?"

Lucille chuffed and walked away.

The booze worked its magic, spreading courage through Doc's body. He got up, crossed to the stage and walked around the side where a poorly lit hallway led to the bathrooms and, at the far end, the dressing rooms. He hesitated at the end of the hall. Should he really be here? Maybe Lucille was right, maybe Stacy wouldn't want to see him again.

No, it didn't matter if she wanted to see him. He spent too many years avoiding this, and not enough time thinking about what she did, what he allowed her to do. After today, how could he go on living with her choice?

This was a night to hang out their penance, his and hers, like matching towels.

Doc strolled through the door and another hallway stretched before him, rooms off to either side. A couple of younger women slipped by as he made his way toward the end where one door stood open. Dull light spilled from it along with the tang of cheap perfume and the dusty smell of body powder.

Stacy sat in front of a simple makeup table wrapped in a white silk robe, her back to the door, stripping the veneer from her face.

Doc stood outside. Stacy's soft muscles ripple beneath the thin fabric as she worked. Would she turn him away, or would she give him a chance? There was only one way to find out, so he tapped on the doorframe and stepped in. "Hi."

Stacy looked at him in the makeup mirror, her warped face stretching as she wiped away the last of her lipstick. She balled a tissue and tossed it on the table, looking down as she did so he could no longer see her eyes. "You know, I've seen you in the crowd over the years. Lucille tells me you come in a few times a month since we... since you abandoned me." She looked up again, her eyes swollen and moist. "Why now?"

He stepped right up behind her, still holding her gaze in the mirror. He didn't know where to start. He came to apologize fifteen years too late. What did he expect? Sorry, honey, can you ever forgive me? No, he didn't think she would accept any atonement tonight. He took her shoulders gently and rubbed. "Can't an old friend stop in to say hi?"

She shook his hands away and stood to face him, tightening her robe around her plump waist. "It's taken you a long time to say hi. Does Rachael know you're here?"

Doc looked her over, unable to meet her eyes again, unable to weather her hateful stare, cold and empty. From a distance, she looked nearly as pure as any of the women around here. Up close Doc's trained eyes could see the subtle changes to her body, alterations only from...

"I'm up here." Stacy pushed his chin up, forcing him to meet her gaze, touching no longer than necessary. "I asked if—"

"She passed on some years back. Bad heart." Doc thrust his hands in the pockets of his blazer. "And yes, when she was alive she knew I came." One hand clenched into a fist, the other wrapped around a scalpel, thumb resting against the plastic cap.

Sympathy crossed Stacy's face like a wish in a windstorm. "Well, I can't say I'm sorry for her. Or you." She sat down again, crossed her legs and arms. "What are you doing here, anyhow? The night's over. I'm not giving you a lap dance. And I'm definitely not going home with you."

Doc turned around and stared at his shoes. Maybe the words would come easier if he didn't have to look into those resistant eyes stained by years of guilt. Maybe she would listen better if she didn't have to see his pathetic weathered features as he spoke words drained of meaning by the passing years. And maybe it would all go quicker if neither one of them saw it coming. "I came to pay my penance. I came so we could pay our penance. Together."

She huffed, and he pictured her blowing a strand of hair from her face, one eye wrinkling more than the other, her nose crinkling. "We? What the hell are you talking about? There is no we here. There is only me, the washed-up stripper who got knocked up by some jackass doctor when she was barely twenty, and though he promised to leave his wife, he never made good. Didn't even have the decency to pay for the clean-up."

Doc's thumb slipped down the protective cover until his nail slid under the edge of the cap. "I said I came to apolo—"

"Don't you fucking say another word to me. I'm not done." The chair scraped as she stood. Her breath pelted the back of his neck as she continued. "Then there's you, the old doctor who seems to finally have grown a conscience over what happened. Well, I got news for you. It's too goddamned late. You could have been a man. It's too late now. You can get the hell out."

Tears stung Doc's eyes as he squeezed them shut, trying to clear them so he could face her once more. He didn't want to cry, this wasn't about crying or making her happy or getting her to forgive him. This wasn't about her at all. He was sure her rage blocked any chance she would understand.

The child he had he didn't want. The child he wanted he didn't have. Those two thoughts made him a horrible father to both children, the living and the dead, and it was to those children he owed some sort of penance.

The cap snapped off the scalpel with a faint click, and his thumb stung as it ran along the blade. He turned to face her, and though the hateful look on her face was almost too much to bear, he held on a little longer. "There were some terrible murders in Washington Heights today. Maybe yesterday. The librarian, some teenagers. Two boys."

Confusion worked its way into Stacy's face, replacing some of the scorn. "Murders? I don't—"

"I had a long day. Autopsies. Bodies stacked up at the clinic. I never finished them. A young woman came in. She had a miscarriage. Then another. And another. Seven by the end of the day, all on the same day. One of them was fifty-three years old. I did her annual last month. No sign of pregnancy, and she's way too old anyhow, and yet there it was. Seven miscarriages, and if I know Washington Heights, for every person I see in the clinic at least two other in the area are suffering from the same thing. Usually, it's when people get some common illness. I think the same thing happened today. I saw just enough dead babies, just what I needed to see, like God was rubbing this in my face, telling me how horrible I am for letting an unborn child die. All those women, and every one of them wore the same sad, empty face, eyes hollow, knowing they've lost something they could never regain. Do you get it?" His tears spilled freely.

Stacy stepped back, bumped into her chair, and stopped. She looked worried, scared. Cornered. "I... what are you telling me?"

"You shouldn't have done it, and I shouldn't have let you. You should have had our baby. Now? You and I? We are damned. Not because it's intrinsically wrong, but because we did it to keep our lives... convenient." Doc pulled the scalpel from his pocket and held it to the side. "It's time you pay the price."

Stacy's eyes widened, and she raised an arm to block his swing. She moved too late. He swept the blade across her throat, opening a deep gash and sending hot arterial spray across his face. She gurgled, looking surprised, confused, and hurt all in one jumbled expression as she groped at her split neck. He stepped back as she dropped to her knees, still trying to stem the flow of blood, staring up at him, her mouth working silently like a suffocating fish.

The fresh blood on his face felt like redemption. He looked down at Stacy, smiling a little, and spoke softly. "It's time I pay the price."

The cold blade burned his neck as he drew it across and let the scalpel fall to the floor. He dropped to his knees, joining Stacy on the floor, catching her before she tumbled over. Clutching his old lover, tilting their heads back so the fresh wounds met, his sins wept from his soul as their blood pumped, mingled, and cascaded to the floor.

LEWIS

June 3, 2008

ewis stood outside the circle of men, his back against the rough sandstone wall of the Lodge basement. When did things go south around here? He should be doing more to stop this bastardized ritual, but the flask in his pocket begged him to take a sip. Bending to its will, he pulled it out and took a big swig.

In the center stood Kyle, wearing a monk's robe and looking like an ass. Everyone else was dressed like any other casual country evening. A young man knelt before him, naked save for his boxer shorts and a blindfold. Jake stood on one side of the initiate looking reluctant and anxious, Davie stood on the other looking eager. Kyle removed the blindfold, popped the clip out of the Ruger, and held it out. The initiate glanced down at the clip. Lewis could almost smell the grimy sweat working its way down the guy's forehead.

"This place is built on trust." Kyle snapped the clip home, the faintest glimmer of a smile on his lips. His smile faded as fast as the gun's click, replaced by the drawn face of a man seeking control over his world.

Lewis couldn't help wonder if he bore the same sad smile. How long would it take them to figure out what he did?

Probably not long. And he was okay with them figuring it out sooner than later. Every man in here was some kind of guilty. They just didn't know it yet.

Kyle looked at the initiate kneeling before him. "Do you trust me?"

Lewis stifled a chuckle. What did Kyle know of trust? Lewis never trusted his son, and the feeling was mutual. Did Kyle really think a gun earned you trust? He should know better. Lewis shook his head and pulled another mouthful of whiskey.

The initiate shot a sidelong glance to a recent member who stood in the circle. Their exchanged looks held more than curiosity.

Kyle tapped the gun against the initiate's cheek. "Don't look at him, look at me. I'm the one asking the question. Do. You. Trust. Me."

The initiate nodded once.

Kyle's face swelled like a balloon full of pig's blood. He pressed the barrel against the poor guy's head. "Earplugs."

The men rustled as they tucked bits of foam in their ears. Davie plugged the initiate's ears, pushing the little scraps in harder than necessary.

Kyle stepped to one side, turned, and aimed the pistol towards the east wall. The men there parted to reveal an empty Maker's Mark bottle on a small wooden table.

The sound of a gunshot and breaking glass echoed throughout the basement. Lewis winced in spite of his plugs as fragments of glass scattered along the east wall, bouncing off the concrete patch he put in almost a year ago. The shards rained down the wall forever, fragments of the past, each only a glimpse into some greater picture shattered beyond repair.

Lewis puffed his chest a little. His boy almost never missed.

The room returned its collective gaze to the two men in the center. Kyle raised the gun, took a few steps back, and pointed it at the young man's head. "One more time. Do you trust me?"

The answer wouldn't matter. Yes or no, they both resulted in the same thing. The initiate checked his friend in the audience one more time, one corner of his lip curling. "Yes."

Kyle took three quick steps forward, pressed the gun to the initiate's forehead, and fired. The gun popped, bloody bits sprayed out the back of the young man's head, and his body slumped to the floor. Kyle stood there with the gun in hand, eyes wide.

Gun smoke swirled in the air as the men slowly removed their earplugs. Lewis let his fall to the floor and pulled another drink from his flask.

Jake stepped away from the body and retched. Davie wiped muck from his pants and whispered, "Nice shot."

The sweat on Lewis's skin froze in place. He should have been out of the building before Kyle fired the second shot. Hell, he should have just handed the gun over and left. Everyone in the room still looked confused. Maybe he could make it before someone realized. He edged toward the stairs, keeping a watch on the men closest to him, waiting for one to stop him. No one did. He reached the steps and began to climb, never looking back.

"Hold it, Pop."

Lewis stopped and peered over his shoulder.

Kyle trembled, gun leveled at Lewis's chest, and for the first time since before Tom left town he was crying. "What did you do?"

"What did I do? You pulled the trigger." Lewis drained his flask, washing away a last morsel of regret, and tossed it aside. "This whole thing was your idea."

"Jesus Christ, did you put live fucking rounds in there? What did you do, oh Jesus, what did you do...?"

The rest of the crowd scuttled toward the stairs, and Kyle waved the gun around, threatening all of them at once. "Don't any of you move. Stay the fuck put until I figure this out." He pressed both hands to the sides of his head and closed his eyes, breathing deeply.

Lewis should have stayed closer to the stairs.

Kyle opened his eyes again. "Okay. Who knows this guy?"

No one answered. No one breathed.

"You're fucking lying, but okay. You're all guilty anyhow. You all saw Pop give me the gun, you all watched me pull the trigger, and none of you did a goddamned thing to stop me. Now get out." Kyle fell to his knees and buried his face in his hands.

Lewis didn't want to see his son crying. Why did the boy have to cry? He should slip out with the rest of the men, but the sound of his child sobbing was too much.

One by one, the men in the room pushed by him and ascended the stairs, and when the room was finally empty, he once more found a small spot in his heart for Kyle. He went to his boy and knelt, taking the robe and lifting it up. "C'mon, let's get this thing off you. It's over. We're done here."

Kyle raised his arms like a toddler undressing for bath time, and Lewis pulled the robe up and over. He wiped errant bits of blood and brains from his hand, took the robe, and covered the body oozing in the middle of the room.

The last footfalls faded and the echo from the great front doors slamming chased itself around the Lodge.

Lewis hugged his son. This was hard on the boy, and no father liked to watch his child suffer. Even so, children needed to be taught, and some lessons were only learned the hard way.

Kyle pushed away and stood up. He looked at the body, hugging himself and rocking. "Why?"

Lewis stood and slung an arm around Kyle's shoulders. There was no backing out now. He'd be lucky if the boy didn't shoot him too. "Because I hate you. Your birth stole the only woman I loved. Your mistake with Alissa made me a killer. You already knew how it felt to be alone and unloved. Now you know how it feels to be a murderer."

Someone across the room cleared his throat, and they both looked up. Jake stood at the bottom of the stairs wringing a ball cap.

Lewis squeezed Kyle, feeling closer to him than he had in years, finally connected with his son. "What is it?"

"Well, no disrespect Mr. Burton, and I don't care much for your family business. You see, Davie makes me do most of the cleanup work, and I thought you might like a hand."

"Mighty nice of you. Get supplies and come back down. Bring me the old dust cover from the piano while you're up there."

Jake nodded then went back upstairs.

Lewis looked at Kyle. "I'll take care of the body. Best if no one else knows where it is. You go on home. We're even now. Maybe tomorrow we can start acting like father and son again."

Kyle shook his head as he started toward the stairs.

Lewis grabbed his shoulder. "Son, best leave the gun with me as well. It's an old piece. I'll stash it with the body, I suppose."

Kyle looked down at his hand, as if only now aware he still held the gun. Blood drained from his face, and he looked as if he might bring it to bear on Lewis. Instead, he steadied himself on the wall, then thrust the Ruger into Lewis's hand. The gun felt warm, alive, as if it wanted more. Kyle ascended the stairs with glazed eyes and a distant look.

Lewis watched him go, then listened as his footfalls crossed the room. There was a long pause, then the front door opened and slammed again.

Lewis sat on the steps and smoked, feeling as hollow and dirty as the basement. When Jake returned, they wrapped the body up, scraping most of the muck onto the thick dust cover with scraps of cardboard. Jake found some twine in the corner and used it to tie off the ends.

Lewis draped the body over his shoulders in a fireman's carry and patted Jake on the back. "You're a good man for helping. Not your problem. You scrub up the mess. Leave everything else as is. I'll be back after I get rid of this. You'll be gone by then, right?"

Jake nodded. "Pardon me for saying... Kyle was right. It's my mess too. It's all of ours." He looked at the dark pool on the floor. "We were all here to see it. I think... maybe we all wanted this to happen."

Lewis looked at the blood as well. "Yeah." The basement felt thick, and he felt hot and itchy as the reality of it all set in. There was nothing more to say. He dragged the body off, leaving Jake to tend to the mess.

Lewis disposed of the corpse, dumping it in the same hidden cave by the river used many years ago to hide another mess. When he returned to the Lodge basement, Jake was gone and the cleaning supplies were put away. He only glanced at the singular dark patch on the concrete. Something else in the room worried him even more.

Lewis went to the middle of the basement to get the only inert object in this whole ordeal. He scooped up the stone, tucked it in a pocket, and went home.

JAKE

The Lodge rose through dithering grays stratified by dark tendrils of black. The very night intensified and collapsed around the building, stretching and accenting angles in peculiar ways. Jake's belly flip-flopped at the sight. The laws of geometry were absent, replaced by the elasticity of dreams.

Jake looked away from the building as they crept up the gravel drive, pebbles popping beneath the tires. "I don't want to go back in there."

"We'll be fine."

The Wrangler drifted by the front porch toward the side lot. The tarnished square and compasses above the door looked carved from coal and the front door itself wore paint the shade of a drowned man's lips. Even the woods behind the Lodge seemed quieter, as if aware of the presence of the condemned.

They pulled around the corner and stopped. Davie wasted no time getting out and pulling the old man from the jeep.

Jake got out and approached the massive front doors of the Lodge. The keys cooled his fingers as he pulled them from a pocket and searched for the right one. The metal felt like the skin of the dead and conjured the image of Lewis Burton laid out in a coffin. What would Lewis think? What would Kyle think? He slid the key in and the lock clicked, but guilt iced him to the porch.

Davie shoved him aside and opened the door. The two men passed him, and Jake wondered what this withered old creature had to do with the events in Washington Heights. Was he a murderer? Maybe. Was he any worse than he or Davie, or any of the other men in the Lodge? Probably not.

The old man became another Lodge brother in Jake's eyes. They all deserved a slice of justice, and did it really matter who served it out? It may as well be Davie and him. Someday another might return the favor.

He followed Davie and their captive into the entryway. The air felt heavy and stagnant, as if the building had trapped the heat of the day in a desperate attempt to fight off the cool night. It pressed against his back, urging him on as he followed them downstairs.

The air in the basement, a few degrees cooler, raised goose flesh on his arms. The bulbs sputtered on, casting harsh light across the concrete floor and sandstone walls.

As Davie reached the bottom step, he shoved the old man to the floor. "You like picking on little boys?" Davie stepped around the old man, waiting for a reaction, as Jake reached the bottom.

The old guy rolled over—pity still in his eyes. Didn't he know what was happening here?

Davie moved to kick again. Jake stepped between the two. "What do you think you're going to do? Beat a confession from him? We should take him in. We could—"

"The question is, what are you going to do? Protect an old child killer, or protect this town?" Davie's eye twitched as his lips curled. He took a step toward Jake, his breath a stale mix of alcohol and cigarettes.

Jake stepped back, his heel nudging up against the old man. He looked down over his shoulder. "Why don't you do something? Run, fight, say something. Don't you know he's gonna kill you?" Jake turned and Davie's fist landed in the hinge of his jaw. Pain streamed out from the cluster of nerves like a bundle of burning wires. He lost balance, caught a foot on the old man's torso, and toppled to the concrete. His chin bounced off the floor, sending a harsh buzz through his head. He tasted blood. Maybe Davie was going to kill both of them.

"Stay out of my way." Davie kicked Jake's feet off the old man.

The dull thuds of body blows blended with the buzz of insects as Jake struggled to pull away from the fray. His fingernails scrabbled across concrete as he inched along, stopping only when he arrived at a stark patch of reddish-brown. He ran his fingers over the stained concrete and felt a matching blemish on his own soul.

The pounding behind him continued. Each punch Davie landed pierced the veil of incessant buzzing. He looked toward the eastern wall, and the room swam as a small concrete patch in the sandstone foundation darkened. Was water trickling through, defying gravity by snaking up the wall?

As the furious sound of insects swelled, he realized the water was made of hundreds, if not thousands, of plump little winged bodies.

Jake flipped over and shouted. "We need to leave. Now."

His friend continued to hammer down on the curled-up drifter, blinded by his own rage and unaware of the swarm of wasps streaming into the basement.

The air hummed as Jake struggled to his feet, the vibrations disorienting him, slowing him down as he sprinted toward his friend. He caught Davie's arm up short. "Look at me. We have to leave."

A deep fire burned in Davie's eyes, only to flicker out. The slick electric hum of insects almost obliterated Davie's reply. "Why?"

Jake pointed to the wall. What could he say?

Davie looked, and the questions on his face washed away.

Both men looked down at the old man on the floor, who unfolded from the fetal position and stood up smiling, unmarked by the barrage of fists. His eyes remained placid ovals as he looked from one captor to the other.

Even now, the old man pitied them.

Then the wasps were upon them.

Stinger after stinger sunk into every inch of Jake's exposed flesh, his hands taking the brunt as he waved them about in weak defense. The insects jabbed with fierce venom and held tight, weighing him down as he watched his friend suffer the same abuse.

Davie fell first as he tried to run for the stairs and tripped up short. The wasps coalesced and buried him in a dark writhing mass of wings and stingers.

Seconds later the air was thick with the hellish insects and Jake no longer knew which way was up. He fell to the ground, hoping the swarm might be trying to move up the stairs in search of an exit.

The weight on his back grew as the bugs continued to land, each no more than a grain of sand, collectively as heavy as a boulder.

He managed to lift a few inches for a final look. The old man remained untouched, the sea of wasps parting to let him pass.

Jake dragged himself across the floor to follow the old man, reaching once again the reddish-brown stain in the concrete, recoiling at the touch. And just before the insects took his eyes, just before they crushed the last breath from his body, he saw the old man stoop at the wall and disappear.

MAC

Mac woke to the scent of jasmine. Cynthia's shampoo. Her hair tickled his nose, one closed eye, his cheek. The dark room felt odd and unfamiliar, and as he slowly lifted from the depth of an already forgotten dream, he remembered. He was not at home.

The fog of sleep slipped away, replaced by the muffled sounds of feet shuffling, voices chattering. Mac sat up in bed and listened. Was it morning already? Couldn't be. Who was in the church at this hour?

What if someone came in?

Mac shook his wife gently, not wanting to scare her. "Wake up." She moaned and rolled over. He dispensed with the niceties, got out of bed, locked the door quietly and flicked on the light.

Victor and Cynthia both cringed at the sudden brightness, neither opening their eyes. He crept back to the bed and began to dress, talking to them in a hoarse whisper. "Don't you hear?"

Victor opened his eyes first and pulled away from Mac's wife, redness consuming his cheeks. "What's going on?"

"Keep it down, and wake her up, will you? Don't you hear?" Mac checked his watch. "Two AM? What in God's name?"

Victor tilted his head, raising first one eyebrow as he listened, then the other as he realized and slipped from the bed. "Who's that?"

"Don't know." Mac finished tucking his shirt in and rocked Cynthia by the shoulders until her eyes opened. "Get dressed."

Cynthia sat up, bed sheet clutched to her chest. "Who—"

"No time." Mac tossed her clothes on the bed. The room stank, thick with the smells of sweat and sex and fear. A sharp nausea swept through him, forcing him to sit on the bed. "Get your clothes on. Did you lock the front doors when you came in earlier?"

She strapped her bra on and let the sheet fall away. Her blouse looked wrinkled—one more thing to hope no one noticed—as she crammed her arms through the sleeves and buttoned up. "I... it was late. Why would I lock the doors?"

Victor sat down to tie his shoes in the room's only chair. "Great. Just what I need."

Mac spun around. "You're worried? What about me? How's this going to look to my congregation?" He buried his face in both hands. What a mess. Maybe they could hide in here. Then again, no one's even supposed to be here. Who knew how long the interlopers might stay? No, he couldn't sit and do nothing. He looked back to find Cynthia and Victor standing side-by-side, waiting, both wearing the same dull expectation he saw each Sunday on most of his congregation. Everyone wanted him to have answers.

He stood and faced them both. Okay. They weren't in any shape to help. "Victor, you stay here. Hide under the bed, or in a corner, or I dunno, just keep out of sight. Cynthia and I will go on out. Everything will be fine." He held up a hand as Victor's face wrinkled. This wasn't the time for arguments.

"Not a word. Whatever is going on out there, I need to deal with it. Just stay put."

Victor nodded, lips pursed, as if struggling to lock in some clever retort. He sat back on the bed. "I'll stay, but I'm not hiding."

Good enough. Mac nodded, took Cynthia by the arm, and led her to the door. "If people ask, it's like old times. We were working late on my sermon." He turned the light off again, enveloping them in darkness. Then he unlocked the door and ushered her into the bright light of the rec room.

The scene in the church basement confused him so much he forgot to shut the door. A wide array of dishes filled the tables—pies of all flavor, cakes, cookies, éclairs, baked beans, little finger sandwiches, green-bean casseroles—almost every potluck or bake-sale dish imaginable. The smell of treats hung low in the air, tainted by something else—a rough and acrid odor he couldn't quiet place. What disoriented him even more than the food were the people. It seemed his entire congregation decided to start the bake-sale in the middle of the night.

Naked.

Great piles of clothes lay strewn around the perimeter of the room. Too many clothes. Way too many.

And what smelled? Gasoline? Where was it coming from? He looked around to see if maybe old Murphy had left an open can down there, unable to find the source of the smell. He couldn't see much through all the food and flesh.

A few of his flock wore pointy paper party hats, most simply munched away wearing nothing at all. Mac looked at his wife. Before he could say anything, a voice called to them from the crowd.

"Pastor! Cynthia! So glad you could join us!" Harriet jiggled her way through a small circle of people. "We were worried when we couldn't get to you through the call tree."

Mac pulled the door shut. He slipped a hand into Cynthia's and held tight, lumpy bags of flesh drawing his attention like a ten-car pile-up.

Harriet held out a conical paper hat. "Didn't have enough for everyone. I saved one for you, though." Her smile flashed to a mock-frown as she turned to Cynthia. "Sorry, dear. Last one." Harriet's smile returned, a grotesque shimmering red, her lipstick smeared well beyond her lips. Her eyes twinkled with a dark light, filling his bowels with lead.

"I... Thank you?" He took the hat. What was it for? The bright-green paper felt cold and hard, somehow a little obscene, as he spun it around to find "Happy Birthday!" written in sweeping white cursive outlined by glitter.

Two women joined Harriet—their names escaping Mac for the moment—neither showing any hint of shame or modesty. The three women cornered him and his wife like wolves, all smiles and teeth, makeup strewn across their faces as if applied by a drunken Picasso.

A day ago, he might have flown into a rage and chased every last one of these people from the church. Things were different now, considering what he did last night. He bit his lip as a reminder to stay pleasant. There must be a reasonable explanation for all of this. "What exactly is going on here? I mean..."

He tried to slip by the three women, pulling Cynthia with him. One stepped in and cut them off. He cleared his throat. "The, uh, bake sale starts tomorrow afternoon. Not this morning. Was there a misprint in the bulletin?"

The third woman tossed her head back and laughed while Harriet and the other exchanged quivering grins.

Harriet slapped one baggy hand against Mac's chest. "No, silly dilly. The bulletin was fine. Who needs a bake sale at a time like this? Don't you see?" She pointed toward the table in the center of the room. On it sat a three-level wedding cake, the typical bride and groom figures replaced with a single number-shaped candle. A zero.

None of this made any sense. Why would these people come to the church in the middle of the night for... a birthday party? He pinched the bridge of his nose, blinked hard, and took a second look. Was he still asleep in the room dreaming this absurdity while nestled between his wife and his lover? "I'm sorry, I don't understand."

Harriet took his hand and led him away from the door. Cynthia, still clutching his other hand, trailed behind like a frightened child. Harriet led them toward the cake-table, bouncing as she walked. "Of all people, I expected you to feel it." She paused and turned to Mac, her makeup twisted into wrinkles of doubt. "You do feel it, don't you?"

Whatever Mac felt, it did not inspire having a naked potluck with his congregation. "I'm sorry. I don't."

Harriet shrugged and continued to a nearby table. "Well, no matter." She cut a slice from the remaining half-moon of a pie and slid it onto a paper plate. "We're gonna light the candle in a minute here. Let me help you." She traded him the pie for the hat. Before Mac could protest, she slipped the birthday cone on his head, snapping the band under his chin. "Dear Mr. Ornthal was first one here, so we're giving him the honor. Unless, of course, you want it."

The smell from the pie, a flaky crust filled with thick juicy chunks of gray, turned Mac's stomach. Harriet gawked at him, and he saw no way to avoid the inevitable. He took the plastic fork from the plate, scooped up a tiny bite, and stuffed it in his mouth. It tasted warm and sour, like meat left too long in the sun. He forced a swallow and fought off the threatening gag-reflex as he set the plate down. "It's a little rich for me."

Harriet deflated. Before she could ask another question, Charlie joined them with a box of fireplace matches. He held them out for Mac and rattled the container. "Pastor. I'm ready to light this up if you are."

The weight in Mac's belly grew heavier. The cake. The matches. And all the clothes stacked around the room—they looked familiar, as clothes of his congregation should. But why so many, and why spread so evenly about?

"Pastor?" Charlie jiggled the box again.

Mac once again smelled the gasoline. It wasn't enough to choke on. Still... "No thanks. Are you sure lighting a candle is a good idea? Don't you smell the gas? I think someone spilled some down here or something. Maybe we should just pack this up tonight. What do you say?"

Charlie nodded. "It's fine. All part of the Lord's plan. Now if you'll excuse me." He raised his voice above the murmuring nudists. "Everyone gather 'round. We're going to light this up."

As the group congregated around the cake, Mac took the opportunity to pull away with Cynthia. He receded into the crowd, doing his best to avoid brushing against anyone and failing miserably. When they emerged from the other side, he wanted more than anything to run home and shower. He forgot the shower as the smell of gas drew him like a hound to a fox. He just wouldn't feel safe until he figured out where Murphy left the gas can.

He led Cynthia toward the edge of the room. "Do you notice something wrong here?"

She let out a small bark of laughter. "Uh, yes dear. We're surrounded by crazy naked people. Is there something more?"

She had to be sarcastic at a time like this? The smell became stronger the closer he got to the clothes. Behind them, the crowd let out a small round of applause. He took a quick look back.

The candle flickered and his congregation of peeled grapes gazed at the glow. They began to sing. They did not sing happy birthday, as he expected. Instead, their voices joined in the well-worn melody of Amazing Grace. Who did they expect to come along and blow out the candle? Where's the birthday boy—or girl? He could no longer deny it—his flock had slipped over the edge. Maybe what he and Cynthia did was wrong—and Victor—but at least there was some logic to it. Then again, wasn't their little love-fest a reaction to something strong and overshadowing, some sudden darkness coating the town like hot tar? Maybe the people here were dealing with it in their own peculiar way. Maybe this was all the result of some mass hysteria, something in the water or something in the air.

Let them serenade the candle. What was the harm?

He and Cynthia continued until they reached the nearest mound of clothes, and he knew why they seemed so familiar. Yes, some belonged to the good people who now stood behind him worshiping some strange birthday cake, waiting for God-knows-what. Most of the clothes came from the donation bin. And the smell of gasoline was nearly overpowering here.

Cynthia reached down and pushed some of the clothes aside, revealing more clothes underneath, damp, as well as some red plastic containers. He yanked her hand away and looked back once more, all thoughts turning to the burning zero in the center or the room.

The assemblage still stood around the cake, singing softly, almost chanting. Charlie was no longer with them. He was in the far corner, separated from Mac by fifty feet of naked people and food. Too much space, too little time.

Charlie touched a match to a pile of gasoline-soaked garments. The flame took to the clothes like sharks in a feeding frenzy, reaching Mac and Cynthia in mere moments.

Mac jerked her away from the flaming rags. Thick smoke undulated toward the ceiling. He grabbed her and turned toward the closed double-doors that led upstairs. They didn't make it far. A well-placed pile of clothes fueled a pillar of flames, blocking their way. Mac felt his blood chill. There was no way through the burning shroud. He pulled Cynthia's hand to his lips and kissed it while the fire devoured their hope of escape. "I've always loved you in my own way."

Cynthia patted him on the arm. "I know."

The congregation's song continued to fill the air, now joined by the soft crackle and sputter of flames interspersed with a few coughs. Mac turned around, searching the room for another way out. Maybe there was a window, or a forgotten maintenance access. The heat grew at their back, the air thickened with dark smoke. Mac looked at the ceiling. Why hadn't the fire alarm gone off? Why weren't the sprinklers running?

Charlie stood next to Mac, slipped an arm around his shoulders, and sang quietly. He forced the couple back into the room, where they joined the rest of the congregation in song. Victor was there as well, clothed, shaking, restrained by sagging older men.

The room filled with smoke, and somewhere behind them came the sound of a small explosion.

Charlie leaned over and whispered, as if sharing a private joke. "I left a stack of rags outside the doors. We soaked the whole building before coming down."

Mac hugged his wife and gazed at Victor through the hot, choking air. There was nothing left to do but sing.

PART III

"And what rough beast, its hour come round at last,
Slouches towards Bethlehem to be born?"

–The Second Coming, William Butler Yeats

KYLE

The summer stars glistened in the clear night over the glen, hypnotizing Kyle as he sat on the balcony gulping bourbon. He wished to God for an answer in those stars, some divine direction on where to go from here, something other than the one he kept mulling over. The evening air and the crystallized pinpoints ignored his wishes, and left him to draw his own conclusions.

Whether what he saw earlier was a real ghost or an image created by his booze-addled brain no longer mattered. The way he saw it, both demanded the same remedy. He tipped the bottle to take another drink, then stopped, angry at the coldness of the woods surrounding his house, the self-inflicted isolation.

"Enough of this shit." He chucked the bottle over the rail. It descended through the blackness and into the trees where it shattered.

He got up and went inside.

Even though the house was clean, he was unable to resist the need for more order. He arranged a few magazines on the coffee table, put the remote into a drawer, and ran a dust cloth over the furniture. He moved on to the kitchen, washing the few dishes in the sink and preparing the coffee machine for the morning.

The phone sat in its cradle—right where it belonged—and though it pained him to move it, he needed to make a call before getting on with his solution. He phoned the office and left a message for his secretary. He wouldn't be in tomorrow.

The bedroom was already pristine, with the bed made and clothes put away. It took some digging before he found an old pair of jeans, a t-shirt, and a pair of work boots—none of them worn in years. They fit comfortably as he dressed, feeling right, as if kept for this very occasion.

Once dressed, Kyle sat on the edge of the bed and lay back to stare at the ceiling. His chest rose and fell in a steady rhythm. "Pop, what in the hell am I doing?"

Then the tears came, unexpected and unwelcome, hitting him hard and fast like a gunshot to the face. Pop was dead, buried in the ground, festering like spoiled meat ill seasoned with secrets. Kyle pressed both palms against his eyes. Maybe he was responsible in some sense. Maybe he could have stopped Pop.

The storm of tears subsided as Kyle rose and went to his closet. He pulled out an old shoebox, too heavy for shoes, and returned to the bed. He couldn't change the past no matter how much of the responsibility was his. He knew it deep in his heart. He also knew there was no sense in thinking too much on the maybes. No, he needed to move forward. He needed to follow Pop's example. Not without a confession first.

The shoebox was an awkward weight in his hands, the lid threatening to slip off several times on his way to the car. Kyle got in the Corvette, placed the box on the passenger seat, and sped off into the night.

This time he needed no ghost to show him the way. Driving as fast as he could, no traffic to slow him down at this hour, he arrived at the Lodge's driveway and stopped in the road. The car idled, once again a patient and obedient beast, as he looked up the gravel drive to where the dark building sat.

Some part of him hoped to see the apparition once more. Maybe she would show up and pull him away from his current course.

If she was there, somewhere in the darkness of the trees overlooking the river, she kept to herself.

Christ, he was so sorry. Sorry for all of it. What pushed the men of the Lodge to do what they did? How could none of them see what was going on? Did any of them see it even now? Probably not. More likely, they were all at home sleeping like angels.

Kyle placed a hand on the shoebox for strength, then put the car in gear and drove on up the road. Minutes later he parked in front of Pop's old house, grabbed the box, and got out. He paused, becoming aware of the dithering orange and red glow on the horizon toward town. Had it been there as he passed around the western edge? It didn't matter. Whatever was happening in Washington Heights tonight had nothing to do with him. Let it burn.

He turned to the house.

Tom might be sleeping, might have even gotten lucky and brought Cassy back here. Kyle didn't care. He popped the lid off the box, letting it fall to the ground, and pulled out a Ruger P90 and a clip one bullet shy of full. Blood stained the handle and barrel. Pop's blood.

"You in there?" Kyle pounded on the front door. "Get out here, big brother. We have to talk."

The clip snapped into place nice and easy.

DORTHEA

The warm water embraced Dorthea as the boy pressed a damp cloth against her forehead. He wasn't so bad once she got used to the smell, and the drink he made... She never tasted anything so wonderful in her life, so filling. So satiating.

The boy pushed Dorthea forward and swabbed her back. Flecks of his skin and crusted blood floated in the tub, mingling with the bubbles. "You have a long night ahead of you, lady. You ready for it?"

"Uh, huh. How are you going to get me there?" Dorthea reached forward and unplugged the drain, sending the water, bubbles, and pieces of the boy on their way to the septic tank. The muffled noise of the front door opening and closing startled her, and she looked to the bathroom door. Jessica was home.

The boy rested his chin on her shoulder and grinned, his teeth looking like perfect little seashells in an ocean of burnt flesh. "Sounds like our ride's home. You leave this to me."

Jessica's voice penetrated the door. "Dorthea? You okay, baby? Were you sick? What's this mess... Jesus, is that blood?" Panic flared in those last words.

Goosebumps rippled over Dorthea as she stood and cradled her belly. The bath brought color back to her skin, and she felt better than she had in days. She stepped onto the tattered bathmat and let the boy wrap a towel around her. "I'm okay. Let me towel off and I'll be right out. The mess is just... A friend stopped by with some health food." The boy brought her a terrycloth robe, and she cradled his face gently before accepting the offering. "One of the neighbor boys."

No, he wasn't so bad at all.

Jessica knocked. "Neighbor boy? Do you realize how late it is?" The doorknob jiggled. "How long have you been in there?"

"I'm okay. Go sit down. We'll be out in a minute." Dorthea snugged the oversized robe around her waist, thick terrycloth sucking the remaining moisture from her skin.

Jessica pounded on the door. "We? You sick, fat little whore. After everything I've done for you. Open this door now!"

The boy hugged Dorthea, kissed her hand, then turned to the door. He grabbed the butcher knife from the sink, drawing it against the porcelain. "Go sit down, you bitch, or I'll cut your girlfriend wide open."

Dorthea stepped back. Would he really cut her? The boy looked over his shoulder, a streak of death in his milky eyes. Though he smiled and shook his head no, she thought he might if pushed hard enough, if denied his requests one too many times. She wrapped the robe tighter, thankful the child inside stayed quiet, and sat down on the toilet. "Jessica, honey, just do as he says. It's the neighbor boy. I needed some help, is all. We'll be right out."

His eyes bit into her. Her help was unwelcome. He tensed, the exposed muscles in his neck and face twitching and flaking.

"Sorry," she whispered.

The muscles relaxed and the tiny row of seashells returned. He lowered the blade. "We don't have long. If you can't convince her, I will."

Dorthea nodded, not wanting to risk any more arguments. The boy unlocked the door and motioned for her to go first. She stepped into the living room.

Jessica sat on the couch, arms folded, her face a mixed sketch of charcoal fear and oily anger. She rose, arms still crossed, and looked over Dorthea. "Who's in there with you? What's going on?"

Dorthea held her hands up. Speaking came hard. She didn't want to lie. She didn't want to risk saying something that would make the boy stick her in the back. She felt the boy standing behind her, so close his breath permeated the robe and tickled her skin. "Listen for a minute, okay? You need to drive me somewhere, and we need to go now. Bring me a dress and some shoes. Don't ask questions. Please?"

Jessica took a step forward, uncrossed her arms, and peered over Dorthea. "No. Not until you tell me what's going on. Whoever is in there better come out now, or I'm calling the cops."

The boy chuckled behind Dorthea, and she felt his hairy breath press harder through the robe. He needled the small of her back with the knife and whispered, "Clock's ticking, lady."

She winced and wished she hadn't. She tried her best to keep cool, to speak with confidence and command, something usually left to Jessica. "We're going to the hospital." The lie rolled off her tongue, burning like bad liquor, tasting right nonetheless. "I told you, it's a neighbor boy here to help. He's a little... deformed. Doesn't want you to see him."

Jessica retreated to the kitchenette and leaned on the table, placing her palm flat on the surface, fingers splayed out. This was her stubborn pose, the one she used when Dorthea was being unreasonable. "Unless you're going into labor, we're not going anywhere."

The boy chuffed then shot out from behind Dorthea. Before she could react, he sprinted to the kitchen table and brought the butcher knife down on Jessica's little finger.

Even from where she stood, Dorthea saw the digit severe neatly from the hand and smelled the fresh blood. The baby kicked.

Jessica stood there silent, eyes like stone wells, blood spurting from the stump where her little finger used to be. She stared at her hand, dry-heaved once, then screamed.

The boy scooped the finger off the table and pointed it at the wounded woman. "Now you listen here, bitch. She's about to have a baby, you understand?" He poked her in the chest with the excommunicated pinky. "You're nothing to the child. Nothing. But we need you to drive, so I'm not gonna kill you." He screamed now as well, pressing hands to both ears, then brandished the knife in her face. "Shut the hell up!"

Jessica's voice cut out, her mouth still open as she cradled the wounded hand with her good one.

The boy turned to Dorthea. "Find something to wrap her hand up, and let's go."

Dorthea moved as quick as she could, returning to the bathroom for a first aid kit, finding only some old gauze and athletic tape. The baby kicked and squirmed. Whether it was the noise or the smell of fresh blood, she couldn't say for sure. She suspected the latter.

She returned to the kitchen.

Jessica sat at the table wincing as the boy poked at her with her own finger. Dorthea pushed the boy aside, and he backed off enough to let her work. She took Jessica's hand and bandaged it up, avoiding eye contact, not wanting to look into those pleading holes. She had to remember this was all for the baby. The boy promised her this was a special baby, a wonderful baby who could set things right again. She didn't know if she believed him. She did know she wanted to believe her child was unique, and nothing else mattered.

She taped off the bandage. Jessica drew her chin up with the wounded hand, forcing them to look each other in the eyes.

"Who is he? Where are we really going?" Jessica's soft breath caressed Dorthea's face, the words falling like whispering rain. "How does he know—"

The baby stretched for what felt like a hundred miles, drawing Dorthea's belly out to where she felt it would pop. A dull roar rose in her ears and she buckled, unable to hear the rest of Jessica's question.

The boy came to her side, and as the noise and pain subsided, she heard him yelling again.

"Get her up. We have to go now. Can't you feel it?" The boy slipped under one arm, and Jessica—sweet Jessica—took her by the other.

She and Jessica came face-to-face as they stood up, and Dorthea wondered at the love still in Jessica's haggard features, even when faced with this inexplicable creature and the unknowable threat ahead. A new pain set in, a tightening sensation low in her abdomen, and she knew the baby was starting his final journey. Sweat poured into her eyes as tears streamed out. "I can't do this," she panted. "I'm not ready... it's too soon. Make it stop, please?"

They struggled to the door, Jessica watching her the whole time. "Okay, baby. We'll get you out of here." Even though some strength returned to Jessica's voice, the usual confidence remained absent and traces of fear tainted each syllable.

From deep in Dorthea's belly, streaks of pain reached out like hungry tentacles. She smelled the blood on Jessica's hand and something deep in her gut bit down. She thought for sure the fucking thing would eat her from the inside out.

The night air struck her face, and the world swam away in mottled darkness as a thousand needles pricked her gut. The three moved down the stairs, Dorthea's feet plunking each step as Jessica and the boy supported her full weight. Rough gravel bit into her bare soles. Another few steps and they stuffed her into the back seat of Jessica's Super Beetle. They snapped her in, the seat belt slicing into her belly, redoubling the sensation of being eaten from the middle out.

The boy crawled in the front and slammed the door. Jessica got in the driver's seat but did not start the car.

The last of Dorthea's strength drained away and, unable to stop it, her head lolled back, the faded and torn ceiling filling her vision, its countless little air holes staring back like a billion dead stars. Her ears filled with the angry throb of kettledrums, and though the boy and Jessica yelled at each other, Dorthea was unable to make out any words.

Jessica screamed once again, and Dorthea thought this time, yes this time the boy stuck her hard, right where it counted, leaving them stranded in this car until the baby came. When it arrived, oh it would come so fast, so ravenous, right out through her belly, gnawing through her gut, mouth full of sharpened teeth dripping with blood and intestines and...

The car lurched forward. Dorthea's head tilted toward the window. The ride smoothed out as they hit the road, and the faint world beyond the Super Beetle bent and wavered like a liquid light show. No one spoke, although Dorthea was sure she heard Jessica whimper between each thundering beat of the contralto drums in her head. The universe swam in and out of focus as Dorthea rode in her German-built chariot, a seasick time traveler unable to gain any bearings.

Metal screamed.

The car changed direction too fast.

Jessica shouted as an air bag erupted. The Beetle thudded to a stop, nose tilted down. Glass peppered the back seat. Dorthea felt the boy scramble over her, pausing to whisper, and out the broken rear window. From somewhere outside, she heard new voices. A gun fired.

And in the last moment before the universe slipped away to total darkness, Dorthea thought she heard the faint mixture of strings and brass and timpani swirling about each other like some forgotten symphony separated from her world by immeasurable amounts of space and time.

TOM

Tom woke from a fading dream, and in those few moments of twilight where the world is thin and the mind does not distinguish between real and unreal, he heard the shaman humming. Then the music was gone, along with the dream, leaving him only the dull shadows of his childhood bedroom and the rhythmic breathing of Cassy next to him.

The room was different from when they fell asleep, and it took a moment to realize a dull orange light flickered through the window. He slipped from the bed, not wanting to disturb her, and pulled on his boxer-briefs. The curtains were already open, giving him a clear view of angrier colors on the horizon, thick smoke billowing into the night sky. The hardwood floor chilled his feet as he stepped over to the window for a closer look.

"What is it?" She sounded sluggish; her words woven with sleep.

"Something in town is on fire." He stared out the window harder. "Something big." Tom turned around, his back itching from imagined heat.

"On fire?" Cassy got up and began to dress. "Jesus. What time is it?"

"Don't know. Early, by the looks of it." He crossed the

room as she finished buttoning her jeans. "I don't hear any sirens. You got your cell? Can you call someone?"

"Uh-huh." Cassy got her phone from the nightstand and placed a call. Tom watched, feeling more and more anxious as the moments passed. She looked up at him, her eyebrows knit. "Burke's not picking up."

Tom bit his cheek and sat on the bed next to her, playing with his necklace as she left a message for the Fire Chief.

She wrinkled her nose. "Burke always answers. Maybe I should call—"

"Shh." Tom put a hand on her knee. "Do you hear a car?"

They sat in silence until Cassy slipped her hand down and intertwined her fingers with his. "I only hear your heart beating."

Tom chuckled. "Is that supposed to be a come on? At a time like this?" He took her hand in both of his, and though he knew they should be doing something, he couldn't resist the feel of her skin against his.

She still looked worried, but she also smiled a little. "It could be." She leaned in and kissed him long and hard. Then she pulled away. "Burke's probably already on his way. Maybe he cut the sirens early. Still... let me make a call to Sheriff—"

"Wait." Tom heard it again—the unmistakable noise of a high-performance engine. He returned to the window and stood in the shadows. What jackass would be racing down route 56 at this hour?

The car slowed—a Corvette, no doubt about it—and turned onto the driveway. Cassy joined him and watched as the car pulled up to the front of the house and stopped out of sight. "Is that...?"

"My brother." Tom listened as Kyle got out of the car and

began to shout. Then his little brother pounded on the door, and he jumped at the noise while Cassy remained motionless. He felt a little foolish and hoped she hadn't noticed.

Cassy rubbed his back. "What do you suppose he wants?"

"Whatever it is can't be good. Stay here."

Her voice betrayed her smirk. "You really think you need to protect me? Especially from him? I mean, it's not like he's dangerous, right?"

More pounding on the door, more yelling.

He didn't know.

"Probably not." No other answer felt right. "I would feel better if you stayed out of sight. Who knows what's going on in his head, and I have no idea how he'd react to you." He hugged her tightly once more, then headed out of the room.

"Fine." She called after him. "I don't have a gun."

Tom shook his head as he walked down the hall. A gun? Why would she need a gun? He couldn't resist. "I thought you law enforcement types always slept with one under the pillow." He paused at the top of the stairs and looked back.

She looked over her shoulder. "We weren't sleeping. Now get rid of him."

Tom nodded and descended the stairs, only then realizing the pounding had stopped. He padded over to the front door and peeked out through the little window. Kyle sat on the front steps, back to the house, head down.

Tom opened the door. "You realize what time it is? What's so important that—" His blood thickened and guts knotted as his brother got up and turned around.

Kyle stood not five feet away, pointing a gun at Tom's chest. "Come on out. We gotta talk."

The world drew away leaving Tom focused only on his little brother who stood at the bottom of the porch steps. The moonlight distorted the minuscule shadows on Kyle's sweat slicked face. Every nerve struck steel to flint, trying to light a fire and get him moving. Tom's body would not respond.

What was Kyle doing with Pop's old Ruger?

Neither man moved as the air between them became dense. Tom thought about charging and taking Kyle down before the gun could go off. He thought twice. Who was he kidding? He wasn't fast enough. Besides, Kyle almost never missed. "Look, I don't know what's gotten into you. Shouldn't the cops have it?"

Kyle glanced at the Ruger. "Why? Pop shot himself. Case closed."

"So, how'd you get it then?" Tom backed into the house the tiniest step, trying to maneuver to a point where he could shut the door or dive off to the side, anything to move out of the line of fire.

"I asked for it, along with the rest of Pop's stuff. The sheriff didn't want it." Kyle poked the barrel at him. "You want to see it?"

He took another step back. Almost there. "No thanks. Would you mind not pointing it at me? You're making me nervous. Why did you bring it here, anyhow?"

Kyle laughed and lowered the gun to his side, shaking his head as a cold smile smeared across his face. "Do you see her? She's right there trying to tell me something." He waved the gun over his shoulder.

Tom looked beyond his brother at an unkempt field mottled with briers and thistle weed. Nothing broke the landscape between them and the Lodge.

Maybe the gun was an empty threat. They were brothers, for Christ's sake, and wasn't this part of what brothers did to each other—threaten and cajole, sometimes lashing out in dangerous ways, when what they really needed was help? Tom still wanted to reconnect, and so he risked stepping out of the door and onto the porch, abandoning his plan to retreat. "No one's there."

Kyle nodded, as if agreeing to some profound truth. "No one's there. Only she is there. She's always been there, just a few yards out. Don't you remember?"

Tom stepped down from the porch and stopped in the dirt a couple of paces from his brother. "I remember. How could I not? Do you think we remember it the same? You see Alissa, don't you? Is that why you're here?"

Tears slithered down Kyle's cheeks. "Why did Pop do it? And how could you leave me here with him, scared and alone?" Moonlight streaked across the Ruger as he pressed the barrel to his temple. "She's right here. I see her plain as day. She doesn't seem mad or sad, but why here? Why now?"

Tom trembled. Please, God, don't take Kyle, too. Another step brought them almost face to face. He laid his hand on the Ruger, searching for the safety and clicking it on. With a firm, gentle grip, he brought the gun down, letting Kyle keep his hold. "It's okay. Tell me what you think happened."

"You were there. You saw him do it. God, there was so much blood." Kyle's shoulders slumped.

"Yes, I saw him do it. Alissa was suffering. In more ways than one."

"Her mother beat her." Kyle swiped his nose with his free hand.

"Alcoholic hag," Tom added. "And the girl had no one to protect her."

"*I* was supposed to protect her. I thought training her to use a gun was the answer."

"We stole Pop's Ruger."

Kyle glanced down at the gun. "This fucking thing. We took her to our little makeshift range down by the creek. Bottles, cans, little plastic army men—whatever we could find." A smile scurried across Kyle's lip. "She was a pretty good shot."

"Yes she was."

"She bled so much. I loved her, you know."

"Pop said she was already dead."

Kyle's face became cold and slack. "He shot her in the fucking head. Put her down like one of his lame fucking lambs. And you're the one who went and got the drunk son-of-a-bitch."

"I never, not in a million years..." Tom nearly gagged on his own breath. Kyle thought he knew what Pop would do? "I swear. I thought he would call the ambulance."

Tom waited for a response. Kyle glared through the tears and remained silent. So, Tom continued, no longer sure what to say. "You wouldn't come out of your room afterward, and dad wouldn't talk. There was nothing more for me here, so I left. Nearly a month with hardly a word from either of you. What was I supposed to do?"

Kyle nodded as his tears dried up. "He talked after you ran away. Told me he was trying to protect us. I was too scared, though. I didn't know what to do. So, I did nothing."

Tom ran out of tears as well. "I'm so sorry."

"They blamed her mom, you know. Town gossip convicted her even though the sheriff couldn't. She slipped away not two weeks after you did."

Tom released the Ruger and took a step back thinking the storm had passed. "Come on inside. We could both use a rest." He turned to go back to the house. He didn't get more than two steps before the safety clicked again.

"I never told anyone." Kyle's voice was so soft and cold. Tom couldn't turn to face his brother. He didn't have to. He suspected what was coming next.

"She was pregnant."

The bottom of Tom's stomach dropped away; pity rushed in like ice water as he spun around. "I didn't know. I—"

"I'm not going in the fucking house." Kyle fired three rounds into a second-story window.

The gunshots left Tom dizzy and disoriented. He turned and ran into the house, believing the worst. He called out for Cassy as he took the stairs two at a time. His head still thrummed, and he was unable to tell if there was any response. The door to his room stood open, and he raced in to find her lying on the floor surrounded by shards of glass, left hand clamped to her right shoulder. He rubbed a finger deep in each ear and shook his head to stop the ringing. "Are you—"

"Caught a bullet." Cassy hissed in a deep breath through her teeth, then trickled it free through her nose. "Hurts like hell." She lifted her palm and a little blood seeped out from under her hand before she clamped it down again. A small crimson pool formed on the floor beneath her shoulder.

Tom squatted and studied her face. She looked pale and worn, but coherent. He touched the hand over her shoulder, withdrawing when she winced. "I... I'll go call the ambulance. Will you be okay?"

She looked up, her eyes moist and bloodshot. "I'll be fine. Bullet went through clean, I think. Maybe grazed. Your brother?"

Tom stood and looked out the shattered window, staying in the shadows. The sickening mixture of moonlight and firelight reflected off the Corvette. "Car's still there. I don't see him. Christ, you think he knew you were up here?"

"Got a first-aid kit? Bandages? Something to stop this bleeding?" She struggled to sit up.

He lifted her gently by the neck and good shoulder until she sat on her own. "Sure. Be right back."

He ran to the bathroom and got the kit from under the sink. He returned and the two of them wrapped her wound with gauze.

She held the gauze in place as he taped it off. "What were you talking about out there?"

Tom should have told her right away. Maybe at the graveside. He certainly should have told her at the diner. Why didn't he? She deserved to know, but now was not the time. He shook his head. "It's a long story. Ask me again in the morning." He made a makeshift sling for her arm. She was lucky. The bullet left a neat path gouged across her shoulder instead of going in.

Cassy took his hand and got to her feet. "I thought I heard you mention my cou—"

Tom sniffed. "Do you smell kerosene?" He didn't wait for an answer. He pulled Cassy through the hall and down the stairs, ignoring her questions. Smoke trickled in from under the front door.

"Get out of there," Kyle yelled from somewhere outside. "I already lit the fucking place."

Tom left Cassy leaning against the banister and opened the front door. The porch was already in flames. The wind outside shifted, wiping smoke and heat into the house like a blast furnace. He slammed the door against the flames and returned to the stairs, taking Cassy by her good arm. "This way." He led her to the kitchen where the back door stood open.

Tom took a last look down the hall. Billows of smoke seeped in under the door, tendrils of pure black hate snaking across the floor. Then he dragged Cassy out the back and toward the pole barn.

He stopped mid-way and turned to watch the flames embrace his childhood home. The paint began to blacken and peel as the fire tumbled around from both sides, closing the loop and cutting off all access to the house. Was this really happening?

"Help me with this." Cassy stuck her hip out. "My cell phone."

As Tom stuck his hand in her pocket, Kyle came around the side of the house, gun raised. "Leave it."

"It's only her cell." Tom pulled the phone slowly from Cassy's pocket and held it out. "You shot her, you fucking idiot, and the house is in flames. We can call it all an accident if you let me use the phone, okay?" Behind him, the house crackled and groaned as the fire took a firm hold and ate into the structure.

The dark smoke swirled and seemed to cling to Kyle's face. "You don't know all of it." He waved them away from the house as he spoke, his voice as quiet and toxic as the fumes from the fire. "I killed a man. Less than two weeks ago. Pop set me up then hid the body. I waited. I watched."

Heat pressed down on Tom. Wood groaned and splintered. Glass shattered somewhere on the far side of the house. The fire raged and huge plumes of thick soot rose into the sky. Even if Kyle let him call, the fire department would never make it in time. He glimpsed the orange reflected in the great plumes of darkness over the town, and the last bit of hope for salvaging what was left of his family dripped away. Burke hadn't answered before. Whatever was happening in town probably had the fire department all wrapped up. No one would make it here in time.

Kyle pressed the gun to Tom's chest and snatched the phone away. "We have a little trip to take, and after I'm done showing you what you need to see, you can come back here and call anyone you like." He tossed the phone into the field. "Now move."

Flames reached up the sides of the house, meeting at the top as more windows blew out on the second floor. Kyle led them to the Hyundai and told Tom to drive. He forced Cassy into the back seat—she cried out as he pushed on her wounded shoulder—then slipped in next to her.

Tom looked in the rearview mirror and saw Kyle holding the Ruger to Cassy's head. He was out of options, seeing no way to regain control of the situation, so he slumped in the driver's seat and started the car. "Where to?"

Kyle met Tom's gaze with cracked and red eyes. "The Lodge. Where else?"

The little Hyundai kicked up a small shower of gravel as Tom shifted into gear and sped down the driveway. He watched in the mirror, unable to take his eyes off the hellish blaze receding behind them, forgetting to slow down as they reached the road. He saw only a brief flash of headlights and a streak of yellow out of the corner of his eye before the world dissolved into screaming metal, breaking glass, and the harsh white punch of an air bag.

Tom coughed out flakes of dust as a dull ache spread across his face. He rubbed his cheek, wincing as he brushed his nose. He cleared his throat, spat red-stained mucus on the deflated airbag, and strained to look into the back seat. "Everyone okay?"

Cassy groaned and nodded. "Fucking shoulder hurts."

Kyle appeared unharmed and looked around wildly. "What the hell happened?"

Tom ignored the question, unsnapped his seatbelt, and coaxed his aching body into climbing out. Before both feet hit the ground, Kyle scrambled out of the back and fired off a round. Tom hustled out and found his brother standing by the back of the car, gun pointed toward the Lodge. "Put the gun away. What are you shooting at?"

"Did you see it? It came out of the other car and ran off toward the Lodge. Jesus, it looked burnt."

Tom took two quick steps intending to tackle Kyle and rip the damned gun from his hands, maybe even whack him a few times with it. No sooner did he move than Kyle stepped forward for a closer look and Cassy threw open the car door. Tom changed course and swung around the back of the car to the other side.

"Is it bad?" Cassy grunted as Tom helped her to the hood.

Tom checked her for wounds. "I don't see anything. Well except for the obvious. How's the shoulder?" He started to lift the bandage. Cassy pulled his hand away.

"No, the other car. How many people?"

Tom looked across the street and saw the ass-end of a rusted yellow Super Beetle sticking up from the drainage ditch like some psychedelic monolith. The rear window was busted out, and he saw a shape in the back seat, motionless. "One, at least. I'll go check. You okay?"

Cassy nodded. "I think your brother's still in shock." She lowered her voice. "See if they have a phone."

As he scurried across the street, a blond woman tumbled out of the driver's door. She saw him, tripped into the ditch and grasped at the dirt to regain her footing. "Is he gone? Oh God, let him be gone. Please, help us. She's—"

The driver erupted in a fit of coughing as Tom bent to help her up. "Are you okay? Do you have a phone?" He hauled her from the ditch and cleaned her face with the bottom of his shirt. The first traces of a bruise ran across the bridge of her nose, blood still trickling from the impact of the steering wheel, and a sloppy bandage around one hand stained with fresh blood.

"No phone. Help her. Please? Dorthea's pregnant."

The woman started to run back to her car. Tom caught her up and dragged her to Cassy. He held her steady as the deputy wrapped an arm around her. "Stay here. I'll go get your friend."

Tom sprinted back to the upended car, pushing away the last pains of the accident, and saw with a bit of relief Dorthea was moving in the back seat, struggling to get herself free. He reached the car and helped her out. He gagged against the thick smell of her sweat, ripe with hormones, as he led her across the street. She mumbled as her eyes fluttered up to show only the whites. She came without resistance.

They reached the Hyundai where Cassy stroked the driver's back. As Tom handed Dorthea to the blond woman, Cassy gave him a confused look and motioned for him to follow her a few paces away.

"Says her name is Jessica. The rest..." Cassy glanced at the other women and shook her head. She looked at Tom, one eyebrow raised. "She said they were being held hostage by some kind of monster. A kid with a knife? I don't know. She's not making any sense. She's missing a finger. Said the kid took it. We need help."

Tom looked back at the women as well. Jessica cried as she held Dorthea. The pregnant woman looked completely lost. They had to be in shock. Hell, maybe he was in shock too and didn't realize it. Regardless, they couldn't all stand around here. They had to get some place safe where they could call for help. He faced Cassy again. "Okay. You go watch them, try to get them calm enough to move. I'll talk to Kyle. Maybe this shook loose whatever crazy bug was eating his brain."

Cassy nodded and returned to the front of the Hyundai.

Tom walked to the rear and stopped beside his brother. "We have a problem."

"You could say." Kyle's gaze remained fixed on the field.

Tom searched for the right words, unsure of what fractured thoughts might be going through Kyle's mind. The wrong thing might bring the gun to bear on any one of them, and the last thing they needed was another gunshot victim. Then something Aunt Harriet said popped into his head. "The past is the past. Can you let it go, at least for a bit? You have the gun. You're in charge. Look at those people back there and tell me you won't help."

Kyle turned a waxy face to him. Christ, he looked as old as Pop. "Sure. There's a phone in the Lodge. Let's go."

"The Lodge? What about the cell phone? It's closer!"

"Like you said, I have the gun. We're going to the Lodge. Besides, a raging house fire's not exactly the best place to take a pregnant woman."

Tom wanted to punch his brother, both for being stubborn and for being right. Kyle must have sensed the hostility because he took a step away and motioned the women over with the gun. Jessica appeared to have settled down enough to walk, and Cassy was strong. Although Dorthea still seemed caught up in a world all her own, mumbling and looking around, her head wobbling erratically as her neck spasmed, she at least walked when the other two women helped. They could be at the Lodge in ten minutes if everyone held it together.

The women reached them and stopped. Cassy huffed as she adjusted her grip on Dorthea. "Tell me we're going back for the phone."

Tom held his hands up. "The Lodge. And don't bother arguing. I think Kyle's right. It's safer there."

Cassy shook her head. "You could run back—"

"No." Kyle wiggled the gun. "Move."

Tom was thankful Cassy let it go, even though he could see the same frustration on her face as he felt only moments before. They trundled across the field in silence—Tom in front, the women between, and Kyle with the Ruger in the rear. The ancient brick building grew closer with each step. At one point, an amorphous shape scurried around the side of the Lodge. Did bobcats still prowl the area?

Within a hundred yards or so, Dorthea buckled over and let out a scream. "He's coming... pushing... oh God, so hard..."

Jessica let go, leaving Cassy to keep Dorthea from falling. She turned on Kyle, screaming. "Why won't you leave us alone? We need help. Is there a doctor in your clubhouse? Is he here? You know what? Don't answer. Even if he were, I wouldn't let him touch her. Just... just..." She threw up her arms. "Just shoot, okay?"

Tom stood still. He saw the surprise and anguish on Kyle's face. "He's not going to shoot you. Help her up."

Jessica returned and helped Dorthea to her feet. They marched the remaining distance in silence broken only by Dorthea's moans.

They reached the Lodge steps at last, and once again, Tom thought he saw a twisted shadow scurry into the woods. Much too large for a bobcat. He let the thought go. What interested him even more was the dark shape jutting out from the side of the Lodge, barely visible from this angle. The tail end of a Jeep. He turned to say something. Cassy held a finger to her lips.

Dorthea spoke, sounding competent for the first time since the accident. "Do you hear the music? So beautiful." She wandered off the porch and headed toward the woods, arms laced under her belly.

Jessica ran and caught up with Dorthea, taking her by the waist. No matter how hard she tried, Jessica could not convince Dorthea to return to the Lodge, so she called back over her shoulder for help.

Tom moved, but Kyle poked him in the ribs with the gun. "No way."

"She's pregnant and probably in shock. We can't—"

"They're not our problem. You're coming with me. If you care so much about two fucked-up chicks, make your call when we're done."

Tom wasn't going to gain control, not yet. He said it himself earlier. He didn't realize how much he believed it until now. Kyle had the gun, so Kyle called the shots. Tom turned to Cassy for help.

The deputy looked defeated and pale, the bandage on her shoulder soaked a dark red. Her eyes glistened with the fuel of contempt. In the end she only offered, "They can't get far. Let's get this over with."

Kyle motioned them into the Lodge, following behind and closing the door. The lights were already on in the foyer, and Tom could see the lights in the basement stairwell. The building felt dense and distorted, as if somehow bigger on the inside. His fingers slipped up to the Huayruro beads. Tom nearly doubled over. Cacophony sliced through his head, as if every instrument in the world played its lowest note at once. He withdrew his hand as if burned. A single low buzzing remained.

Tom looked to Cassy once again. Had she heard it too?

She met his gaze and raised an eyebrow. He never got the chance to ask.

"Down there." Kyle swung the gun toward Cassy. "Ladies first."

Tom followed as she descended the stairs, drawing closer to the buzzing noise. Whatever was down there sounded like the dark side of insanity, and he wanted nothing to do with it. He stopped halfway and turned to Kyle. "The place was unlocked. The lights were on. There's probably someone here. Maybe—"

"Keep moving. I don't care who's here." Kyle thumped him on the side of the head with the Ruger.

Tom lost his balance and tumbled the rest of the way down the stairs, barely missing Cassy as he rolled from the last step. His head felt split clean in two, and the buzzing invaded every molecule of his body, making it difficult to focus. He rolled over, expecting to see Kyle towering over him ready to end this with a single bullet. Instead, Kyle and Cassy stood side-by-side, mouths dropped open as they stared farther into the room.

Cassy reached down her good arm to help Tom up, and Kyle reached down as well. He took their hands and stood, not wanting to turn around and see what made the awful buzzing, yet unable to resist. Whatever was in the basement seemed to make Kyle forget the situation, and Cassy too.

He let Kyle's hand slip away. He held tight to Cassy's as he turned around. Two feet from where he landed lay a partially masticated corpse, and another lay near the center of the room. Clumps of mud daubers worked here and there on both, and a thick curtain of them hung on the eastern wall. He squeezed Cassy's hand. The faint sound of the shaman's humming breached the incessant buzzing, superseded by an orchestral version before slipping away again. His throat dried out, leaving his voice cracked and decayed. "Is this what you wanted to show me?"

Kyle backed away. "No. I don't know what this is." He fled up the stairs.

Tom looked at Cassy. Her face was a blank. He tugged her hand, chasing the disbelief from her eyes. "I think we better go."

Cassy pulled away. "Go ahead. I'll be up in a moment."

Before Tom could protest, she crept over to the nearest body, knelt, and began searching its pockets with her good hand. She looked over her shoulder and whispered, "Either leave or come help." Then she resumed patting down the corpse.

Of course—the Jeep. He moved to the other body, stepping as lightly as possible, and began to search the pockets, taking care not to disturb the feeding insects. He found a wallet in one back pocket and was about to roll the body over when Cassy whispered again.

"Got it. Let's go."

DORTHEA

orthea looked over her shoulder and saw Jessica's car poking into the sky like some distant sun-filled skyscraper. She felt the forward motion, the hairs on her skin wavering in a slight breeze, but felt no ground under her feet.

On her left was sweet Jessica, face bruised and bloodied. Dorthea tried to speak—"Where are we going?"—but the words tripped out of her mouth. Jessica smiled through two streams of dried crimson tears.

Dorthea looked to her right, expecting to see the boy. Instead, she saw an unknown woman whose features looked rigid and angular. This woman ignored her entirely, which was just as well as Dorthea was starting to get a little sick at the way the landscape swirled and shifted in the background.

In front of her was a dark form—a man maybe?—who led the way toward some dense presence towering over them in the distance. Yet he wasn't really leading. She sensed aimlessness and ambiguity in the shape she followed. And though she had not seen anyone behind her when she looked before, she felt a clump of sorrow and regret tagging along, a shameful form threatening the rest of the group, driving them toward the solid structure.

Where was the boy? She could not get a bearing on him even though she sensed him. She certainly could not see him since the surrounding land now billowed like a tattered sail.

As the group drew near the structure, the kettledrums began again, this time softer, almost pleasant, like the heartbeat of an old man near the end of his life. The drums went unaccompanied, striking in steady rhythm. She listened closely, counting them like sheep, their sound changed from the foundation of a symphony to a warning to all who heard. War drums.

The women stopped her. She felt the structure, now only a few feet away, still unable to see anything beyond her companions with any clarity, only certain of the building's reality in her plastic surroundings. It pressed down on her, twisting in impossible and unseen angles, surrounding her, suffocating her, and as she began to think the weight of its being would crush her flat—her *and* her baby—a singular note called out, piercing the darkness with razor clarity, stripping away the unnecessary forms around her. The boy waited at the edge of the woods, only he no longer appeared as a charred mass of flesh. Instead, he was a collection of dark crystal, a finely chiseled obsidian statue, beckoning to her.

"Do you hear the music? So beautiful." She spoke to no one in particular and expected no response. And as she spoke, she moved toward the boy, stepping back to the earth, feeling the drums coming from the earth—no not from there, of there. The drums were the earth, the drums were her heartbeat, and the singular note blossomed into the full-blown sounds of an ethereal orchestra emanating from all around. Still one note pierced through it all, and she thought at first the boy was singing to her. She was wrong. The note came from beyond the boy, and at the same time from below her, and she could see—she could see! A beautiful winding trail of white wove into the woods, and she followed it, not caring where it led or who followed.

Dorthea floated along the earth, surfing on a single note of white, until a shackle around her waist stopped her once more. Jessica held her tight and begged her to stop, telling her to think of the baby, those woods were dangerous, and would she please, please, please come back to the building so they could call someone.

"This is for the baby." Dorthea's words trickled out and dissipated, swept away by the tide of music surrounding them. She pulled free of her lover's lock and continued on, willing to let nothing stand between her and the end of the road.

The boy disappeared into the woods. Dorthea didn't mind. She wasn't concerned with him anymore. She saw the path on her own, heard the music, and felt in her heart this streak was hers alone. The beam led her to the woods, an old path covered with decaying leaves and creeping myrtle, the trees parting and bowing as she pushed through.

The trail dropped at a steep pitch. Her feet found solid footholds with no trouble, taking her to an opening in the ravine where a mass of deadfall lay piled to one side. The beam twisted down the slope and into the cave, and the boy stared at her from within, his shriveled eyes like tight little diamonds sparkling in the cold night.

Jessica caught her once more, screaming at her to stop and come back, this place smelled of death, and she could see the boy in there, waiting.

Why couldn't Jessica understand? This was exactly where Dorthea needed to be. As if in agreement, she felt the baby tumble and turn, head down, facing the cave entrance. And she swore her baby smiled, a bright grin full of teeth, not sharpened fangs like she felt before but little chips of ivory cast between ruby lips, the centerpiece of a symmetrical face with features mapped out in perfection. Even though she knew babies didn't have teeth, the image felt true, and so she held onto it as the obsidian statue sprang from the cave and Jessica fell away in a curtain of red.

An oily, flaky paw took her hand and led her into the opening, through the darkness for what felt like an eternity, until they arrived in a chamber hewn from solid rock, glowing faintly of its own accord as the ceiling writhed and hummed.

Another statue, cast from muddy alabaster and smudged emerald, stood opposite Dorthea, separated from her by a circular stone table.

Voices spilled from the tunnel, the music torn to discord by the jagged noise.

The alabaster moved, and she saw now four wings attached to the statue, two folded about the body and two raised in flight. The face spun in a blur, showing a lion, an eagle, and a bull, stopping once again on the fractured visage of an old man. He smiled at her, a gentle, sad gesture. She wanted to cry until the world stopped turning.

The boy, still holding her hand, led her around the table to the old man, and the two of them helped her onto the altar, stripping her bare and stretching her out. The cold stone beneath her sent icicles through her skin, but it was okay, this was all okay, because the music kept playing and she could see now the sky through the roof. The heavens moved and squirmed and writhed with the rhythm, anticipating the coming child.

She laid her head to the side as three shadows entered the chamber, and though all three were as dark as the living night, only one was the unwelcomed emptiness of a black hole. The other two were shimmering pools of obsidian, and a feverish joy overtook her, though she didn't quite understand why.

The old man bent over her, his face shifting with each whispered word. "Will you offer yourself completely?" Lion, Eagle, Bull, Man. "Will you give your life for this child?"

She nodded, wanting nothing more than to give her life meaning in this last act. The end of the road was a beautiful place and she would dwell in its final moments forever.

The ceiling swirled in tiny drops of muddy gold, descending on her, filling her mouth with the taste of stale honey and vinegar. Choking her. She let them enter and surrendered her breath as her body began to rip and rip and rip...

TOM

The buzzing receded as Tom climbed the stairs, following Cassy back into the Lodge foyer, joining her at the top landing.

Kyle held the front door open, gun still in hand. "Took you long enough. Come on. We're heading out back."

He grabbed Kyle's arm. "Isn't this enough? Didn't you see the mess down there? We need to get some help." What was wrong with his brother? Why was he being so stubborn?

Kyle's eyes narrowed. Tom withdrew his hand.

"What mess? It's just a basement. There's nothing down there." Kyle poked the gun in Tom's chest. "Now let's move."

Tom leaned into the gun. "This is far enough. We're not going anywhere until you let us call someone." He took the barrel of the gun and held it tight. "Either shoot or get the hell out of my way."

Kyle pulled the gun back. "Yeah, I won't shoot you." He swung it around to Cassy. "She's a different story, though. Willing to risk it?"

Cassy placed a hand on Tom's arm and spoke to Kyle. "We're coming. No need to threaten us." She looked at him and nodded lightly. "Isn't that right?"

Of course, she was right. Why stir up Kyle when they could all walk out together. "Sure. I have your word we get to leave once you show us?"

Kyle nodded, then waved them on with the gun. The three stepped back onto the porch and into the enveloping night. He pointed toward the woods. "You first, brother. You'll find a little path leading down the side of the ravine."

Tom led, Cassy came next, and Kyle brought up the rear. They passed the Jeep, but no one mentioned it. Either Kyle didn't notice or he didn't care. Either one was fine by Tom.

He reached the woods and stopped. Kyle and Cassy flanked him on either side. He turned to his brother. "Where to now?"

"Down. Follow the path until you reach a pile of wood and brush. Once you get there, stop and wait, or so help me, I'll put one in her."

The woods yawned before him, and Tom hesitated. The path they faced felt threatening, as if they stood on the edge of some deeper, darker secret than even Kyle intended. He wanted to grab Cassy and make a break for the Jeep, but the weight of his brother's frustration—or was it guilt?—was almost palpable, so he stepped into the woods and the thickening darkness. The crunch of leaves and underbrush echoed behind him as Cassy and Kyle followed. "A flashlight would be nice." It was a stupid thing to say.

Kyle handed him one. "Here. I grabbed it from the Lodge."

The path fell to a steep slope as Tom moved forward. How many groundhog burrows? How many rabbit holes? He tried not to dwell on all the hazards crouching in the shadows as he worked his way down the bank. Moonlight filtering through the trees and the soft glow of the flashlight provided enough light to walk by while still leaving doubt about what was shadow and what was not.

Tom approached a tremendous pile of deadfall next to an opening in the ravine and cried out as he almost tripped over Jessica's body. Cassy caught him with her good arm as he stumbled back.

Kyle stepped up next to them. "I knew it." He knelt and took a closer look. "Throat's cut. Nasty. What do you want to bet the other woman isn't really pregnant?"

Even in the dim moonlight, the redness showed on Cassy's face. "What are you talking about? You think Dorthea did this? You can't be... After what we saw in the Lodge, and now this? You're—"

Kyle nudged the body with his foot. "Yeah, it's clear to me now. I don't know how they pulled it off—the ghost, the accident, leading us here—but they did. Mirrors, maybe. No honor among fucking thieves, right?" He laughed, an eerie mixture of glee and stress.

Tom took Cassy's arm and began to back away, then stopped as a soft, low thrum began to drift from the cave entrance.

Kyle swung around. "She's in there. Stupid bitch knew all along." He took the flashlight from Tom, moved toward the opening, then stopped and motioned for them to follow. "We're almost there. Cassy, you can solve a murder and bag yourself an extortionist." He chuckled again, then disappeared into the cave. His voice echoed out at them. "Two birds, one stone. In the bush. The burning bush of birds. Tweet, tweet!"

Tom's feet wouldn't respond. Even the strange night in the Peruvian woods with Hruesco's tribe paled in comparison to this. Kyle was mad. He expected them to follow him into a cave? With a gun? And his laugh? One hand moved to his necklace, the other clasped Cassy's hand, and the world froze.

He saw no vision, heard no voices. The air simply fell

dead, and the night creatures ceased their chatter, as if Mother Nature paused to take a breath. Then the world resumed. Somehow, during the silence Tom managed to abandon his reluctance and remember why he came home. Crazy or not, Kyle was his brother. He needed to follow the man through to whatever grisly end lay ahead.

Kyle popped out of the cave waved the gun. "Well? You two coming?"

Tom pulled Cassy along. She resisted at first. He pulled harder. "We'll be okay. He needs me to see, and I owe him." She furrowed her brow, and he almost spilled the whole story about Alissa. Almost. But not yet.

Kyle took Tom's free hand as they entered the cave. "Damn straight, he owes me. Take off on me for ten years, leave me with her blood on my—"

"Please." Tom squeezed Kyle's hand, then let go. "Not now. Let's just get—"

"Who's blood?" Cassy let go of Tom's other hand, and the three paused in the glow of the flashlight.

Tom shifted from one foot to the other. "It's not important right—"

"You didn't tell her? I figured you told her. I mean, you're the chicken shit who ran away." The shadows accented Kyle's exaggerated smile. "I can't fucking believe it."

A sudden distance washed over Cassy's face as she studied him. "Back at the house. Before the fire. I heard right, didn't I. You two were talking about Alissa."

Tom wished she had not come home with him. He wished he had not come home at all. "Yes."

Kyle wrapped an arm around each of them. "Oh, get over it you two. Pop killed your cousin. Your boyfriend here skipped town 'cause he wasn't man enough to deal with it.

Don't be mad at him, though. I'm the one who shot her first." He nodded at Cassy, his mouth twisted with mock concern. "An accident, of course." He released them and continued deeper into the cave. "Now where's that corpse? Here, little corpse! That's a good corpse. Come on out, we won't bite."

Even as the light receded with Kyle, Tom saw the hurt in Cassy's eyes. "I wanted to tell you." He reached out for her hand. She would not take it.

She followed Kyle. "Come on."

Tom joined her. She would not look at him. They followed Kyle, listening to him babble on about the corpse, until a soft glow illuminated the cave in front of them.

Kyle clicked off the flashlight, his shadow framed by light from an archway. "What the..."

Tom and Cassy flanked Kyle. Before them, Dorthea lay naked on a circular stone altar, her belly swollen, sweating even in the damp coolness. An old man, dirty tank top, olive-green khakis, and skin the color of the finest alabaster, leaned over her whispering. Next to him crouched a charred mess of a child, grinning at them with ivory teeth and flashing a butcher knife.

The ceiling writhed with mud daubers. Their buzzing filled the chamber and rattled Tom's teeth. He scooted around his brother and took Cassy's hand. She accepted it this time, and he was grateful. They were not meant to see the events unfolding before them, and if he was about to die, he didn't want to be alone. He reached for Kyle's hand as well and found nothing. His brother no longer stood beside them. He was moving slowly around the chamber toward the old man.

The mud daubers bulged down over Dorthea, one by one dropping down into the woman's mouth, filling her up, extending her belly beyond its limits. She began to split, her eyes glazed and mouth spread wide, as if she'd reached an epiphany of some sort. The old man straightened up, watching the pregnancy come to term.

Had he noticed them? Tom squeezed Cassy's hand and looked at her. She stared into the chamber, eyes heavy with pain and lips pressed together in a white line. He began to back out, once again pulling her along without resistance. Before he took even two steps, a shroud of insects descended from the ceiling directly above and draped over the passageway like a thick muslin curtain.

Too many things happened at once for him to know which came first.

The charred boy brandished the knife and dashed around the altar toward Kyle, who leveled the gun at the old man, both wearing twisted caricatures of smiles. They were mirror images, madness clashing against madness, meeting with simultaneous shouts of incoherence.

Dorthea unzipped from throat to crotch, mud daubers pouring out of the seam in thick clouds. The old man reached in and pulled a small form from her twitching corpse, a mewling child covered in blood and amniotic fluid, a thick bluish-white cord trailing back into its mother's body. Insects peppered the baby, touching down then lighting off again right away.

The boy plunged the knife down into Kyle's chest as he fired the gun, and both fell to the floor, hidden by the altar.

Cassy took a step back into the shroud of insects covering the door, her hand slipping from Tom's hand. She let out a single gasp, then became a thrashing mess of arms, bashing his back as she swatted at the mud daubers.

Tom ran to his brother, uncertain of what else to do, and found him face up, the twisted creature lying on top. None of this made sense, but none of it mattered. He only saw a sudden finality to his family, the end of secrets, and an utter loss of any chance to forgive the past. He knelt next to Kyle and pushed the boy away, revealing the hilt of the knife sticking out of his brother's chest. The wound was deep. Too deep.

Kyle coughed, thick dark blood bubbling from his mouth, and held the gun out.

Tom wept. "You'll be fine." He grabbed the knife handle, trying to believe his words.

Kyle winced, coughed again, and pushed Tom's hand away. He strained as he spoke, the wound bubbling and hissing as he sucked in deep breaths every other word. "You don't get it. You never asked me to go the first time you left town. I never expected to go anywhere this time. Take it." He pulled Tom's hand from the knife and slipped the gun into it. "Just go."

The old man spoke in a harsh, guttural language, his words ricocheting off the chamber walls like bullets. Tom grasped the gun and looked up, only to see the old man transformed into a statue of stained alabaster clad with wings and enveloped by a pillar of blinding golden light, face a spinning mosaic of creatures. He slipped his free hand, still sticky with Kyle's blood, up to the Huayruro seeds, and the sound in the chamber faded to soft orchestral tones undercut by Hruesco's humming. The statue fell quiet and turned to him, its spinning face stopping at the visage of a lion, the surrounding light flickering and fading.

Cassy cried out from behind. Whether she called for help or called for him to shoot, Tom couldn't tell. Instinct answered for him, and the chamber roared with the sound of unabated gunfire as he pumped the remaining rounds into the horrible hallucination.

The light shattered, the vision dissipated, and the old man stood before Tom once again, chest pockmarked with bullet wounds. The child slipped from his hands and landed in Dorthea's soft remains, sending up a cloud of mud daubers disturbed from their feast.

Cassy crouched beside Tom, shouting in his ear, her voice cutting through the dull roaring aftermath of the gunshots. "Get the child!"

The old man still stood over the baby, deep lines of rage chiseled across his face. Where was the blood that should be spilling out of his chest? There were only angry little puckers winking out through frayed holes in his tank top.

Tom moved anyhow. The child was the only innocent actor in this one-act play, and it deserved to get out of there as much as any of them.

The old man opened his mouth and let loose a keening wail, the cries of innumerable voices. He stared at Tom but made no move to stop him from taking the baby. Tom slipped around the altar and reached for the child. The old man raised his arms summoning the insects into a swirling funnel cloud.

Mud Daubers pelted Tom, nipping exposed flesh. He dug both hands into warm innards and pulled the baby free. Its umbilical cord snaked down and caught on a piece of bone jutting out of the corpse. Tom slipped it free, gathered both baby and placenta, and backed away.

The old man remained rooted to the ground, his incessant cry shaking the very air about them. Tom retreated to Cassy, who now held the flashlight, and took her by the arm. Together they fled the room, jumping through the mass of insects barring the door. As they raced down the passageway, chasing the beam of light bobbing against the walls, the old man's cry died out. He called after them in his guttural language, archaic syllables booming down the passageway like cannonballs. As they reached the entrance and emerged once again into the night, the tunnel behind them filled with the angry drone of insects, pushing the very air out behind them.

The swarm was coming.

Cassy held the flashlight in one hand and led Tom back up the path with her other. "Don't look back. Keep moving."

Tom resisted as long as he could. Once they reached the top and slipped from the woods, the temptation was too great. As Cassy dashed for the Jeep, ditching the flashlight to dig the keys from her pocket, he paused and looked back down the path.

Hissing darkness consumed the trail and trees. Behind him, a door slammed and the Jeep's engine rumbled to life. Still the pitch-black mass approached, consuming Tom's attention. How nice the emptiness might feel, how pleasant and forgiving. Someone shouted from far away, but the words fell aside, unable to penetrate the inky nirvana looming before him.

Cassy's hand fell on his shoulder and spun him around. "Move."

Tom shook his head. Were they going somewhere? What was this wriggling mess in his arms? Where was the cape of dreams, the silence of the dead staring him down moments before? Behind him. Wasn't there something...

The baby.

The swarm.

Tom broke into a run, clutching the child and its afterbirth close to his chest. Cassy caught up to him at the Jeep, and they both jumped in, closing the door as the swarm passed by, insects mashing against the windows.

As Cassy threw the Jeep into gear, Tom climbed into the

back seat. He took his shirt off, wrapped the baby up, and looked around for something to cut the cord. The Jeep bounced as Cassy drove them across the field to the highway.

Tom found a rusty utility knife, an emergency blanket, and some twine in the Jeep's bay. They would have to do. He clipped a piece of string free, tied off the cord, and severed the child from its spent lifeline. The placenta quivered like thick pudding as he scooped it up and tossed it in the back. No way in hell was he going to roll a window down.

The Jeep gave a final hop as it passed over the drainage ditch and onto the road. As they sped down Route 56, Tom cleaned the baby with the emergency blanket.

A boy. Skin the color of ivory. Eyes a color of blue found only in hot stars or rare gems. A full head of hair, fine platinum threads. All smiles.

Tom forgot everything while lost in the child's beauty. His hand worked with an unrecognized skill, swaddling the boy up, clutching the baby to his chest. The swarm outside broke away from the Jeep, leaving them draped only in the cool night air. As Tom watched, the insects rose over the trees in a tear-shaped stream, heading for whatever remained of Washington Heights.

The boy laughed, a sound of pure innocence, and Tom could only smile back. He leaned up between the front seats. "Keep heading south."

Cassy glanced at him, one eyebrow raised. "South? We have to take it—"

"It's a boy. And take him where? There's nothing left here. Who would believe us? Do you want to dump him at some orphanage?" Tom looked down at the child. The boy stuck his little tongue out and smiled, blinking. "No. He stays with me. Take us as far south as you want." Tom met Cassy's gaze. "I know where we can go. If you're not busy, you're welcome to join us."

Cassy turned her attention back to the road, her face a blank slate imposing cold distance between them. They drove in silence for several minutes before she finally answered. "You'll tell me everything about Alissa?" Cassy looked at him once more, and he saw the need in her eyes. She deserved the truth.

"Yes."

Her lower lip quivered as she faced the road once again. "Okay. I'll come. What about money? We're low on gas. How will we eat? Where will we stay?"

Tom pulled Jake's wallet from his back pocket. "You got the keys. I must have slipped this in my pocket by mistake."

Cassy smiled and huffed. "By mistake. Sure. Where to, then?"

"Florida."

LEWIS

June 10, 2008

Lewis sat on his lawn chair sipping bourbon and staring east toward the Lodge, where only a week ago his son put a bullet in some poor man's head. Behind him, the bloated sun made its way down the sky casting long shadows into the field. A composition notebook sat in his lap, one of those black and white things used by college kids and artsy types. He bought it on a whim the day after the shooting, probably knowing even then how he would end this madness. So far, he only managed to scribble his son's name across the cover.

As darkness stretched across a flock of resting sheep, a voice drifted down from behind and a gnarled hand settled on one shoulder. "Mind if I join you?"

Lewis shrugged the hand from his shoulder. "You know, I've been wondering if you'd show up. There's another chair in the pole barn if you like."

An old man dressed in a clean white tank top and fresh olive cargo pants stepped around him, and even in the darkness his yellow and brown teeth stood out as he smiled. "Thanks. I don't need a chair, though." The old man squatted on the ground, folding his legs neatly over each other lotus-style, and squared his shoulders toward Lewis as he rested a hand on each knee. "Let's start with why you were expecting me."

Lewis considered the odd figure before him, unsure if what he saw was real or imagined. He took another swallow of bourbon and set the glass on the ground. "I haven't decided to do it yet, you know. You might be wasting your time."

The old man's brow wrinkled in mock confusion. "Haven't decided to do what?"

"You know." Lewis slid the composition book aside to reveal his Ruger P90. "End it." The old man continued to look perplexed, and Lewis tensed as his blood pressure rose. Was it not enough he was going to surrender his life? What more did this thing want? "Goddamn it, I haven't decided to kill myself."

The old man smiled again, broad and knowing. "Ah. Well then, who exactly do you think I am?"

A cool breeze blew in from across the field, bringing with it the raw smells of livestock and damp earth. Lewis shielded his eyes. He swore the lines on the old man's face shifted as the breeze petered out. "Well, it's obvious, isn't it? You're the angel of death."

"The angel of death." Shadows enveloped them as the sun dropped another notch, and the old man appeared less substantial than he had mere moments before. "I like that, but no. You and me, we met before once. Long ago."

The old man's face solidified again as Lewis studied it for an answer. He found a slight familiarity in the list of the old man's lips, the crooked nose, the alabaster skin, but he couldn't quite place him.

As if sensing Lewis's struggle, the old man added, "We met in the Lodge."

A memory surfaced, faded and worn. Lewis barely recognized it as his own. Before he was old enough to join the Lodge, he attended a Christmas party with his father. The old man before him now was there, dressed in the standard black tuxedo, passing through town on a visit. "It's been over half a century, and you haven't aged a day. I must be losing it."

The old man shook his head. "You're fine. Least as fine as a man in your shoes can be." He craned his neck around to look at the Lodge across the field. "Been a while for you. Not for me. Now I have to ask, then, knowing I'm not the angel of death, were you or weren't you expecting me?" The old man turned back around. His smile evaporated.

"No. I wasn't."

"I didn't think so." The old man's gaze cut Lewis to the soul, leaving him naked and exposed. "Now, let's get on with your business. You bought a notebook to leave a confession. You have a gun to end your life. And the rock..." The old man reached out and plucked the stone from underneath Lewis's chair. "...you intend to bury way out in your field where no one else can find it."

Lewis nodded, realizing sometime during the conversation he had started crying. "I can't live with all of this anymore. I've seen things... *done* things. Where did I go so wrong?" He swiped at the tears with the front of his shirt then reached for his bourbon.

The old man snatched Lewis by the wrist. "No more booze. Great in moderation. Lousy for the spirit."

Raw power emanated from the old man's touch, a stifling presence as if a great creature loomed beyond vision ready to pounce. Lewis felt himself shrink in his chair, unable to move, as the world around him melted away like a cheap plastic toy on a hot stove. Wildfire spread from the old man's touch throughout his body, rushing in like back draft then withdrawing, taking the essence of Lewis Burton with it.

The landscape reemerged, only everything was in the wrong place. Lewis now sat on the ground, legs crossed, and palms flat on each knee, still unable to move. He watched, helpless, as his own body leaned forward and whispered in bourbon and stale cigarettes.

"We're taking over for now. We have to finish what you started. Finish it the right way. Don't worry. This'll all be over soon enough. Pretty much the way you planned."

Lewis's body began to scribble in the notebook. He tried to scream, willing this new body to bend to his will. As he fought, thrashing his spirit against the flesh imprisonment, he became aware of others in there with him, trapped and broken, writhing in pain at the disruption his new soul brought. He concentrated as hard as he could, shouting on the inside, screaming for help.

What's going on here?

(go back to sleep)

Why won't you help me move?

(there is no place to go)

"There, all done." Lewis's body stood, tucked the notebook under one arm, and slipped the Ruger into a pocket before bending to retrieve the stone.

Who are you all?

(we are one-hundred and forty-four thousand)

His body walked toward the pole barn and called back over its shoulder. "Aren't you coming?"

The old man's body moved, as if on autopilot, Lewis trapped inside still unable to gain any control.

Why won't one of you stop this?

(why would we the end is near repent)

Lewis followed himself into the pole barn, past the tractor, to the little workbench at the back. His body knelt on the ground, placing the notebook to one side. It clutched the stone in one hand and the Ruger in the other.

Not like this please God not how I wanted to go.

(we all gotta go with the nowhere man)

He sobbed inside, his continued cries for help unanswered.

His body lifted the Ruger and pressed it under its chin. His own voice called out. "Would you mind giving me a hand?"

The old man's hand reached out and wrapped over Lewis's so both held the gun.

Who are you?

His body answered, the old man's body answered, and every voice inside with him, the countless trapped spirits, answered as well. They rang out a single name as his soul slipped back into his own body in time to catch the bullet.

"Lazarus."

TOM

September 29, 2008

A cool summer breeze drifted through the tent. Tom smelled the ancient stones of Machu Picchu, their hard fragrance carried for miles on lazy winds sweeping down the southern terraces and across Rio Urubamba. Even though the night sang its rhythmic lullaby, sleep stayed at arm's length denying Tom any hint of peace. He rolled over to face Cassy and the baby, both deep asleep, holding their own secret counsel with their imaginations.

One month to make it here, and another two living among Hruesco's tribe, hoping they would take Cassy on her own journey. How long would they wait this out? Was this trip really worth selling his boat and the favors he traded? It seemed so when they started, felt like the right thing to do, but the nocturnal forest sounds and the remote village made fertile ground for doubts.

The baby snorted, cooed once, then fell silent again. He needed a name, one fitting of him. Tom had his buddy put Kyle Lewis Burton on the birth certificate. Even then, he knew the name didn't fit. Though Cassy scrunched her face at the time, she remained silent on the matter.

Tom supposed when the time was right, an adequate name would come to them. Not a great name, nothing truly reflective of how the child made him feel, but a sufficient name, a simple label of uniqueness to carry the little boy through his unforeseeable future.

A joint would taste pretty good. Or even just a beer. Something to take the edge off. How could Cassy sleep so soundly each night? She must harbor fears of her own. Especially now.

The tent flap rustled, and a tanned head capped with jet-black hair poked in.

"Is time." Hruesco motioned for Tom to wake Cassy, then slipped back out.

Tom sat up, ran both hands through his hair, then crawled from his cot and lit a small lantern. Cassy remained undisturbed as he knelt over her. Her hair fell in loose strands around her face, longer now than ever, dull from their time in the forest. Why did she ever agree to this? He ran a hand across her cheek, bent down and kissed her lips, once again almost hearing a distant thrum of music, always out of reach.

"That's nice." She smiled then opened her eyes. "What time is it?"

"Does it matter?" Tom brushed a stray hair from her face and did his best to smile. "He's waiting outside."

Cassy's lips trembled then strengthened into a firm, joyless grin. "Okay. So, how's this work?"

Tom shook his head. "You just go. We'll be here when you get back, and in the morning, we can choose what to do next. Maybe California. Maybe Canada. Or maybe we stay here."

Tears formed in Cassy's eyes and pooled in the rims of her lids. She rubbed them away with an arm, nodded, then got out of bed. She wore jeans and a t-shirt, the same as every night since they arrived, in anticipation of the coming event.

Her belly bulged slightly. The attractive and endearing bump made Tom want to pull her down and hold her tight. He placed his hand over her bellybutton. "I'm not so sure..." He looked into eyes once again damp with anxiety.

Cassy nodded. "It'll be fine."

Hruesco poked his head in once again. "Now. Or never."

Cassy patted Tom's hand then pulled it away from her belly. "We'll be fine." She straightened up, smoothed her shirt, and disappeared into the night, leaving Tom and the baby to wait.

ACKNOWLEDGEMENTS

A lot of work goes into writing a novel, and it's not all by the author. For me, there was a wide cast of characters who each played a role in helping make this book what it is.

None of this would have been possible without my wife, Denna, and my sons, Logan and Dylan. Denna makes an excellent first reader and critic. My sons too young to read this as it's being written, provide endless inspiration and are a constant reminder of what's important. I love you so much.

Tearstone served as my thesis for Seton Hill University's Master's program in Writing Popular Fiction. A big thank you to two friends and mentors from the program, Scott A. Johnson and Tim Waggoner. Both provided insightful feedback and persistent encouragement as I worked on the novel. Without their guidance, I may never have produced the book you hold in your hands now.

I also worked with several critique partners at Seton Hill who each provided excellent feedback. Thank you, Eric Spery, Stephanie Harbulak, Craig Grossman, Jared Vickery, Elsa Carruthers, Venessa Giunta, and Jennifer Della'Zanna for all your help in refining Tearstone. Seton Hill is full of wonderful, supportive people who made me feel welcome. Thank you, Calie Voorhis, Erica McEachern, Genevieve Eldredge, Todd Harlan, David Johnston, Kristin Dearborn, Paul Popeil, Sheldon Higdon, Ron Gavalik, Carla Anderton, John Dixon, and Chris Shearer, just to name a few. Your countless hours of conversation (some light, some deep) helped make me a better writer. I could fill several pages and still not cover everyone. For those I missed, just know that if we met while at Seton Hill, if even for just a few minutes, you influenced me for the better and I appreciate it. I can only hope I did the same for you.

Thank you to all my Beta Readers. Two deserve special mention. Tara Paider and Richard Lee know me through my day job. Both took time out of their busy lives to give this work a careful read and provide thoughtful feedback. While I couldn't use all their suggestions (for various reasons), I tucked them away to help guide me in my future work. When it comes to writing fiction, for me there's nothing more valuable than the mind of an avid reader. Thank you, Tara and Richard.

My deepest thanks to Tim McWhorter and Manta Press. Tim took big a risk and placed a lot of faith in my work by offering to release this 10-year Anniversary Edition of Tearstone in anticipation of the sequel. I've written and rewritten the sequel several times over the past ten years, never quite feeling like I got it right. Tim, thank you for encouraging me, for placing your trust in me, and for your friendship.

And finally thank you. You're also taking a risk. You're looking for something. Maybe you know what it is and maybe you don't. That's okay. This is entertainment, but it doesn't have to be meaningless. My job is to provide something meaningful for you, something that pays off for the hours it will take to read this book. I hope you walk away from here feeling satisfied, that your money was well spent, and that you're a little better off for having invested your time here. And I hope you'll come back for more.

About the Author

David L. Day is a writer, coder, and thinker. (Perhaps an overthinker?) He has an MA in Writing Popular Fiction from Seton Hill University. His unpublished novel, *The Galvanized Man*, was the official runner up of The Columbus Creative Cooperative's The Great Novel Competition in 2015. In addition to a growing stack of unpublished novels, David has published a handful of short stories over the years. He lives in central Ohio with his wife, children, two obnoxious but adorable cats, and one very loyal and loving rescued Pit Bull.

"Emptiness"
a short story

Jaipur, India. 1999.

The old converted school bus bounced along the pitted dirt road, jostling my jaw every few seconds. The countryside scrolled by: bland desert, bland shrubs, bland sky, a collage of dirty yellows and tans.

James, my long-time cohort, sat next to me, thin hands fidgeting, elfin brow knitting a furious bow. "We should be heading to that gig in Mysore, Paulette. We need the money."

His cowardice was a flea in my ear. "We're going exactly where we should be going. Talitha is out there." I affixed the zoom lens to my Canon, aimed at nothing out the dingy window.

"You have no way of knowing for sure. And besides, what if she is there? We need to eat. Do you think she's going to invite us in and feed us?" His tone scratched like sand in the shoes.

"We'll eat millet." I dropped the camera, cradled it, wished I still had Mom's old Pentax instead.

"We'll starve, more likely." He crossed his arms, crossed his legs, crossed his whole body.

"Did we starve in Bogotá when that so-called gig you lined up turned south and our so-called client stole my camera?" Mom's Pentax was dead weight on my heart.

James deflated in his seat. "That was years ago. How many times do I have to apologize? Look, we get off at the next stop, head back to Mysore, and after the shoot, I'll buy you a new camera. A digital one."

"I don't want a digital camera." My gut wrenched at the thought of not using real film. "I want to find Tali. I want to do what I want for once instead of what you think you need," I said, hurling words like stones.

"She's not there. Malta, Cairo, Gobekli Tepe, Kandahar," he fired back, each place a chuffed bullet. "She's never been there."

My last nerve, taut and strained, snapped. "She is." I yanked the newspaper clipping from my pocket. One I'd found that morning, along with the 20-year-old photo of her, shoved them both in his face. "Tell me that isn't her."

"You showed me a dozen times already." He pushed them away. "Sure, looks like her." He grew louder, his voice rising on waves of fear. "But those pictures were taken decades apart. No way she'd be the same age."

"She's already dead. Dead. She wouldn't age." My voice rose on the tides of anger along with his. The old local couple across the aisle stared at us, hugging their suitcases like life preservers.

"Are you feeling okay, sir?" the man hazarded.

James let go of his poker-hot anxiety for a moment. "Oui. Fine, thank you." Then he gripped his helplessness again, turned it on me in a pleading whisper. "Let's go to Mysore. Or we could go anywhere. We could go home. Back to France. Not Colmar, of course, but maybe somewhere south like

Carcasonne, near Rennes-le-Château, where she went after…"
He stopped, eyes wide and helpless, lips locked in fear. He
couldn't say it.

I said it for him. "After grandfather killed himself. Yes.
But this is a picture of her here in India, not France." I tucked
the photo away but raised the clipping and held it where we
both could see. "That's her. Living among the Mahakali
devotees. Being worshiped by them as Kali's avatar."

He sank into his seat, out of arguments, out of energy.
"We'll get murdered. Or worse."

I tasted a germ of remorse, tucked the clipping away, then
put an arm around his shoulders. "You're scared, and that's
okay. But trust me. Haven't I always taken care of you?"

Colmar, France. 1980.

Paulette is 16, and though rolling hills covered in lush
grape vines should be a paradise, living on Grandpa's
struggling vineyard was exactly the opposite. When he wasn't
complaining about his "slut of an ex-wife" or how his "whore
of a daughter" burdened him with Paulette, he was drinking his
stock away.

Or worse.

Much worse.

Unbearably worse.

Her first day of summer she rose early, gathered her
mother's old camera, a 1970 Pentax Spotmatic, and left before
Grandpa emerged from the fog of wine. She trekked out into
the sprawling vineyard with a light lunch and several spare
rolls of film stowed in her backpack.

The grapes were near the end of fruit set, veraison just around the corner, that treasured point in the lifecycle of grapes when their plump, rich greens show the first signs of darkening. She spent hours wandering among the rows, shooting whatever caught her eye, eating up two rolls of cheap film bought with what little she earned from chores around the farm.

Legs aching, stomach growling, Paulette wandered toward the end of a row where she planned to sit and have her lunch. But when she drew near, she spied a figure through the tessellations of shadow and vine.

A slender girl about Paulette's age lay supine in the next row, face skyward. Sunlight sparked in the oval lenses of her sunglasses. She was trim, if not just a little bony. Her long obsidian hair lay splayed out around her head like black rays of sunshine. Her skin hinted at Mediterranean.

Startled but curious, Paulette raised the Pentax instinctively, found a clear spot in the vines, and snapped a photo.

"It's rude to take a picture without permission," the girl said, her tone flippant. Her French was flawless but carried an indeterminate accent. She turned her head, stared back at Paulette through the lens. "Who are you?"

Paulette lowered her camera, stepped around the end of her row and into the next, stopped at the girl's feet. "It's rude to lie around in someone else's vineyard," she volleyed back. "I'm Paulette. Who are you? What are you doing?"

The girl, chin to chest, graced Paulette with a pixie grin. "Talitha. It's biblical, you know. But you can call me Tali. I'm a corpse, and I'm doing what corpses do."

"A what?" Paulette sat down in the dusty row, crossed her legs, cradled her camera. She liked the way this girl joked, felt the warmth of instant connection, connection she'd never felt before.

"A corpse. I'm dead. A sorcerer stole my soul, and now I'm just a corpse held together by magic." The girl sat up, mirrored Paulette's posture. They stared at each other, two unflinching stones in a zen garden.

The joke soured into a thick, hard dread, dread that replaced the warmth inside Paulette. A wellspring of sorrow blossomed from nowhere, as it so often had over the past year. "That's not funny. My mom died recently."

Tali's smile dissolved into dolefulness. She leaned forward, took Paulette's hands, pressed them between her own chill fingers. "I'm so sorry. Death isn't funny." Then Tali leaned in, quick and unexpected, and hugged Paulette tightly. "Death isn't funny at all. My mother's dead, too. And my father."

Paulette cried salty tears on Tali's shoulder. Tears for the memory of her mother's coffin. Tears for the gaping hole of never knowing her father. Tears for the aching inadequacy of her grandfather's disapproval.

Tali let her spill her sorrow until the spring dried up, and when Paulette was done, she clung to the girl, heart pumping, head thumping. The connection was back, as if they had somehow known each other for a long, long time.

Paulette pulled away, mouth dry, throat aching. "Thanks. My grandfather gets so mad when I cry. He gets mad when I do anything, but especially when I cry." She looked down at her camera. "This is all I have left of my mom."

"Does he hurt you, this angry grandfather of yours?"

Paulette looked up, stared at her reflections in Tali's lenses, twins of embarrassment and brokenness. Embarrassment that knotted in her gut, brokenness that blossomed into pain lower down. She'd just met this girl, wanted to tell her, needed to tell someone, but putting words to her truth nauseated her like a belly full of sour meat.

"It's okay. I can see it in your eyes." Tali spoke softly, her words a blanket of snow. Cooling. Covering. Comforting. "You don't need to say anything. I've known bad men. Bad women, too." She brushed Paulette's cheek with the back of her hand, skin icy and soothing. Her voice fell to the ghost of a breeze. "He's the reason your mother is dead, isn't he?"

Paulette felt understood for the first time. Felt loved. Wanted. She nodded, uttered a meek, "Yes."

"I can help, if you want. Take me to him."

Tali smelled of lavender, jasmine, something earthier, odors that drew Paulette close, so close their lips touched, and Paulette stole a kiss without realizing what she was doing.

"I'm so sorry," she whispered, her voice the color of embarrassment. Her head swam with a fresh gallon of grief, and she scooted back.

Tali touched Paulette's cheek, stopped her from getting up. "It's okay. It's hard being so alone." And then Tali leaned in and returned the kiss, a quick peck, but enough to charge up the wiring inside Paulette's heart.

"Now, take me to your grandfather."

Thar Desert, India. 1999.

The shanty town lay spread out before us, a festering wound of aged plywood, corrugated steel, and yellowing plastic. A thick coat of dust and dirt covered everything, even the people milling about in the alleys and doorways, rivaled only by the heady odors of goats and chickens and forgetfulness.

We were the last passengers on the bus, the only ones to come this far into the desert. When our feet hit the dirt, it pulled away behind us as if running from its own shadow. We were stranded a few hundred kilometers from modern civilization.

"Well, now what?" James heaved his duffel over a shoulder. "Should we grab a nice steak dinner, or should we check in and go for a swim in the Olympic-sized pool?" he said, tone iron-tight and biting.

"We find the head honcho. The pujari." I wandered toward the closest shacks, leaving him and his sarcasm behind.

"Goddammit, Paulette. Wait up." He scurried like a roach in sudden sunlight, caught up and matched my stride. "We're gonna get killed," he muttered.

I stopped short, grabbed his arm, and faced him. "These aren't savages. They're a religious sect. The worst-case scenario, they tell us to go away."

"No, they kill us," James said, the conviction gone from his voice.

The people wore traditional dhotis, all shades of gray and black. Apart from an occasional side eye, we walked among the hovels, ignored.

"See," I said, smug and secure. "No problem. They just don't care."

"Yeah, right." James squirmed like he'd just been caught shoplifting. "That guy and his goons look like they care."

A husky man with deeply tanned skin and a black bushy beard power-walked toward us. Two younger, firmer men followed him. All wore the blackest of dhotis, and the lead man wore a beautiful black turban, wrapped with the utmost care, signifying his position as pujari.

James and I both stopped, frozen by the approaching storm. But when the three reached us, their expressions were not full of scorn or anger. They were not full of contempt or hatred.

They were not full of anything.

The pujari pressed his hands together, bowed slightly. "Namaste." Then his companions did likewise. James and I returned the gesture.

The pujari spoke rapidly, weaving a masterful tapestry of syllables from a language I didn't understand. I leaned into James, not wanting to surrender, but having no choice. Languages were always his thing. "What did he say?"

James drilled holes through me with his glare, then jutted his jaw in irritation, turned to the pujari, spoke briefly. The only word I caught was "Mahakali", so I chimed in. "Her name's Tali. Or Talitha."

"Okay," the pujari said in French, cutting short another of James' irritated looks. He waved off his companions. "There is no one here named Tali or Talitha. Only the Mahakali."

I stepped in front of James, taking control again. "That's her. I'm sorry. The Mahakali. Can I see her? Please?"

An expression at last from the man, the faintest brush strokes of confusion tinted with hesitation. But his emotions disappeared just as quickly, his features falling once more to bland disinterest.

"Follow me." He turned around, headed back the way he came with an unhurried stride.

"Now?" My heart shoveled out blood in hot, thick scoops. I wanted to see her, but I didn't expect it to happen so easily.

The pujari stopped, stood for a moment, then glanced at us over his shoulder. "Follow me, or don't follow me. It doesn't matter." Then he continued on his way.

We followed him through the town. The inhabitants continued to pay us little attention, but glimpses of their faces told a story. They were at peace of some sort. Quiet. Mindful of their activities. A woman grinding millet, solely focused on the stones. Two men repairing the wall of a shack, no words shared, just a mechanical ballet. A young boy by himself, not playing, but sitting still, being patient.

A kind of peace, but the kind that scared me. The kind that comes from having nothing to look forward to. I wondered if James saw it, too. A quick look at his furrowed brow and slight frown said he did.

The pujari ushered us into a well-lit shack. Sunlight seeped in through several plastic windows and a chorus of candles shimmered throughout. He took a spot in the middle of the room, knelt, motioned for us to do the same.

We both knelt as well, hard-packed dirt instantly making my knees ache.

He looked at us, tilted his head. "Why are you here?"

"I told you. To see Tali. The Mahakali, I mean. I met her once, when I was about 16."

He nodded, full of knowing, full of understanding. "Of course. But, you do not see the Mahakali without joining us in Sunyata. Do you understand?"

"This place has a name?" I looked to James for help. I didn't understand.

James cocked his head, raised an inquisitive eyebrow. "So, I have to agree to become a member of this cult in order to see her? No way."

I gripped James' arm, squeezed my insecurity into his bicep. "Don't ruin this for me. Just agree. They can't possibly keep us here. That bus comes every day."

The pujari nodded again, fresh traces of confusion rippling across his face. "Correct. We won't keep you here. The bus comes often. But I think you misunderstand. To see the Mahakali is to join us in Sunyata, to live in the great emptiness. I'm not asking you to agree to one to do the other. I'm asking you to understand they are one and the same."

Skepticism and suspicion creased James' eyebrows. He studied the pujari for the space of a breath, then nodded. "Okay."

Colmar, France. 1980.

Cyrille Hachette was a large man by any measure, thick-necked and thick-headed. A man hardened by countless years of toiling in isolation. A man who believed the world owed him, and he owed nothing to no one.

Paulette and Tali reached the house, followed the banging and swearing to the barn, and entered from the rear. They found Cyrille elbow-deep in his precious McCormick V80, man and tractor wrestling in the swath of sunshine spilling in through the front sliding doors.

Tali motioned for Paulette to wait, then proceeded through the cool shadows of the barn alone, still wearing her specs. "Excuse me, sir. I'd like to speak with you about your Paulette." She spoke with all the respect he didn't deserve, paused at the edge of the square of sunlight.

Cyrille peeked over his shoulder. "What's that sack of shit done now?" His words slammed Paulette like stones. Fresh lumps of terror coagulated in her chest, and she took a hurried step back.

Tali was unperturbed, cleared her throat. "Sir, it's not what she's done, it's what you've done." Her words dripped with rotten honey.

Fury flared across the large man's face, a wildfire burning out of control. He rose, a mountain standing on tree trunks, and tossed a wrench into a metal toolbox, punctuating his aggression with a clang.

"I don't like the tone of your voice, young woman. Who are you? Did Paulette send you here? Where is she?" Cyrille planted two meaty fists on his hips. "Why don't you come into the light where I can see you?"

Paulette couldn't see Tali's face, but in the momentary pause, she imagined that same impish grin from before. And it terrified her.

A cold wind swept through the barn, and Tali stepped into the sunlight as if driven by it. "Here I am. And I have something to show you." Tali removed her glasses, held them at her side. "Look closely. Your dead daughter is here."

Cold confusion settled on Cyrille's face, the same confusion squeezing Paulette's heart. She inched forward, cautious, cat-like, until she stood just outside the light watching her angry grandfather over Tali's shoulder.

The man bent before Tali, peered into her eyes. His puzzled expression exploded into frozen panic. "It's empty. So empty. Full of nothing and nothingness." And there was nothing for him to hold on to. Only emptiness. He collapsed to his knees, buried his head in his hands.

Then the large, angry grandfather who owed nothing to no one wept at all the emptiness. Emptiness surrounding him. Emptiness filling him. Emptiness taking him down.

Thar Desert, India. 1999.

The pujari led James and me deeper into the endless sea of shacks. He walked at the pace of a man with no destination in mind. "Talitha isn't a name. It's from the Christian bible. Sometimes it's used to refer to the raising of Jarius' daughter. I have a Ph.D. in religious studies from the University of Deli. I only mention it because most who visit us do so under the presumption that we're uneducated people. That this way of life is a reflection of ignorance."

A twinge tickled my stomach, a suspicion that he was leading us on a snipe hunt. "I'm sorry if we've offended you."

James' face reddened. "We don't think you're uneducated at all."

The pujari led us to the entrance of an unassuming shack, held aside the sheet of plastic covering the entrance. "I speak seven languages fluently. We are doctors, lawyers, teachers, and even a low-ranking politician or two. All are welcome here." Then he bowed. "She's been expecting you."

Tali sat lotus-style in the center of the shack, the same Tali I'd met in the vineyard decades ago, same rays of black hair, same shimmering sunglasses, the shade of her skin finely tuned by the desert sun. Behind her loomed a make-shift altar, flowers and jewelry and candles covering every square inch of its rickety shelves. Incense smoldered quietly on either side of her, decorating the air with ribbons of smoke.

She smiled, wide and gracious. "It's been awhile. Please join me." Then the joy faded, leaving her grin uncertain. "I see you brought a friend."

James and I sat down cross-legged before her. A snake of anxiety gripped my gut and sank fangs into my heart. "I wouldn't exactly call him a friend. He's more of a companion." I missed her and didn't want James' presence to make her uncomfortable.

She tilted her head, curious but detached. "Why are you here?"

"I wanted to see you again. I wanted to know if what happened was real. The memories are dusty and dull, and I'm left with only feelings." James eyed me, the lines of helplessness and betrayal clear on his face. "Grief and sorrow and shame and powerlessness. I want to know what you showed my grandfather before he killed himself. You showed him something, then you ran away and left me alone."

Tali's expression fell, her revulsion at my request almost palpable. "It would kill you."

But the cobra in my belly billowed its cape, rose up, blinded me. Tali held a truth I couldn't see, a truth about my mother, a truth about my grandpa. A truth about me. I lurched forward, slapped the glasses from her face, held her head steady.

I looked into her eyes, deep wells of darkness, and I saw the emptiness beyond nothingness, the emptiness at the end of the universe. It seared me, seared me to the bone, to the soul, a flame of extinction. I cried and withered and hurt and numbed and crumbled.

Paulette faded. James faded. Both gone. But I was still here. I closed my eyes tight and hard like bulkheads on a ship in a storm before the emptiness could reach me, too.

"I put my glasses back on, Paul James Hachette." Her words smiled at me through the darkness.

Tali and I were alone. Eyes closed. In the dark. In the empty. And I could tell her. "There was one more feeling I've carried this whole time," I whispered, as if bearing a truth that could break the world. "Love. For you. I've looked for you ever since that day."

"Would you like to stay with me?" Her words, though gentle and serene, sent shivers of nervous anticipation through me. "Paulette and James were nothing, and returned to nothing. But you, you are real. You will not die."

I slowly opened my eyes, greeted by my sullen reflections in the mirrors of her sunglasses, no longer of brokenness and embarrassment but an older, singular version of the young boy who'd looked into those mirrors two decades ago. "Will it hurt?"

She shook her head slowly.

"May I have a kiss first?"

Her cheeks shaded with playful embarrassment. "You may." Then she leaned forward, pressed her lips to mine, just a quick peck, but enough to ignite the wiring of my heart for the second time in my life.

She leaned back, and I lingered in the scents of lavender, jasmine, something much, much earthier. Then I gently lifted the glasses from her face, set them in my lap, and looked into the emptiness. There, I found my truth.

There, I found Sunyata.

~ The End ~

<u>ALSO FROM MANTA PRESS, LTD.</u>

THE BUTTERFLY CIRCLE
MARY CARROLL LEOSON

GONE WHERE THE GOBLINS GO
MATT BETTS

MANDATE: THIRTEEN
JOSEPH J. DOWLING

THE MOUTH IS A COVEN
LIZ WORTH

HOLBURN
TIM JEFFREYS

WHO HOLDS THE DEVIL
MICHAEL DITTMAN

THE MUD MAN
DONNA MARIE WEST

THE OPENING
TIM MCWHORTER

BONE WHITE
TIM MCWHORTER

SHADOWS REMAIN
TIM MCWHORTER